Death at the Oast

by

Peter Chegwidden

www.publishnation.co.uk

Author's note

As I mention with my previous crime novels the police officers and their behaviours, their ranks, police procedures, and so on, are products of my imagination and are simply to suit the story. They are certainly not a reflection of the real Kent Police for whom I have the utmost respect.

I do not carry out research in the pursuit of authenticity.

Most of the places (towns, cities and villages, attractions and countryside) are real, but the characters and their actual homes are fictional.

I do try and invent names for the main participants but this is not always practical and I apologise to anyone who shares a name with a character.

The story is set in Kent, my home county, a county I am very proud of. I love the miles of unspoilt countryside of which there is still so very much. Please see my Afterthoughts at the end of the book.

If you have read and enjoyed "The Chortleford Mystery" you may well enjoy this work which is presented in a similar vein, yet is, of course, quite different in content.

Both books are as much about the characters themselves and developing events as about the crimes. They are written in a more gentle style with humour and satire, pathos and poignancy, and the absolute minimum of slightly unpleasant language.

Most of my books are based in Kent including:

- **Kindale**
- **Sheppey Short Stories**
- **Tom Investigates**
- **Tom Vanishes**
- **No Shelter for the Wicked**
- **The Chortleford Mystery**
- And coming soon **'The Master of Downsland'**

Please see "Other books by Peter Chegwidden" at end of this work for more details.

Chapter One

Yet another birthday

His birthday passed more or less unmarked, which was the way he liked it.

Plenty of cards, two texts, brief phone calls from family and a longer call from an old friend, this one being particularly welcome, they being best mates.

Otherwise Ernest Pawden allowed his 86th birthday to slip quietly by, uncelebrated save for three cans of chilled Holsten Pils lager, his favourite. He'd gazed longingly at the photo of his dear departed Edna, his wife of fifty-three years, and allowed a tear to escape undoing his determination to keep a 'stiff upper lip'. Grown men don't cry. Not in his generation, that is.

He spent the day alone which was his choice and the way he preferred it.

For the first time there was no card or call from his younger sister, Kathleen, as she'd passed away four months previously. A widow by many years at least she'd had children, a joy denied Ernest and Edna, and Naomi and Stephan had grown-up children of their own now, so the chance of great-great-nieces-and-nephews was on the cards.

Something to look forward to.

The trouble was that today families didn't stay together in one area, Naomi and husband Richard living in Fleetwood, Lancashire, and Stephan and his wife Patricia living in Shrewsbury. In total there were five offspring who, as adults, had spread their wings far and wide with one emigrating to Canada and another working in Portugal.

To Ernest Shrewsbury seemed quite far enough, let alone Fleetwood, never mind Ottawa.

However, none of this was on his mind as the evening approached.

He'd prepared a roast dinner which was to be followed by a couple of DVDs accompanied by the lager. An episode of *Foyle's War* and another from his *Cadfael* collection would be his entertainment to start his 87th year on planet earth.

Another appreciable delight had been the call from Cedric Pugh-Calford, his friend from way back when, and they nattered about this and that, shared some laughter, put the world to rights and spoke seriously on matters they considered to be serious. Cedric knew Ernest would want to be alone and wouldn't have dreamed of imposing himself and so, having ascertained his friend had a busy and enjoyable evening lined up, bade him happy birthday and goodnight.

Mr Pugh-Calford was not a fan of any sort of TV drama, and certainly not crime drama, his idea of an enjoyable night in being to immerse himself in a good book with music playing quietly in the background. This evening he left Ernest to his own devices and settled down with George Eliot's *Daniel Deronda* accompanied by Mozart's 39th Symphony and felt he was all the better for it.

Whatever did that man see in fictional crime, he wondered as he shook his head in mock despair and permitted a gentle and affectionate smile to put in a brief appearance on his face. And murder too! Always murder. He had often thought Ernest might have seen himself as a kind of Miss Marple, solving a really baffling killing while the police looked on appreciatively and gratefully.

As if that ever happened in real life!

So was it an escape from the real world, from real life perhaps?

After all, twas just fiction. But then so was *Daniel Deronda*! Had Cedric answered his own question?

And so these two good friends settled down to their diverse and pleasurable evenings deep in the Kent countryside totally unaware that a real life crime drama was about to be played out nearby, and too close for comfort into the bargain.

Chapter Two

Waiting in the Wings

DCI Sheelagh Mehedren did not suffer fools gladly, nor indeed did she tolerate them with any other adverbs.

In the company DS Willoughby 'Willie' Broughton she was putting the finishing touches to her report on the investigation into a group of cowboys who had been plaguing older people in east Kent. Three arrests but not before they had fleeced over twelve individuals by persuading them that (unnecessary) work was required on their property.

A great deal of money had been handed over. None of it recoverable.

Some victims hadn't come forward, no doubt too embarrassed to do so. None of the victims was a fool in Sheelagh's eyes; they had simply been conned by convincing and cunning criminals preying on the elderly.

She sat back and tapped her pen against various teeth in her mouth, the knocking sound causing Willie to look up and stare over the top of his glasses.

"Can you play a tune on them, Ma'am?" he enquired in a manner that might have been considered by some to be insolent and certainly insubordinate, but the DCI dismissed his question with a few salty comments largely relating to other oral activities and the resultant pleasures they might bring the Detective Sergeant. He smiled in reply.

This was typical banter between the two, paying no heed to political correctness and even less to worries about 'harassment'. Their respect for each other rose above such contemplations, with both knowing how far they could go, acknowledging the boundaries, but permitting themselves a degree of leeway when the opportunity presented itself.

"Besides," she added, sporting a lecherous leer, "the way you look over those glasses, mate, you look like a dirty old man."

"One out of three right, Ma'am. Definitely all man, my only known deficiency being hyperopia."

"I don't like the idea of a man being hyper anything, let alone hyper-active."

"Well, I must admit to suffering a little from attention deficit at the mo."

"You'll get all too much attention from my right hand before long if you start that nonsense."

Sheelagh chuckled slightly and leaned back in her chair which groaned having to cope with the strain of such a manoeuvre. Willie smiled and told her she'd break the chair one day. She ignored him.

"You know what, Willie, I'd like something to really get my teeth into." Sensing the most likely response that was forming in his mind was almost ready for despatch to his mouth she swiftly interjected. "That's enough of that, mate. Right now I'd even look into a burglary for something different to do."

"Ma'am, ma'am, ma'am, you mean do something the paying public actually wants done? Tut-tut, wouldn't please 'em upstairs, y'know." They shared mischievous grins and returned to the work presently decorating their desks oblivious to a matter for the DCI's eager teeth lurking just around the corner.

***

Audrey Modlum was pottering around in her front garden totally absorbed in the paradise she believed her garden to be. Pausing for a moment she placed her hands on her hips, stretched to her full height, gazed up at the blue May sky, took an immensely deep breath and smiled with the sheer happiness and contentment of it all.

5

Paradise indeed.

And by what stroke of good fortune it had come to them!

When husband Gareth retired three years earlier they had chanced upon this idyllic converted oast house planted right next to a hop garden here in one of their favourite corners of their beloved Kent. They couldn't believe it. Sadly they couldn't afford it either.

But fate played a welcome hand.

Audrey's auntie Phoebe died without prior notice but fortunately not intestate, and Audrey was left a modest bequest which proved to be sufficiently *immodest* to make up the difference between the value of their property and the cost of the oast house. Auntie Phoebe, a childless widow, had not figured very much in the lives of the Modlums and the bequest came as a complete surprise.

Overcome by guilty feelings (they hadn't even attended the funeral) they planted a flowering cherry tree in the back garden and dedicated it to the late relative. And that was that. Guilt extinguished.

It was Audrey's custom to explain to anyone who asked that they lived in the countryside south of Faversham, this being an adequately vague and satisfactorily large geographical location to hopefully put off unexpected and unwanted visitors. Since Satnav, in all its glory, would've dumped the unsuspecting a mile up the road Audrey's desire to remain hidden away was as close to reality as might be hoped.

They were not quite solitary people. They had some good friends, precious few close relations, and were on excellent terms with the nearest neighbours. They socialised but preferred their own company most of the time. Their retirement home was their escape and they wanted it kept special.

Audrey played golf which was her prime escape from Gareth, not that he needed escaping from, and in his turn he went fishing leaving his wife to her own devices, mainly the garden and the kitchen.

Thus had their three years of retirement played out, Gareth little realising he now had hours rather than days of it left to enjoy.

Weekends were usually spent at home, the couple rejoicing in their togetherness, but there were odd exceptions such as when they had a night or two away at a B&B, or when Audrey rose early Sunday for a round of golf with her friend Rosemary Wandon. And it was this weekend that she had such an arrangement.

***

Molly Penderman fed Tom, her rescue cat, and watched him slip out to spend the night doing whatsoever he might please, wheresoever he might choose. He was a cat and, as Molly knew, cats are in charge! You don't have a cat, the cat very obligingly chooses you and expects you, as his or her servant, to cater for his or her every need.

She smiled and looked at Felicity, her other cat, a marmalade, the one she'd had from its kittenhood, who was both a home-lover and a day-lover. Felicity came when called, spent much of each day indoors or in the garden, and slept on Molly's bed at night.

Miss Penderman had always adored feline pets, preferring them to men, although she had to admit that Tom displayed many of the facets that made the male of the human species so undesirable. But she loved him dearly for all that.

7

The two pets got on well enough which might be attributed to the fact they spent so little time together when awake.

Molly had lived in and around this part of Kent all her life, having been born in Doddington and having moved with her parents to other settlements prior to their settling in Faversham itself. Her career, if it could be called that, progressed from being a plain typist to the dizzy heights of becoming a secretary, ultimately joining a firm where she had a lady manager.

This was a time of notable pleasure and she could imagine no situation arising to mar this heavenly existence. So she allowed the approach of her autumn years to wash soothingly over her as she dreamed of modest retirement.

The hammer-blows came one after the other.

Her father passed away, and almost immediately her post was made redundant when the company closed. She struggled to find any sort of employment for much had changed in the world as she soon discovered. Her age was against her despite the fact it should not have been.

Eventually she found work here and there and even tried her hand in a supermarket, but was clearly not cut out for the tills. And then her mother died.

With no siblings Molly inherited the house and decided at once she would move back to the country from whence she came. Within a few short years she reached retirement age and settled back in her country cottage to accept whatever else life might throw at her, good or bad.

She was on good terms with Ernest Pawden who lived about half a mile up the road, considering him to be one of the old school, a real gentleman, and she had taken to the Modlums who had bought Constance Hemden's oast, about half a mile the other direction. Molly had never been comfortable with Constance and they had rarely socialised together.

For one thing Constance detested cats which condemned her in Molly's eyes to the role of one of very low standing. So Molly was delighted when she moved out, bound for Hertfordshire or somewhere, and the Modlums moved in. Nice people, the Modlums. And they liked cats.

However, the Modlums were about to impact on her life in a way she would've rather avoided if at all possible.

**

Ananya Ghatik and her partner Clayton Mainstreet lived in the country mainly because it suited their environmental credentials. Here they could grow their own vegetables and breathe the fresh air, or so they presumed it to be. They bought a small cottage (with a large garden) not too far from the M2 and rail services to London and rejoiced in the concept of being away from it all.

Clayton was an architect, Ananya a builder, and they harboured a dream of converting their cottage into a much larger eco-home, a dream which, it later transpired, was not shared by the local planning authority.

Once again Ananya thought herself a victim.

She had suffered from three or four –isms, the worst, in her eyes, being sexism. A fellow builder, glowing with sarcasm and confident of his wit, once asked her if she knew what an RSJ was. She briefly explained the manufacturing process, the reasons why they were used, and then enlightened him as to the unpleasant consequences of her inserting one into him.

At least he had the good grace in acknowledging defeat to say "well at least it'll keep me back straight".

Ananya and Clayton were vegetarians, and he a vanitarian if there is such a word. Extensive preening, often conducted in

9

front of a mirror, confirmed him as a typical example of the male of almost any species. When home he would shower three or four times a day, tried to ensure he was perfectly clean shaven all day and there was not a hair out of place.

One of the things they had not been prepared for was the fact they were not on main drainage, having not given it a moment's consideration when studying the property details. Their showers, coupled with the frequent use of the dishwasher, and the employment of the washing machine, led to the cesspool having to be emptied far too often for their liking.

There was another drawback to their eco proposals: they had no knowledge of how to grow vegetables or the application to carry out the work. Digging the garden was anathema and Clayton was not one for getting dirty. The upshot was that they decided to take on a gardener believing that the county might be alive with retired people happy to earn a few bob.

So it was that Ananya walked down the road one day to talk to their nearest neighbour as they must surely employ someone to tend their beautifully kept garden, and she was astonished to discover that Audrey and Gareth Modlum did their own gardening. Well, that is, it was Audrey's pride and joy, she led the operation with her husband as gofer, do-fer and general handyman.

Nonetheless the enquiry started a friendship and produced a successful outcome.

Audrey took Gareth for a day's slog in Ananya's garden and a transformation was begun. In the two years the four had known each other the garden became a vegetable patch of appreciable size as the Modlums spent the occasional day at labour. And Ananya and Clayton at last enjoyed the fruits of the efforts of others and felt truly environmentally friendly. The intrepid gardeners would accept no payment in cash and settled for some veg instead.

It amazed the Modlums that their neighbours' desire to save the planet did not extend to their cars. Both had large, expensive gas-guzzling models which did not sit comfortably with the idea of preserving polar bears, and which did not often sit comfortably on the country lanes. Clayton, in particular, believed these minor roads could and should be taken at motorway speeds.

Being a keep-fit fanatic he also used the lanes as his personal running track. In winter he would set off in the pitch dark attired in reflective yellow sportswear which would be adorned with flashing lights front and rear. This was in the belief the greatest risk came from vehicles on the road.

His only accident to date had not involved a vehicle but a fox. He never saw it, but it had emerged ahead of him and filled the silence with a loud vulpine bark. Taken by surprise when sprinting at full career Clayton, unsure in that split second what was happening, leaped with a squeal of shock and fell headlong into a muddy ditch.

Returning home he was a full two hours in the bathroom restoring his cleanliness in both bath and shower, thus ensuring the cesspool would need emptying quicker than usual. Using so much water never seemed to square itself with his environmental philosophy.

During their two years at Earth Cottage as they renamed it they also became friendly with the couple who lived a couple of hundred yards in the opposite direction to the Modlums.

Eric Furness and his partner Gerald Samuels dwelled peacefully in the more aptly named Rose Cottage and were country people by birth and heart. Eric came from the village of Stalisfield and Gerald from Eastling and if there was one thing above all else that gave them most pleasure it was walking the footpaths of Kent.

Their next planned walk, a local one this coming Sunday, was to have unexpected drama thrown in for good measure.

Chapter Three

A Hole in One

If April can be a month of promise May is the month of delivery.

The days are about as long as they can be, the weather is often pleasant enough, an aperitif to the summer now reaching across the country, and a wealth of plants, trees and shrubs are blossoming or preparing to explode into their full seasonal regalia.

Of course, it can equally be a washout, but this particular year was not destined to suffer thus, so May was in full swing, confident it marked the start of a real summer.

Ananya Ghatik was worried that long, hot, dry summers indicated the worst effects of developing climate change and the disaster she saw around the corner, a tragedy seemingly being too easily ignored everywhere. Especially by politicians, keen to display their green qualifications while paying this major issue lip service only and doing silly things like planting trees on grass verges that had all but been destroyed by vehicles.

Where was the sense in that?

She was annoyed to learn that the hops grown down the lane were used for ornamental purposes rather than the brewing of beer. It was a problem she had to constantly wrestle with as she was teetotal anyway and did not approve of the drinking of alcohol, much to Clayton's chagrin. He'd been so madly in love with her he fell in willingly with her beliefs without paying any attention whatsoever to the long-term consequences for him and their relationship.

Even now, surrounded by hundreds of sheep he was beginning to see beyond their woolly coats to the lamb chops beyond, not a reasonable state of mind for a committed vegetarian. Was this to be the first sign of a crack appearing in their partnership?

When he was staying away on business he was not above having a pint before dinner, wine with his meal, and a liqueur afterwards, and all on expenses. It troubled his conscience but he eradicated his qualms with ease, always making sure he thoroughly cleaned his teeth several times before reaching home.

On his last night away, in Leicester, he had thrown caution to the wind, eschewed the vegetarian options on the hotel's menu, and tucked into a sirloin steak well done, washed down with a particularly distinguished Chablis. He fretted later, but not much.

He had long felt that Ananya would view his behaviour as a dreadful and unforgiveable act of unfaithfulness to her, and that he stood an improved chance of absolution if he had a fling with another woman rather than eat meat and drink wine. Having said that he'd never entertained the possibility of intimacy with another girl, as from the moment Ananya had seduced him so beautifully, so enchantingly, so purposefully, so determinedly, so satisfyingly in that magical woodland near Smarden he'd surrendered heart, soul and mind, and knew he would never look elsewhere.

Their bedroom was a shrine to the exquisiteness of true love where they could lie entwined, lost in blissful happiness and, when the mood took them, embark on something more vigorous and explosive. And afterwards settle together, wrapped in each others' arms, warm and content and in love.

As Saturday evening drew to a close Audrey and Gareth Modlum were also wrapped in each others' arms as they lay quietly in bed, listening to and enjoying a silence only broken by an occasional owl's hoot or lamb's baa-ing, the sound reaching them through open windows. They knew that for them they had reached the age where anything that could be termed vigorous and explosive might carry serious health risks.

13

Audrey had set the alarm as she had an early start for her morning's golf with Rosemary. It had been a good day, shared with her husband who was an ace helper in their garden. He was good at doing what he was told, and he executed his duties well and entirely to Audrey's satisfaction.

After a ham salad dinner they had read in the garden, relaxing on their hammock, swinging gently backwards and forwards as birds serenaded them with delightful songs while the sheep and their lambs added the tenor and baritone parts.

Not far away Eric Furness had been studying the computer and drawing up a route for the walk next day. Kent County Council has an excellent inter-active mapping system on their website enabling walkers to find footpaths and plan walks, and Eric was taking full advantage while Gerald prepared the packed lunches they would take.

The weekends were their special times and preserved for togetherness.

During the week Eric worked as an electrician for a large company and travelled extensively throughout Kent, for which purpose he had a company car, whereas Gerald worked for the local Faversham brewers, Shepherd Neame, and cycled to and fro the town centre brewery. Oddly enough, perhaps, Gerald drank little beer, his preferred tipples being gin and tonic, rose wine and cognac, the latter only when he thought he deserved it and could afford it.

Eric loved Shepherd Neame's beer, but it had not always been so. He detested the stuff when he was young but it had improved to his liking in the ensuring years, so it wasn't unusual to find him nursing a pint of *Spitfire* or *Whitstable Bay* these days.

He met Gerald in a pub, the Dover Castle at Teynham, and their friendship grew to be followed later by affection which deepened unbid into love.

Eric knew Kent inside out, was a good map reader (who needs Satnav, he would say) and always planned their excursions leaving the food side of things to keen chef Gerald, he being able to conjure up all kinds of dishes from their favourites to original and innovative creations.

Tomorrow they would set off down the lane, turning left just before they reached the Modlums oast house and take the footpath that ran across the adjacent hop garden. At least that was the design.

About the same time that warm May evening, as darkness was engulfing the land, Molly Penderman fed Tom and saw him saunter off down the back garden, pausing now and then for a scratch and a lick, as was his wont. She turned in time to see Felicity skipping upstairs ready to claim her prime position on the bed, and with a smile she switched off the downstairs lights and followed her cat to the bedroom.

Ernest Pawden was back home having been at Cedric's for their customary Saturday night game of chess, accompanied by cheese and biscuits, and a pot of strong brewed coffee. Ernest was at peace with the world. He was happy. He shone the torch a short way ahead of him to light his way even though it was still twilight.

The game was the finale of a fine evening enjoyed by two dear friends who could talk for England. But their conversation was, as always, wide ranging, intelligent and bright, thoughtful and deep, but with plenty of room for humour and mirth. They talked and listened, never talking over each other or interrupting when one was speaking. They argued from time to time, having different opinions on certain matters, but their arguments were well reasoned and discussed, and presented quietly and pleasantly for perusal and consideration.

They never fell out. They were true friends.

There was an element of routine about Saturday nights in this small portion of rural Kent, a rustic community woven together by location and the enjoyment of its environment by the residents despite their diverse nature. Yes, from time to time Ananya and Clayton would go out and dine at a good restaurant, such as Read's near Faversham; Audrey and Gareth might have a night away, their favourite being the sensational Brambles B&B at Eythorne, but basically here they all were in their remote homes leading their chosen lives.

Saturday night was Saturday night, and they spent it how they saw fit.

And in due course, as the planet turned, Sunday arrived in the wee hours and eventually Audrey's alarm went off, signalling, had she but known it, a very different Sunday to the one those residents were used to.

***

In Minster on the isle of Sheppey another alarm erupted causing such shock that one person fell out of the bed while the other knocked a glass of water over trying to extinguish the throbbing noise.

Twas still dark and Sheelagh Mehedren fumbled hopelessly and helplessly for both the damned light switch and the damned knob to turn the damned alarm off. Once over the initial surprise and with the light glowing bright both women collapsed in fits of giggles.

Katie Parchant slipped into her dressing gown and went off to fix breakfast leaving Sheelagh to clear up the mess and dress. The DCI was on duty this morning, hence the rude awakening.

They were an interesting couple, Katie being a bus driver with Arriva, Sheelagh a police officer now of high rank. But love

16

knows no bounds. They met years ago in the aftermath of a road accident when Sheelagh, in a more lowly position, was taking statements from witnesses and Katie had seen the crash take place right in front of her bus. She was quite shaken but Sheelagh was comforting and yet professional and the comforting continued later that evening when she called on Katie to see if she was alright.

Katie was, in fact, fully recovered in spirits especially when she learned that there had been no serious injuries, but she still accepted some of Sheelagh's comfort, this being much to her fancy.

The only difficulty their blossoming romance ran into was that both were on shift work and working odd hours. Even today they could be like ships that pass in the night, seeing each briefly from time to time, and yet it made their relationship all the more healthier and fun, for they so surely made the most of any periods spent together. The difficulty was thus turned into the catalyst for a thriving partnership which remained as beautiful and tender as it became all those years ago. Once again, true love conquers all.

Elsewhere Molly Penderman had been woken, as she always was, by Tom activating the cat flap on his way in from his night of feline adventures, and duly delivered a much longed for meal for the tabby. Felicity was having a lie in, as ever.

It was early but Molly was conscious of a car moving slowly on the road outside. She looked out of the window but didn't recognise the car as it drifted slowly past, anymore than she recognised the driver who for a couple seconds stared back at her. Must be lost and looking for someone she reasoned. Nonetheless she shivered involuntarily as the vehicle pulled away.

She had to admit she didn't like the look of the driver. Shifty was her opinion, an opinion formed from the merest glance. Since throughout her life most men had appeared shifty to Molly perhaps this wasn't a surprise. What she didn't realise was that

17

the driver was a deal more than just shifty and her observations would later put her life in danger.

Right now Tom was at her feet pleading for more food and she dismissed the encounter with the car and its shifty driver, returning to the kitchen to feed the cat.

Further along the road Rosemary Wandon had previously called to collect Audrey Modlum.

Two people, two sets of golf clubs, one car. Surely not a problem?

Unfortunately Rosemary had a vintage 1978 Mini Cooper and it was a remarkable feat just getting the clubs in the back, but having achieved their target the two ladies sat in the front and Rosemary crunched into first and set off.

Being fairly low the car made the most of any rough surface, including the pot-holes, and Audrey felt that her teeth were being shaken free of the gums, and that constantly banging her head on the roof was the precursor to a headache. She had a much larger car, a Ford Focus of 2018 vintage, much more capable of the job, and certainly more comfortable, but it was Rosemary's turn to drive and Rosemary insisted.

So Audrey kindly put up with it.

Rosemary was enthusiastic about the original Minis, and she had laid her hands on this one five years ago. It roared and bellowed, thanks to an exhaust system she had fitted herself, and could 'go like the clappers' as she described it when let loose on an open road. In addition to the basic headlight arrangement four other lights could be found on the front, Rosemary's only sadness being that she couldn't have a flashing blue light on the top.

Possibly just as well Audrey had always believed.

Shaken, stirred, battered, bruised, Audrey was delivered to the golf course where she had more difficulty getting out of the car than they had getting the clubs out. I am in no fit state to play, she said to herself adding, silently and wickedly, that maybe that was the idea; to render your opponent useless and claim an easy victory.

In fact, Rosemary was, by a country mile, the worst of the two players and rarely ever won except when Audrey deliberately lost in order to keep her friend's spirits up.

Back home Gareth Modlum had enjoyed his lie-in and had now risen, wandered to the bathroom, back to the bedroom to dress, thence downstairs to prepare a simple breakfast he would not eat. His last meal did indeed turn out to be the last supper.

Having had all her internal organs re-arranged by a ride in Rosemary's Mini Audrey was not in the mood for conceding defeat cheaply and consequently had the round comfortably wrapped up in her favour before the last two holes. Then something extraordinary occurred. At the 17th she tucked away a hole in one, putting the result beyond any reasonable doubt.

She stood transfixed. There was nowhere else the ball could be. Both ladies had watched it bounce three times on the green and roll towards to flag where it vanished. Rosemary let out a scream (not, as it turned out, the only one of the day) and Audrey dropped her club as her eyes bulged and her mouth dropped wide open.

Four other golfers dashed over thinking something dreadful had happened and were much relieved to discover that not only all was well and good, but that a fellow member, and a lady to boot, had achieved an amazing success. Her name would be added to the Honours Board, the drinks were on her, she would be talked about for years to come. The accolades poured forth in profusion.

Overcome with praise and personal disbelief she set off for the green, pausing briefly en route to let Rosemary take her second shot, an effort that put her ball into some rough a good distance to the right. In truth Rosemary took three more shots to reach the green, but once there an impatient Audrey was able to retrieve her ball and accept that she had *done* it, she really had.

***

About the time Audrey was experiencing ecstasy and glory at the 17th, Eric and Gerald were making final preparations for their walk. Late risers, they had taken a light and healthy breakfast at the table on the lawn in the back garden, and flicked through the Sundays, their papers being delivered, the only day they partook of such luxury.

Eric grumbled unnecessarily about snippets he gleaned from the Mail on Sunday, issues that bothered neither of them, while Gerald cast his eyes over the sports pages and the football in particular, and did so without comment.

Ernest drove down to Cedric's and the two set off for Teynham to get their respective papers, their normal Sunday morning routine. They would return to Cedric's for morning coffee.

Molly had washed and dressed and eaten a bowl of fresh fruit salad washed down with herbal tea. Tom and Felicity were asleep on her bed. What a lovely picture they made! But suddenly her mind returned to Mr Shifty and once more she shivered. My goodness, she muttered under her breath, a goose has just run over my grave. And she shivered again as another thought crossed her mind, no, not my grave, somebody else's.

What on earth made me think that, she asked herself, suddenly feeling rather upset, cold and very alone. The sensation passed as swiftly as it had come, but it haunted her for some time and came back to frighten her yet again later on.

Ananya and Clayton were still in bed.

The bedclothes were strewn hither and thither but it troubled the occupants not one jot. The only thing that mattered was each other. It was Sunday morning and that was 'me' time for the pair of them, except that 'me' meant 'us', of course.

And so the scattered residents of this part of rural, unspoilt Kent, continued with their varied lives without the knowledge that one of their number was no longer alive.

Audrey arrived home, seriously jarred, and invited Rosemary in for coffee.

She opened the front door and was unable to take in the vision in front of her. Rosemary stepped in behind her, saw the blood-drenched body in the hall and let out a scream that might've been heard in East Sussex. It was heard by Eric and Gerald who were nearby and who dashed to the Modlum's Oast house from whence the scream appeared to have emanated.

Audrey was utterly transfixed. Her husband was lying dead in front of her, Rosemary was having an attack of the screaming abdabs, and it took Gerald to cast a calming aura about them. Audrey fainted and Eric tended her.

Looking at the screaming Rosemary Eric asked unhelpfully, "Should I slap her?"
"Good God, no. Not in this day and age anyway," Gerald responded as he applied his first aid training to trying to locate life where there as none to be found.

"I think he's dead. I'll call 999," he said softly with a coolness typical of the man, "and then we must remove ourselves. This is now a crime scene."

They carried Audrey to the lounge and a sofa, and manhandled Rosemary to an armchair. She was still beside herself but the worst of the storm had passed. Audrey was

21

coming round and neither man knew how to deal with the situation. However, Audrey was made of strong and sensible material.

"My husband," she muttered, "what of my husband?" Gerald chanced his arm and hoped he was doing it right.

"I'm afraid he's dead, Audrey, but I have called the police and sent for an ambulance." He stood, rooted to the spot, dreading what eruption might follow. He need not have worried.

"Thank you. I knew he was. Thank you for what you're doing. Oh for God's sake, Rosemary, shut up. Gareth's dead and you should be comforting me, not going to pieces." Rosemary stopped disintegrating and moved to sit next to the widow, but carried on wailing all the same even if in a quieter mode. Eric exchanged looks with Gerald.

And thus the police and ambulance crews came upon them shortly.

Chapter Four

Eric and Gerald to the Rescue

Eric gallantly dashed home, collected his car and came and drove Audrey and Rosemary back to his place, Gerald following behind in the Mini, thus achieving a lifetime ambition. Better to drive a Mini Cooper half a mile than go to your grave having never driven one at all, he reasoned.

A paramedic had checked the widow over, decided shock was more likely to manifest itself in time and the police agreed she should be moved at once to a place of nearby refuge. The paramedic attended her further at Eric and Gerald's and also administered medication to the distraught Rosemary, whom the police initially thought to be the widow, such was her vociferous and painful suffering.

Now things were settling down, Rosemary becalmed and Eric and Gerald proving to be good comforters completely, if quietly and modestly, in control. The paramedic departed convinced both ladies were in very good hands, having explained what should be done if an emergency arose and advising Audrey to see her doctor in due course.

In fact she was presently staring ahead seeing nothing in particular, nursing a now cold cup of tea in her lap. Her friend was sitting next to her murmuring and making other odd noises as the sedative took effect.

Between everyone involved it had been ascertained Audrey had no close relatives, certainly no children, and the conclusion was reached that there was nobody to be immediately notified. Besides, Eric and Gerald, clearly in their element, were more than capable of dealing with such matters should the need arise in the foreseeable future.

In fact, Gerald had telephoned Mr Wandon, explained what had happened and Rosemary's resultant plight and assured him she was being well looked after, and was where she needed to be, that is, by Audrey's side. Rosemary's husband agreed this position with a degree of meek acceptance, in Gerald's opinion, and said he would drive over later. He gave the impression to his caller that his wife was often to be found at the heart of all manner of difficulties, that it wasn't unusual for him to have to rescue her, so presumably being caught up in a murder was, to use a golfing term, par for the course.

The first visitor was DCI Sheelagh Mehedren.

Preliminary observations had suggested Gareth had been stabbed with a large double-sided knife but no more could be established prior to the post mortem, other than a rough idea of time of death which, unsurprisingly, fell between Audrey's departure and return. The forensic team was swarming over the oast house and its environs.

The murder weapon had yet to be found but the DCI thought the killer had almost certainly taken it with him or her, perhaps to discard it elsewhere. There were no obvious signs of forced entry but much more investigation was needed. At the moment it appeared Gareth Modlum opened the door to his killer, either someone he knew or a complete stranger. Already officers had been despatched to neighbouring properties, and Willie Broughton was about to arrive at Molly's home and discover a possible clue.

***

Having thoroughly scrutinised DS Broughton's ID and admitted him to her home Molly Penderman impatiently launched herself into a hundred and one questions about what had happened up the road. And all this before they reached the lounge and the sanctuary of a seat.

24

"Oh Sergeant, I'm so sorry, whatever must you think. Please sit down anywhere you wish. My manners have deserted me, I'm so very sorry, but I'm dying to find out what's going on." He sat next to the fireplace and she located herself in the matching armchair just a couple of feet away.

"Your name please ma'am?" he enquired in a rather languid way, realising this was going to be just another interview with a near-neighbour of the deceased, and knowing it was his job, someone had to do it, and he'd be expected to answer questions rather than the other way round.

"Miss Penderman, Sergeant, Miss Molly Penderman."

"Well, Miss Penderman, I'm afraid that at the moment I cannot disclose any details except to say that a serious crime appears to have been committed where Mr and Mrs Modlum live, and we are conducting house to house enquiries as a matter of routine."

He knew it wouldn't do, knew it was hopelessly inadequate, knew he could say no more, not even in the knowledge the story would be on the news any time soon.

"We're hoping to find someone who perhaps saw something unusual, maybe a stranger, first thing this morning, anything like that Miss Penderman, anything that might turn out to be useful to us." It was his normal approach, and he was approaching boredom, watching her sitting eagerly on the edge of her seat longing to ask all the questions.

Except that she didn't. When she spoke it Willie Broughton who involuntarily sat up straight.

"Well Sergeant, do you know, funny you should say that, but there was a shifty fellow up here first thing, well I don't know, probably around eight o'clock. He pulled up outside, stared at me and drove off in the direction of the Modlum's house, and I thought to myself, well Molly, I thought, there's a shifty character if ever there was one".

"Could you describe him?" an incredulous Willie asked, rather taken aback by the revelation.

"Shifty," came the response, "definitely shifty."

"Mmmm ..... could you describe what you mean by shifty, Miss Penderman?"

"Well, shifty, you know .... shifty." He was wearing an expression that might have said 'this is going to be a long day' and after a brief pause tried again.

"Beard or clean shaven, long or short hair, how old would you say he was? That sort of thing."

"Oh right. Well, clean shaven probably, not sure about his hair, and I'm no good at judging peoples ages, but I'd guess anywhere between twenty and forty, and definitely shifty."

Broughton pondered the issue, considering his best line of attack, trying to weigh up the lady sitting close to him. She had short grey hair, high cheek bones and excited blue eyes, and her lips were moving as if ready to fire the answers to each of his questions. She wore a high-buttoned white blouse with a pale blue cardigan, a bright reddish-brown tartan skirt to just below the knees, no stockings but sensible shoes, exactly how he imagined someone's 'maiden aunt' might look!

To add to this impression her home 'The Dahlias' was, in his opinion, olde-worlde and therefore quirky. It was far from tidy and, he concluded, something in the air suggested it was home to pets as well.

"Miss Penderman, can you explain precisely why you thought he looked shifty? Was it something about his face, or facial features, perhaps?"

"Yes, that's it Sergeant. His face was shifty." Broughton sucked in his lips as if trying to seal them to prevent what he really wanted to say escaping which might then make him appear offensive and rude.

"Did he look .... evil, maybe?"

"Yes, evil. Evil and shifty."

Time to change tack.

"What can you tell me about the car? Make, model, colour....?"

"Ooooh, Sergeant, I'm sorry I know nothing about cars."

"Size, colour, how many doors, did it look new or old."

"Mmmm, well, I think it was a dark colour, very dark blue, and I think it had four doors. It looked big to me, well that is, it didn't look small, and I think it might have been quite new, definitely not old."

"If I showed you some photos of cars do you think it might help?"

"I'd be only too pleased to try."

As exasperated DS pulled out his all-singing, all-dancing phone, played around with it and located pictures of cars which he presented to Molly in hope rather than anticipation. His lack of belief in this procedure was well founded as she failed to positively identify *one*, instead pointing to several that might fit her bill and all it did was illustrate a range of vehicles from small to medium to large. She realised it wasn't helpful at all.

"Please forgive me Sergeant, I'm not very good at this, but I tell you what, why don't you ask my friend Mr Pawden just along the road? He may have seen the same car and its shifty driver, and he could be really useful to you. You see, he loves all those TV murder mysteries and has a library full of crime novels, and I'm sure he'd love to be involved. You never know, he might even solve your crime for you."

It would be difficult to describe DS Broughton's feelings coming upon such intelligence. His mind was a mixture of horror, despair, sarcasm, fear, humour, resignation and disbelief, all the ingredients stirred into a horrible concoction that might've produced a fuse in a lesser mortal.

"We'll be talking to him," he stammered, nearly choking as the words found their way from his throat to Molly's ears. Gawd, he thought, an amateur sleuth, just about all we need.

***

With tenderness and a sympathetic approach DCI Mehedren had been able to ask questions of a surprisingly calm Audrey, and by this medium had learned that Rosemary had been admitted to the Modlum's house at around 6 a.m. There was certainly no body in the hall at that stage, a fact confirmed by a simple nod from Mrs Wandon. The ladies returned five hours later.

Obviously Audrey did not commit the crime, not unless she and Rosemary were in it together, of course. That was most unlikely since the pathologist had made the preliminary observation that death occurred approximately between eight and ten, or maybe seven-thirty and ten thirty at a push.

Possibly.

Nothing more definite until the post mortem was completed.

Mehedren had received the DS's radioed report on the car sighted by Molly Penderman and enquiries were already underway, with the forensic team checking for tyre-prints around the Hop Pickers Oast in any case. It was presumed unlikely the killer was on foot. Meanwhile Willie Broughton had walked down the road to Ernest Pawden's abode and was standing transfixed by the gate, mouth agape.

No, it could not be so. Of course it couldn't. But yes it was, yes indeedee. The property was called 'Whodunit' according to the nameplates on the gate and front door. Oh please God, he pleaded to a higher authority, please don't let this happen to me!

He needn't have worried.

28

The small, neatly kept bungalow, symmetrical with its centrally positioned front door and matching windows either side, overlooking a smart, well-tended garden of postage stamp proportions, seemed strangely welcoming in a way Willie couldn't put his finger on.

The man who opened the front door was equally welcoming. Ernest Pawden was about five feet nine in old money, pleasantly attired with shirt and tie, buttoned cardigan and grey trousers sporting a crease you could cut a cake with. He escorted the Sergeant to the small but perfectly formed lounge and bade him sit in an armchair not dissimilar to the one he occupied at Molly Penderman's.

A job lot for the elderly, he wondered.

The uniformed officer who had already spoken to Ernest had reported the gentleman had nothing to offer but Willie was obliged to follow up each call along this stretch of the highway, a meandering byway that twisted this way and that for no obvious reason, its passage marked by an occasional residence, its progress dogged by potholes.

To describe the interior of 'Whodunit' as quaint would be to do it a mischief. Obviously clean, decor in good order, a place for everything and everything in its place. No clutter. And yet, and yet ... it exuded a strangeness that was hard to define, a friendliness that grabbed you and made you feel warm and wanted, an aura that cried out 'this is home'. It was undoubtedly a place of peace and calm.

Ernest, being Ernest, was watching the Sergeant's reaction closely and assessing what sort of man he had before him. It was some little while until Willie spoke, so taken was he by his surroundings, a fact not lost on the gentleman opposite him.

"Mr Pawden, I believe?" A simple nodded response was sufficient. Broughton continued. "I know you've told us that you saw nothing in this vicinity but you did drive out for a paper in

29

the company of ... let me see ... Mr Pugh-Calford of 'The Vines' just along the road." He looked up from his notes to observe another single nod. "What time would that've been, sir?"

"Mmm ... I set off around ten, picked up Mr Pugh-Calford immediately afterwards, drove to Teynham, and probably arrived back at the Vines, oh I don't know, probably between ten forty-five and eleven o'clock."

"Did you see any vehicles or people in this area during your drive, sir?"

"No, nobody, officer, I'm sorry, nobody at all, and we encountered no vehicles at all except in the region of Teynham, that being a rather busy place on the roads."

"Well, thank you sir. And as we always say if something should come to mind don't hesitate to give us a call, no matter how insignificant the matter might appear."

Willie found himself, for reasons that escaped him, making a further comment he might've preferred to avoid had he not felt driven to mention it.

"Talking to Miss Penderman at 'The Dahlias' she happened to mention that you enjoy TV crime shows, and the books and all that. Is that so, sir?"

"Yes, it is my one weakness and one passion, officer. But I can separate fiction from reality. The novels I read, the television programmes I watch, well, they're simply stories aren't they, officer? I love a good read and a well-told story is engrossing even if it's far-fetched and not like real life at all. The TV murder mysteries are the same: they're simply entertainment and I don't suppose they pay too much attention to factual police work. I expect they get on your nerves sometimes, officer!"

"To tell you truth, sir, I rarely watch anything like that and I'm not a reader, but from what I hear you could well be right where accuracy is concerned. Still, mustn't let facts get in the way of a good tale, eh?" He wasn't sure why he'd added that, but both men smiled and chuckled, and in that moment Willie discovered he'd quite taken to Ernest Pawden without understanding why.

***

While DS Broughton was unwittingly taking a shine to Ernest Pawden Molly Penderman's dark blue car had been located and its driver eliminated from police enquiries.

It had transpired that the vehicle she had seen was the newsagent's. He had brought the Sundays along for Gerald and Eric and had never been that way before, the delivery usually being made by an assistant, but today he was compelled to make the journey himself. And he had a dark blue Ford Fiesta. And he'd stopped outside Molly's to check the address.

What he would have made of being described as 'shifty' is anyone's guess.

But by believing they had identified the car and driver they had fallen into a trap, and a trap that might lead to fatal consequences for an innocent and unsuspecting lady.

Willie had wandered down to the Vines and chatted to Cedric who merely affirmed Ernest's account of their perambulation to Teynham and back, devoid of humans and cars as it was at the country end. One more visit to make and that was to Earth Cottage. The uniform who had attended there rudely referred to the occupants as tree-hugging, save-the-planet types and received an admonishing riposte from the Sergeant, complete with a light-hearted warning about future conduct.

Nonetheless it had been an eye-opening day for Willoughby Broughton, not least thanks to his encounters with Molly and Ernest, the latter proving an unnerving experience without obvious explanation. Added to that he hadn't been expecting a murder, and certainly not one out here amidst Kent's remaining unspoilt and gloriously rural rolling English countryside.

It didn't feel right. It didn't fit 'proper' and it disturbed him. And Earth Cottage was about to disturb him further had he but realised it.

As he walked past the Modlum's 'Hop Pickers Oast' he felt a sad pang. A life had been ended there, ended violently and horribly, and the victim's wife was left to find the body of her beloved husband. It was terrible. But life was becoming all too cheap these days. Mr Modlum could just as easily have upset someone in the high street and been fatally wounded with a knife. Knives were drawn at the slightest provocation, the morons believing their chances of capture were slender, and if caught there was actually little to fear.

Broughton could understand why they might believe that.

But he would do his best, as always, because that was why he joined in the first place. And with such thoughts in mind he suddenly found himself at Earth Cottage.

Chapter Five

Dahlias, Beetroot Tea, Forgotten Sugar and Two Pints of Beer

Sheelagh Mehedren spoke briefly to Willie Broughton and then made her way back to base to get things organised. She could trust Willie to play his part, and now she needed to really start the ball rolling.

At Rose Cottage Audrey had decided she needed some fresh air. Gerald offered to accompany her but she wanted to be alone. He accepted this but asked if he could just linger about, keep a distance, but be there should she require him. She preferred not, but reluctantly gave in without being pestered to do so.

Rosemary was now snoring soundly on the sofa, her attempts at providing comfort reduced to the efficiency and practicality of a chocolate teapot. Eric was chatting to the uniformed officer who had taken their own initial statements and who was now required to remain at the premises.

Frankly, Eric was rather absorbed by the young woman whom he found noticeably attractive, particularly, he felt, in her smart uniform and with her obviously long auburn hair tied back under her hat. All very fetching. They conversed at length, finding each other easy to talk to, and discussed a wide range of issues as well as explaining their backgrounds to each other.

By this medium Eric learned Louisa Scarnett had been born in Walthamstow, east London, and had moved to Kent as a child when her father's job relocated to Maidstone, the county town. Louisa had always wanted to be a police officer but had originally been turned down. A very, very determined lady she had not let the matter rest there and in due course was accepted thanks to hard work, enthusiasm and commitment, an object lesson, Eric decided, for too many youngsters today.

33

He also learned that the murder was now in the public domain.

A short way away, at Earth Cottage, the occupants Sunday lie-in had been disrupted by a plethora of sirens and the startling realisation that something, probably serious, was going on at their neighbours less than half a mile down the road. Both were standing naked in their bedroom watching through net curtains and trying to fathom what all the fuss might be, when a policeman emerged on the lane from behind overgrown vegetation and made for their front door.

Panic ensued. Clayton ripped a pair of pants in his desperation and nearly twisted his ankle in the process, tripping and falling to the floor amidst a flurry of filthy language. Ananya put her top on back to front and demonstrated that she had an unpleasant vocabulary to match her partner's.

Eventually, and looking sort-of dressed, they dashed downstairs and opened the door. The picture before him adequately explained to the Constable why he had been kept waiting.

"Hope I'm not troubling you," he quoth, barely managing to conceal his mirth and joy at having broken up what he assumed was an intimate occasion. Coitus Interruptus, he thought, and that consideration merely added to his enjoyment of spoiling their pleasurable pursuits.

"There's been a serious incident at 'Hop Pickers Oast' and I'd like to ask some questions please. If it's con-ven-ient." He emphasised the last word, dragging it out slowly so as to endorse the view that he hoped it was inconvenient, the true meaning not lost on Ananya and Clayton, the former resolving that once again she was a victim of an –ism, although she wasn't sure which one just yet.

Back at The Dahlias Molly Penderman had finally been appraised of the truth behind all the police activity and had collapsed into an armchair eyes agog, her whole body temporarily paralysed by the shock. The kindly policeman who had brought the news, and who been trained to deal with imparting sensitive and dreadful information, acted perfectly well in the circumstances and gradually Molly regained her composure even if her eyes remained truly wide open.

Once assured she was somewhat recovered the officer went and made a nice pot of tea and sat down to partake a cup with the bewildered and shaken Miss Penderman. Tea, the cure for all ails.

Cedric Pugh-Calford had hurried up the road to Ernest's as soon as the facts were made known and the two sat down to debate the situation. Gareth Modlum, stabbed to death in his home, his body discovered by his wife. Right here in the Kent countryside. Right here on their doorstep. Right here where sheep grazed, hops grew, skylarks sang, tractors ploughed the fields. Right here where so little happened the weekly waste collection was an event.

Knowing his friend's fascination for fictional crime Cedric asked if Ernest had any theories and was taken aback by the answer.

"Oh, Cedric, it's all stuff and nonsense. It's fiction and it's entertainment and it's all written as such. I wouldn't have a clue, if you'll forgive the pun, where to start speculating, I really wouldn't. Besides, you and I know so very little about it anyway." A sudden thought struck him. "Cedric, my dear chap, I've just realised. Miss Penderman is all alone. Good grief, we should make all haste and see if she's alright."

Cedric leaped to his feet, a slight exaggeration, but he moved as swiftly as he could.

"Ernest, you are quite right. Our place is with our neighbour. Let us depart at once, my dear sir." And the two gentlemen with a combined age of a hundred and sixty something checked their appearances in the hall mirror, decided all was right and proper, and set off for The Dahlias.

***

DS Broughton's reception at Earth Cottage had been different from that of his colleague.

For one thing the pair of them were better attired and had gathered their senses and were eager to discover more. He was offered beetroot tea which he had no trouble politely declining.

"We're vegetarians," declared Ms Ghatik with enthusiasm, "and we're hoping to, like, become vegans shortly," she added all rather unnecessarily. Willie noted Mr Mainstreet's involuntary wince. She continued.

"There's no time to lose. Climate change is real and we must all do our part," she disclosed. Willie thought back to the two large top-of-the-range cars, flash jobs, parked in the drive and decided the end of the world might well be nearer than these two believed. Sitting down as invited he conveyed the news as tenderly as he could.

"Do you know the Modlums very well?"
"Oh yes," replied Ananya, "they've helped us with our garden which is now given over exclusively to vegetables, and we have an astonishing range growing this year."
"Well, I have some sad and unpleasant news, and you should prepare yourselves for a shock. I am so very sorry but Mr Modlum has been found dead this morning and foul play is suspected."

He watched the reaction, the colour drain from their cheeks, the wordless lips moving silently, the incredulous look on their faces as the sheer horror sunk in.

"We ... we ... we," spluttered Clayton in a weak and hoarse voice, "we were told there had been a crime but ... but ... but..."

"I'm sorry sir, but we couldn't give further information until we had the situation more in hand and had a better idea of what was going on."

Willie continued with his enquiries but he knew they had seen and heard nothing of any value, especially as they had been abed and immersed in each other most of the morning, well, since they had been awake. It was Clayton who now dissolved into floods of tears, emitting sickly sort of moaning noises while Ananya ignored him.

"Sorry Sergeant, he's the sensitive, emotional one. I'm the strong one, like, in this house. One of us has to be. He saw a dog run over once and cried for five days, and it was all like Oh-Mi-God, y'know, too emotionally distraught to go to work even. He'll be alright soon. Take no notice."

Broughton was speechless. Was this what was meant by a snowflake?

Leaving Earth Cottage a bemused Detective Sergeant stood alone in the lane and tried to remember where he left his car. Must be at the Modlums. He hoped he was right as it was only a short walk. What a collection of characters he'd met today, and that was without having to interview Eric and Gerald.

But he was pleased that Ernest Pawden hadn't turned out to be an interfering busy-body, an amateur sleuth all too ready to get in their way.

He was astonished to see Audrey Modlum walking from the other direction. Surely she hadn't been back to her house? But no, she hadn't, had just needed some fresh air, she explained, and had ambled along the road and back again, not going close to Hop-Pickers Oast. She was fine now, she told him in answer to his query, and strode off in the direction of Earth Cottage and her destination, Rose Cottage beyond. He noticed Gerald Samuels just along the way and presumed he was keeping a long-range eye on the widow.

***

Ernest and Cedric arrived at The Dahlias to be greeted by a policeman who led them inside and announced their arrival. Molly wept with joy as she embraced both.

"Oh, thank goodness you've come. Thank you both so very much," she wailed, overcome with a mixture of delight and grief. "The constable has been excellent and first class company, but I can't tell you how pleased I am to see you. I've not long been told what's happened and it's so ghastly it's unimaginable. That poor, poor woman, and poor dear Mr Modlum. Whatever had he done to deserve that? Do you have any ideas yet, Mr Pawden, I know you're very up on police investigations."

He disappointed her.

"Sorry Miss Penderman, I have no theories, and I am no expert. Sorry." She looked a little crestfallen.

The three subsequently sat and mulled the situation over without reaching any reasonable conclusions, Miss Penderman clearly still very distressed. The arrival of two good friends had calmed and cheered her and now Felicity strolled in to complete the picture of revival, jumping onto Molly's lap to be cuddled and made an extraordinary fuss of. The cat lapped it up as cats do.

The policeman entered and volunteered to make tea and managed to locate a larger pot to brew it in, and he re-emerged a little later with a large tray, the pot, tea-strainer, cups and saucers, jug of milk and a plate of chocolate digestive biscuits.

"Hope you don't mind, ma-am," he offered, "but I thought you might like a biscuit or two. Sorry if I've taken a liberty..."

"No, no, no, of course not, officer, and I can't thank you enough for your kindness and thoughtfulness. It's very sweet of you, and good of you to trouble. So please don't think I'm being in any way critical," Molly added in a critical way, "but you have forgotten the sugar."

All four laughed and a blushing PC nipped back to the kitchen for the missing item and returned within seconds.

"If you're fine now, Miss Penderman, I can be on my way."
"Oh won't you have a cuppa first, officer?"
"No, really, it's time to be moving, and I can see now you're in the best possible company."

"Well, officer, thank you for all you have done. What a marvellous advertisement for a caring force. You've been my absolute angel and I will write and say thank you to the powers that be. My very best wishes for your career; you deserve credit as does your force. You hear so much condemnation for the police these days but I daresay it's not the foot-soldiers who are to blame.

"You have been excellent in looking after this old lady at a time when I might have been overcome by shock without your support."

The Constable's cheeks, which had been a light pink when the discrepancy over the sugar had been drawn to his attention, now turned a deep red.

"Only doing m'job, ma-am. Only doing my job, and it's been a pleasure. And now I'll say goodbye to you good folk and set off. Been a pleasure meeting you all." Molly, Ernest and Cedric rose as one to shake the officer's hand and bid him farewell. After he'd departed Molly mused on the encounter.

"What a lovely young man. Restores your faith in the young, doesn't it?" Both men nodded.

And with that they returned to their tea and biscuits and the subject of the murder of Gareth Modlum, Ernest keen to hear about the shifty driver. If Molly might've been close to being overcome with shock she was now fully recovered in every sense and eager to talk about the day and find out if Ernest did actually harbour any theories.

***

In due course Rosemary's husband, a weary looking object with untidy hair to match his untidy clothes, turned up at Rose Cottage exuding an air of weariness to equal his appearance.

Audrey was back from her brief perambulation with Gerald in tow, and Rosemary was back from her lengthy nap but barely coherent. Not that it bothered Desmond Wandon, for he gave the impression it was pretty much her normal state. In fact, his wife sounded every inch as weary as he did and Eric humorously considered the possibility their lethargic conversation might send both of them to sleep.

The upshot of their tedious discourse was that he would drive Rosemary and Audrey back to their home where Mrs Modlum could stay as long as she wished, and where the police could access her when necessary. Gerald readily agreed to drive the Mini, his enthusiasm just about under control given the sad circumstances of the day, and Eric would come and pick him up.

Rosemary insisted Audrey was to stay with them and found no opposition, Eric and Gerald having no spare bed anyway, and Desmond being inclined to do whatever his wife wanted, as was always the case. It may have been a lifetime of such subservience had led to his resigned and wearied approach to all things.

A quick check with the police and the procedure was carried out, an over-excited Gerald behind the wheel of the noisy Mini Cooper following Mr Wandon and his seemingly spaced-out wife who promptly fell asleep in the back seat. Audrey was in the front and staring aimlessly out of the window. The three cars,

40

Eric in the rear, took a circuitous route to remain well clear of the Hop Pickers Oast, not that the road was open in the vicinity anyway. Closure, they had been informed, could well be prolonged.

And in the fullness of time Ospringe opened its arms and welcomed them one and all.

***

Clayton Mainstreet appeared preoccupied with grief, real and imagined, and suffered in his own over-emotional way while Ananya Ghatik studiously and determinedly disregarded him. He liked the Modlums and was distraught over Gareth's killing, and desperately sorry for poor Audrey. Added to this was the news that his partner intended to make them vegans in the foreseeable future and he was beginning to question his own commitment to the cause.

Time for tears indeed.

Time for reflection on his relationship with Ananya.

He wasn't even sure he wanted to be a vegetarian much longer, let alone take another step along this road. It could be a pathway to a kind of hell, he reasoned. When he also considered that alcohol was a banned substance he had to agree with himself that he had abandoned much in his pursuit of the fair Ananya, his princess, his goddess of love, his heart's desire.

She had won him with her heart and mind, and she had won him with her body, not with fruit juice and lettuce leaves. It was all starting to play on his mind as he sat quietly coming to terms with the ghastly crime committed just along their country lane. Suddenly his partner was standing in front of him.

"What can I do to cheer you up, you miserable sod?" she asked in a manner devoid of sympathy and sensitivity. Clayton looked up and wondered what he did want. Did he want to be

41

taken to bed and ravished to the point where he didn't know what day it was? Not at the moment, he felt. Did he just want to talk about the whole shocking business of the murder? No, Ananya wouldn't approve. Did he simply want to be hugged and cuddled and made to feel wanted? No, Ananya could not achieve that without being overtaken by lust.

"I'd like a pint of beer," he whimpered, and closed his eyes to await the tempest that must certainly follow.

"How about two pints?" she asked. He opened his eyes and saw her smiling face, her own eyes seducing him and destroying any defences he had left. "I have two bottles I've been saving for a treat, my darling. Would you like them now or after I've taken you to the bedroom, like, and ripped all your clothes off and set about your macho body?"

After a second or two the laughter came to both of them. She plopped down on his lap and smothered his lips with hers. He vainly tried to splutter some sort of response through their urgent kisses but failed miserably, and knew in that instant he would love and adore her forever, and would surrender to her every whim. He would follow her to the ends of the earth, believe in everything she believed in, and would worship her in any he could.

Especially if she surprised him with two pints of beer now and then.

***

Molly was recounting the early morning for the benefit of the eager ears of Ernest and Cedric.

"A car came here first thing, you know. A very shifty looking driver. I saw him through my window and told the police all about it. They seemed to think it very important." And a sudden thought, a thought of darkness and menace, flooded her mind. "Oh, do you think I may have seen the killer himself? It's very

42

strange, you know, but I remember now that after he'd driven away I shuddered and said that a goose had just run over my grave. In that moment, and I don't know why, I thought no, not my grave. Oh crumbs, do you think I should tell the police?"

Ernest was comforting.

"No my dear Miss Penderman, there's no need, I'm sure. Your intuition may be quite correct but the police would regard your goose as pure supposition." All three chuckled lightly. "If you have told them all you know about the man driving past then they will definitely pursue that. What exactly were you able to tell them, do please tell us?"

"Well, the car almost stopped outside. He was so shifty, the driver, so shifty. It was obvious he was looking for somewhere in particular and was not familiar with the area. But I'm afraid the police will not think I was much help, more of a hindrance I expect."

"Miss Penderman, I'm certain that's not the case. Were you able to tell them about the driver and the car itself?"
"That's just it, Mr Pawden, that's just it. I was so vague. I put his age between twenty and forty but I may have been wrong, and I knew he was clean shaven and shifty looking. But I was hopeless with the car. Hopeless. I know nothing about cars. That Sergeant Broughton was so kind and patient but must've thought me a useless old dear...."
"Perish the thought, Miss Penderman," Ernest interjected soothingly, "Perish the thought. Please go on."

"He showed me so many photos of cars I became quite confused. I think I said it was dark blue and had four doors but I appear to have identified cars of all shapes and sizes, silly me."

"And what time was this?"

"Ah, now that I'm more sure of. It was around eight o'clock."
"And did you see him drive back?"

43

"No I didn't. The police asked me that, too."

Cedric, who had been listening intently, moved to the edge of his chair to ask his question.

"Did they offer to do an e-fit or whatever it's called, perhaps use a police artist, to try and get a picture of the driver?"

"They did consider it, Mr Pugh-Calford, but dismissed it as my description was so vague, not that they said so, of course."

"Just a thought, Miss Penderman, I used to be an illustrator for a magazine. Would you agree to sit with me for a while sometime and we'll start with a blank sheet of paper and my pencils and however long it takes try and put together some sort of picture?"

"Oh Mr Pugh-Calford, what a splendid idea, yes I would, yes I would."

Ernest threw another suggestion into the melting pot.

"You two might even be able to do something with the car. What about it, Cedric?" And Cedric and Molly showed their enthusiasm, Molly having completely dispensed with her distress. "Miss Penderman, would you do me the favour of calling me Ernest, please? In the circumstances it would be much easier."

"Oh Mr Pawden, I mean Ernest, thank you, and I am Molly."

"And I'm Cedric," cried Mr Pugh-Calford keen not to be left out of this new familiarity.

At this stage they were unaware the car and its shifty driver had been all but eliminated from police enquiries. They were equally unaware that the outcome of Molly and Cedric working together might put Molly's life in danger.

For the present they were distracted by Felicity ambling into the room again clearly in the mood for being fed, and this being a priority of the highest order it took precedence over the murder putting paid to further discussion on the topic.

44

***

In Ospringe on the outskirts of Faversham Audrey was being settled into what was to be her temporary home and not liking it much.

For one thing she had no change of clothes, no night clothes, no personal things, nothing.

Nobody had thought about that aspect. Rosemary, still dazed but improving, offered to lend her whatever she needed pro tem and they would arrange with the police to collect her own stuff as soon as possible. Desmond fussed around both women like a mother hen, an action that annoyed Audrey even more. She hated being treated like a child, and Desmond added to his offence by calling her sweetheart in a most condescending and patronising way.

Why don't you pat me on the head, she thought to herself, and say 'there, there'.

Rosemary was a different size and shape to Audrey and her clothes would not fit. Audrey did manage a private laugh at the prospect of Rosemary's knickers sliding down to Audrey's ankles in the middle of Faversham town centre. No it wasn't funny, but it provided some light relief for the new widow.

She was shown to her bedroom, fussed over extensively, given an assortment her hostess's clothes to try on, furnished with toiletries, towels and heaven knows what else besides and finally left alone 'to rest'. Her ears were singing with the incessant chatter of the Wandons. And then there was silence.

For the first time she'd been left truly alone.

Silence at last. She was in her own space, and it was shared with nobody else. No Gerald lurking up the lane. No police officers to question her or watch over her. No paramedic to examine her. No Rosemary and Desmond to proverbially pat her head.

Gently, slowly, carefully, Audrey lowered herself onto the bed amidst the abrupt arrival of peace and tranquillity, and as she sat there came the pain.

Came the pain, came the horrific realisation, came the stunning memory of Gareth lying dead on the floor. The agony took control of her body and she flung herself face down on the bed with a pillow over her head lest the Wandons should hear her.

She was torn apart, all her senses shattered, and she wished to be dead so the fearsome, unbearable anguish might subside.

She wept violently and called silently to her husband to come back to her knowing he could not answer her call, and never would. And her wretched pain was complete.

Chapter Six

Yawn, Stretch, Scratch

Sheelagh Mehedren and Willie Broughton were looking for motives without success.

"No sign of a struggle, unless the post mortem suggests otherwise, no sign of any ransacking, no obvious signs of searching. Unfortunately, Willie, only Audrey Modlum can tell us if anything's missing, and we need her to do that urgently."

After a brief silence marked by head shaking the DCI continued.

"We've found his wallet, mobile phone, laptop, cheque book .... absolutely everything you'd associate with straight-forward theft .... all there, all untouched. Unless, of course, Audrey tells us otherwise. Their main computer, jewellery, small items of value, even an unlocked cash-box containing twenty seven pounds forty pence. All undisturbed.

"If you were a merciless robber you'd take what you wanted after knifing the bloke, wouldn't you?"
"Unless he or she was disturbed, ma-am; always a possibility Gareth shouted or screamed and the killer thought they heard someone coming in response."

The two detectives pondered the mental pictures before them, the DCI once again tapping her teeth with her pen.

"Thing is, Willie, a desperate thief might still grab a handful of stuff if they believed, knife in hand, last victim dying on the floor, that they had little to fear. Somebody else's life wouldn't matter to them. How we doing with prints?"

47

"Mostly Gareth's and, we assume, Audrey's, although we're waiting to get hers."

"And forensics? What's the latest?"

"No tyre tracks in the lane directly outside, nothing on the drive, no footprints. Just a great big zero. We've obviously eliminated Mrs Wandon's car – she used the drive. Gerald Samuels and Eric Furness came to collect the ladies and Mrs Wandon's Mini, and we've eliminated them, of course."

More teeth tapping, more head shaking, and an increase in sighing which had hitherto been scarcely noticeable.

"We need Audrey's prints, and sadly we need her to ferret through her house, ideally scour it thoroughly, but that really ain't the easy part, Willie, definitely not for her to have to face. What do we know about Gareth Modlum?"

"Well ma-am, he was an engineer, that is, a gas engineer. Retired three years. Worked for British Gas doing mainly domestic stuff, servicing boilers and that sort of thing. They moved here from Allington where they'd been for fifteen years. Before that Snodland. We'll be finding out more tomorrow when the world yawns, stretches and scratches and gets out of bed for another Monday morning. Not got any other gen on Audrey other than what you learned yesterday, mainly that she hasn't had to work for years."

"That Mrs Wandon was a handful. Don't suppose, do you Willie, there's any chance she was having an affair with Gareth? Still, wouldn't add up really. After all it would be more likely that Audrey would kill her rather than her own husband. But, thinking about it, maybe I'm wrong. You know, hell hath no fury and all that."

"Don't know much about scorned women, ma-am...."

"And don't bother finding out. You won't like it!"

Next they considered other factors, the Detective Sergeant going first.

48

"We thought we had one big, big clue. Miss Penderman and her shifty driver! Wow that was a performance I could do without revisiting..."

"Don't be rude about council tax payers, Willie..."

"She did her best but then we learned about the newsagent and that wrote that potential clue off as a non-starter. Nobody else saw or heard anything. The newsagent saw no other vehicle or person in the area. Perhaps the killer was on foot; plenty of well-marked footpaths criss-cross that part of the countryside."

"Mmm ... I follow that. Find out where the nearest other roads are where someone could park and take a relatively short walk. Those two guys, Samuels and Furness, they're keen walkers, have a chat with them. They were just setting off through the hop field..."

"Hop garden, ma-am..."

"You'll hop if I get hold of you in a minute. Facetious git. Anyway, talk to them. I don't think you've had the pleasure."

She concluded her comments with another one of her smouldering leers in Willie's direction, and he returned her look with an unpleasant kind of knowing smirk. Willie had, from time to time, wondered what it would be like if Sheelagh ever got hold of him and concluded that in any case it might be an experience he'd not lightly recover from with any alacrity. Pleasure or pain? Could go either way, he felt.

***

After being summoned for a sandwich she didn't want, and for that matter didn't eat, Audrey was allowed to take a bath. This was how she imagined life in a care home might be. Behind the locked door she ran a particularly deep bath and into it poured copious quantities of all the different body washes and shower gels she could readily find.

The result was a glorious mass of bubbles that overflowed everywhere. She giggled manically as if to say this was her revenge on the fussers as she now called them. Testing the water

49

and finding it to be not quite hot enough she ran some more, and giggled again as she heard water running down the overflow. More revenge.

She stepped in, sank down quickly and watched as bubbles and water slurped over the top before the overflow could get a grip. And she giggled at the spectacle. Her thoughts turned to the early years of the marriage as she luxuriated in her bath, warmed by its soothing hug, freshened by its cleansing properties.

Audrey might have liked a family and was confident she could've withstood childbirth. It was child-making that was so disagreeable. Such an unpleasant way to create something so wondrous as new life. Gareth had been her only love and he seemed all too keen on child-making in those early days but gradually, thanks to her lack of interest, he tried less and less. She had assumed that it was a masculine thing and that once you had seen off the initial frenzy of activity a husband and wife could settle down to an enjoyable existence.

Totally unbeknown to Audrey Gareth had started taking his frenzy elsewhere, his occupation giving him appreciable scope to make contact with like minded individuals. It had proved a happy hunting ground and he developed unwritten slogans along the lines of "The gas man's coming" and "Now we're cooking on gas" with which to amuse his associates in frenzy.

But with the passage of time and the advancing years Gareth slowed up and eventually phased frenzy out of his life altogether, a spent man indeed. Thus it was that he came to appreciate life with Audrey all the more, taking to retirement like a duck to water, and between them they made their relationship precious, fun and rewarding.

Now it was all over and more tears fell as the water's tender embrace slowly morphed into a grip of imprisonment. She pulled herself together, washed swiftly and emerged to wrap herself in the large, thick white towel Rosemary had provided. Dry, she stood in front of the full-length mirror. This is what a widow looks like, she muttered to herself, and pulled on her friend's nightdress which was rather similar, she thought, to climbing into a tent.

And with that her mild humour, her defence against all the horrors, returned. Donning an oversize dressing gown and slippers that actually did fit, she went downstairs to face the fussers and a mug of Horlicks, an almost inevitable mug of Horlicks.

Apologising, she made her excuses before they could set about fussing her and headed back to the sanctuary of her bedroom with her drink, and hopefully to the comfort of blessed sleep.

And in the darkness of this part of rustic Kent slowly but surely Sunday made its way towards midnight and the coming of Monday.

***

The lane being closed Gerald Samuels faced an uninviting and extended journey to work on his bike so Eric Furness drove him to Faversham, he not being on duty until late morning.

Ananya Ghatik had been away early in order to reach the outskirts of Brighton in good time to attend a site meeting, whereas a happy Clayton Mainstreet was busy preening himself as the rush hour passed him by. He was working from home today prior to driving down to Bristol Tuesday where his latest project was taking shape. No doubt he was encouraged, in his present mood, by the prospect of two nights away.

Ernest and Cedric had left The Dahlias early evening, content in the knowledge that Molly was settled, and had promised to meet at her premises for morning coffee Monday. She had both their phone numbers and strict instructions to call without hesitation if any concerns arose or she became frightened or worried. As it happened the only event of any note was Tom

51

coming home at daybreak with a mouse dangling from his mouth.

After Audrey had retired her friends the fussers had spent the next hour and a half discussing what they might do with her to make her life more bearable, without realising that not being fussed over was top of Audrey's list.

In the morning Desmond had taken Audrey tea in bed at an ungodly time and informed her breakfast was in three-quarters of an hour. His guest wanted neither tea nor to be instructed on culinary arrangements in the household. Being left alone after a restless night would've fitted the bill perfectly.

But she dragged herself downstairs wearing a baggy top and the only pair of trousers that kept up by themselves, her hair undone, her face devoid of make-up despite the fact Rosemary had supplied a generous quantity and variety of items for the purpose. She arrived in the kitchen.

"My sweetheart, come and sit here, come and sit here," cried an over-zealous Desmond, full of bonhomie and fuss, waving his arms unnecessarily as he forfeited his seat at the table, and guiding her into position, patting her shoulder as she sat down as if to praise her for completing the feat. My goodness me, Audrey thought, if I'd been a dog and just fetched a ball he couldn't have done that any better.

Rosemary fussed over the breakfast menu, recommending the full English, complemented by toast and marmalade and steaming hot ground coffee, and refused to accept Audrey's request for a bowl of cornflakes and nothing else.

"I'll do you some bacon and egg anyway. Desmond will get the cornflakes, won't you Desmond? And I'm doing plenty of toast. Just have what you fancy, dear. But you must eat my pet. Do try and force something down."

As it happened it was all Audrey could do to chew and swallow the cornflakes. She wasn't interested and what aggrieved her rather more was Desmond sitting at her side unsuccessfully encouraging her every mouthful she took. In the end she feigned sickness and rushed to the downstairs loo where she slammed the door, made a throwing-up noise and sat down on the seat contemplating murder.

Not a million miles away DCI Mehedren's incident room was taking shape and Willie Broughton had just arrived with a large bacon bap to hand which he had no trouble enthusiastically chewing and swallowing.

"God, that's disgusting, Willie. An orange would do you much more good."

"An orange, ma-am? Give me the pip, that would...."

"Might make you a better peeler. Peeler, peeler .... geddit, geddit?"

"Oh very witty."

"Wassmatter, boy, you had a bad night?"

"No, a late one if you remember, ma-am. Oh no, of course you don't, you weren't here. You left me in charge and went home to bed..."

"Privilege of rank, Sergeant. One day, when you're a DCI, *you'll* be able to go home to bed. Anyway, what time's the team meeting set for Willie?"

"Eleven pm last night. You missed it, my beloved one of high rank."

"Another remark like that and your rank will be lowered to Constable!"

He touched his forelock, knelt on the floor at her feet, begged forgiveness and advised the time for the team meeting.

"Like a man to beg, Willie. On his knees even better. You're learning. Now, give me an update."

"Well, ma-am, no more info from forensics and the post mortem is at ten this morning. The search of the area started again at seven, and I've been studying the Kent County Council website which gives detailed data on footpaths. I'll show you the results when you're ready. No other news, apart from the fact it's *on* the news, and our PR people want a media conference."

"F-f-f-fudge, of course they do. Okay, I'll check with them, leave it to me. Now I want to know everything we can learn about Gareth Modlum right down to what day he changed his underwear."

"Ma-am, ma-am, too much telly, that sounds ever-so Sweeney."

"You're too young to remember the Sweeney, and come to think of it, so am I."

But murder is too serious to be sidelined by humour, and within seconds the mood had changed in the incident room as more officers arrived for the meeting.

"Another thing, Willie. We're talking Sunday morning in the country here. Was it important that Gareth was alone, was it mere coincidence, did the killer know Audrey was out? All that sort of thing. At the moment I'm not buying into a theft gone wrong. One part of me thinks it's pure murder and that Gareth was the intended target. Keep our options open nonetheless.

"Lack of forensics says we could even be dealing with a pro. Who knows? I don't want to push Audrey for obvious reasons but the sooner we know if anything at all has been stolen the better. And we can get her prints in the meantime."

***

Ernest had taken Cedric to Teynham for the papers, Molly had asked for two, the Telegraph and the Mirror (odd bedfellows Cedric felt), and they were heading for The Dahlias full of anticipation tinged with sadness over the killing.

They were still shocked, upset and full of compassion for their neighbour, Audrey, but their emotions were experiencing a degree of excitement they couldn't yet explain.

54

The papers took some searching. Ernest examined his Daily Mail, turning the pages as he scrutinised each item if only briefly, and ruefully concluded that it was many a long year since such a killing made front page news. Murder, especially through knife crime, was becoming too commonplace.

But he located it on page seven. It was a similar situation in the other papers.

The two men had been surprised when reaching Molly's to discover that a reporter had called in person not twenty minutes earlier, but otherwise there seemed little sign of media activity apart from a helicopter circling just after first light. Ernest had been able to confirm it was not the police or the air ambulance.

"What would we do without you, Ernest?" Molly gushed with over-active adoration. "Now, I must tell you I told the journalist about the dark blue car and the shifty driver, and he wanted more details which sadly I couldn't give him. He was quite disappointed but he said he'd get more information from the police if he needed it.

"He said he'd spoken to the gentleman at Earth Cottage this morning, now what was his name? Oh yes, Mr High Street or something, and he hadn't seen or heard anything."

"Jolly good, Molly, we were talking about all our neighbours the other side of Hop Pickers Oast on the way to Teynham, weren't we Cedric?"
"Oh yes, I'll say so. And it sounds as if we may be able to walk that way even though the road's closed to traffic. Do you think we ought to have a stroll in that direction, Ernest?"
"What a splendid idea," chirruped Molly, almost clapping her hands together. Ernest poured cold water on the plan.

"There really isn't any point, my dear friends, in fact it might make us look rather ghoulish. After all, there's nothing we can do and we would be passing a house where a man was brutally murdered only yesterday. I'm sorry, but it still makes me shudder. And just suppose Mrs Modlum was there for any reason? We'd be sightseers. Not the done thing."

"Ernest, you are quite right, of course. We are in danger of not behaving at all properly." confessed a disappointed and saddened Miss Penderman. "It wouldn't be neighbourly at all. It's just that I thought you were so good at crime, Ernest, and you might want to try and find some more clues."

"Thank you, Molly," a modest Ernest said in accepting such high praise, adding his own caveat, "but as much as I enjoy the books and films I have no special skills. Better leave it to the professionals, my dear Molly. But thank you again for the accolade."

"In all the years I've known you, Ernest, I've always felt that you fancied yourself as a bit of a detective, and now you're being very self-effacing if I may say so." Cedric's comment was delivered with a gentle smile that spelled respect allied to a little leg-pulling. The three laughed as was becoming their way; Molly was, in that regard, fully accepted, and evidently shared their humour.

About a mile along the lane Clayton Mainstreet had been busy on three projects, the prime source of employment being the work related to his forthcoming trip to Bristol. The second project had been personal grooming; he was always like this the day before he set off for anywhere. The word 'pristine' could've been invented just for him. He had to be pristine.

The third matter had been triggered by the reporter's visit.

He was puzzling the killing and had given in to another burst of tears in front of the hack in the hope it might get his picture in the papers, unlikely as there was nobody with a camera. He liked the Modlums and was really broken up by the awful slaying of a man he considered, with very good reason, to be a friend.

What if there was a madman out there and he was the next victim? He looked out the window but there was no police officer there to guard him. He was alone, just like Gareth Modlum yesterday, and he managed to work himself into a lather of distress dreading another ring at the doorbell.

Help! He was a prisoner, he dare not go out! The killer might be lurking in the undergrowth or hiding behind the raspberry canes in his own garden. And his partner wasn't due home until late in the evening. It was a long day to be alone and afraid. Thus did Clayton reduce himself to a nervous wreck, a situation that played merry havoc with his work and put him way behind schedule.

Drink! He needed a steadying drink. Now, how to get one without leaving the house? He now had a fourth project on his mind, wishing he had a bottle of whisky tucked away where Ananya might not easily find it. One for the future that. When the phone rang he screamed and jumped a foot in the air before pulling himself together. It's only the phone, it's only the phone he told himself, and wept with joy when he saw it was Ananya's number.

"Just a quickie like, darling," she rattled down the line, and was stopped dead as Clayton gabbled away his sorry tale at the rate of nineteen to the dozen. "Whoa, whoa, lover boy, take it easy, only got a couple of seconds, just time to say love-you, really. Sorry, got to go, pleased you're okay and see you tonight. Bye." And she gone leaving her partner clutching the receiver and mumbling all the things he wanted to say and hadn't had time to do so.

But the call had given him some courage, or at least the call plus his desire for alcohol had done so, and he grabbed his wallet and car keys and made a dash for it, shaking with fear as he spun out of the driveway and accelerated away, free and safe at last.

***

DS Lucy Panshaw had arrived at the Ospringe residence of Mr and Mrs Wandon tasked with assessing Audrey Modlum in the hope of escorting her back home.

Rosemary would insist on sitting next to the widow and clasping her hand during the ensuing interview, but Desmond had taken the hint and vanished, with luck forever Audrey prayed.

Lucy chatted calmly to Audrey, ignoring unnecessary interruptions by the hand-clasper alongside, and combined the appropriate air of sympathy with a display of simple common-sense and friendliness, without being overbearing, patronising and over-talkative. By this medium she won Audrey over and quickly ascertained Audrey wanted to get her own clothes and things, and had no obvious qualms about going to Hop Pickers Oast. Quite the reverse.

"I'm level-headed, Lucy, and I will cope. I want to get my initial reaction, whatever it proves to be, over and done with. I want to stand at the spot where I found Gareth and I want to come to terms with it if I can." Unsurprisingly this frankness and determination undid Rosemary who was once again in floods of tears and full of wail. "Besides," Audrey added markedly, "I need some air and some space."

The comment wasn't lost on the DS who realised at once the meaning behind Audrey's words.

Rosemary wanted to go with them and couldn't be dissuaded, but Lucy did succeed in packing her off to find Desmond to put him in the picture. In her absence, a brief moment, Audrey was blunt.

"They mean well, they are good friends, but they are fussers and I am up to here with being fussed and nursed and patted like a good dog. When we get home I would be more grateful than you could imagine if you could engineer some purpose for Rosemary to get her away from me for a while. I'll be alright,

Lucy. I just want to be alone there. It's something I have to do. I'm a strong person. I may be overcome but I may not be." Lucy nodded and said she'd sort something out.

Mr and Mrs Wandon returned together and gave the Sergeant a perfect demonstration of how to fuss, nurse and dog-pat a bereaved person. Gor, Lucy thought, what a pair of thoughtless prats.

And so the three women set off in Lucy's car, with Audrey, by this time, being the one doing the dog-patting to Rosemary so distraught was the latter. The DCI was right, Lucy decided, Mrs Wandon is behaving as if it's her husband who's perished.

***

More to please his friends than because he wished to do so, Ernest Pawden had started making some notes when in truth there was so little to note. In fact when they watched an early afternoon news bulletin he faced having to cross some notes *out*. The police, it was reported, had eliminated a car and driver seen by a witness in the area.

"Well, really," exclaimed Molly, sounding very hurt and indignant, "and he was such a shifty man."

Cedric sighed, almost sad that his artistic skills would not be needed and it was left to Ernest to save the day.

"Speaking as a would-be detective, and with all my knowledge of criminal investigations, such as you believe I have, may I suggest this." Molly and Cedric showed the signs of people listening intently and being oblivious to Ernest's deprecating humouring. "Please, if it's convenient to you both, why not go ahead with the artwork together? We may be able to ask the police if the result matches the vehicle and driver they've eliminated."

"My dear sir, what a marvellous idea. What do you say, Molly?"

"Ernest, Ernest, what a treasure you are! Oh Cedric, I knew Ernest would have the right idea. I think he's been hiding his light under a bushel, too modest to admit his talents, don't you Cedric?"

"I couldn't agree more, dear lady."

Molly had, by arrangement, prepared some sandwiches for their earlier lunch and not all had been devoured. By common consent, and in celebration of the euphoria that had surrounded the three of them, the unconsumed remnants of lunch were brought out, enhanced by a selection of biscuits, to be enjoyed with a delicious cup of tea.

Meanwhile Clayton Mainstreet was enjoying a different sort of delicious beverage and overcoming his fear and making a pig's dinner of his work.

Not used to drinking neat whisky the drink was having a marked effect on his ability to do whatever it is architects have to do, and do with great accuracy, and he was finding his failure all rather funny. Not a good time to take a phone call from DS Broughton especially when, without looking, he didn't bother to check the call-identifier and presumed it was his partner.

"Hello darling, my cute little living sex doll," he slurred down the phone.

"Good afternoon, Kent Police here sir, is that Mr Mainstreet?" It took a while for Clayton to adjust to this unexpected intelligence.

"Whooozzat?" his blurred voice scrunched into Willie Broughton's ear.

"DS Broughton sir. Mr Mainstreet? Earth Cottage?" Realisation was with Clayton who was now wholeheartedly embarrassed.

"Yuzzz, it's me, off ... off ... off ... shargent. Shorry. Shorry."

60

"If you're home sir, would it be alright to come and see you? I'm in your area and another word would be appreciated. Is Ms Ghatik at home too?"

"Nose .... she ... she ... *away*. But I'm here."

"If it's inconvenient......"

"No, no, no, come when you're ready and have a dwink."

Willie ended the call. He knew when someone was inebriated.

The visit to Earth cottage was every bit as pointless as he knew it would be. He trudged along to Rose Cottage believing Mr Mainstreet faced a fate worse than death when Ms Ghatik arrived home, envied him not a jot, and grinned at the light-hearted prospect of Clayton being the next murder victim.

He knew Messers Samuels and Furness would not be home but decided to knock anyway since he was in that neck of the woods, and it was on his way out of the front garden that he noticed something.

Chapter Seven

A strong woman, a nasty weapon and footpaths galore

DS Lucy Panshaw arrived at Hop Pickers Oast and was waved into the driveway by a fellow officer.

Audrey commented on the event.

"Wondered what it was like to be allowed to pass that blue and white police tape and now I know." Lucy dismissed the remark as a kind of throw-away line that was part of Audrey's defence mechanism, whereas Rosemary debated it openly and at length.

"Oh shut up do," an exasperated Audrey grumbled, leading to an outburst of tears and indignation by Mrs Wandon. "Rosemary, bless you for your kindness, but for heaven's sake woman, much as I appreciate all you are doing for me, the kindest consideration you could offer me now we are here is to take my arm and simply be quiet." Hurt, Rosemary complied with some reluctance, and resolved to inflict her pain on Desmond later that day.

The three women entered the house and without incident passed through the hall into the front lounge where they sat for the time being to enable Audrey to gather her thoughts and emotions. The hall had been totally cleaned and the blood-stained carpet removed for forensic examination.

Audrey was pleased she was coping. She had secretly dreaded seeing blood but there was none to be seen.

Of course, it was impossible for Rosemary to either sit still or keep her mouth still. Eventually she just had to speak, she just had to.

"What do you want us to do, Lucy?" she asked emphasising great impatience. The officer was not about to be deflected from her pre-determined course of action.

"When Audrey is ready, and not before, I'd like to take her finger-prints and then we can all decide what we want to do. Audrey, we need to know if anything is missing. If you don't feel up to it today that's fine. If you do you can go around the house at your own pace also collecting the things you want to take to Rosemary's. We won't disturb you unless you need our help. I'll sit here with Rosemary." This was music to Audrey's ears, and a terrible put-down for Mrs Wandon.

"I'm fine, thank you Lucy. You may have my prints now and then I'll tour the house as you've suggested. If you can give me a notebook and pen I'll note anything out of place as I go and I'll certainly let you know if anything's missing." Rosemary was dumbstruck though whether because she was being sidelined or because Audrey was so self-confident was not recorded.

***

DS Broughton radioed in and asked if the search had reached as far as Rose Cottage to be told yes, it had, inclusive of the garden. He found himself looking at something glinting in a rose bush that on closer inspection appeared to be a knife, a large knife. He summoned help.

There was something of a quandary here as either the knife, assuming it to be the murder weapon, had been missed or it had been placed there later in the day after the hunt. It was a thick bush and he could quite understand nobody wanting to rummage around in it without the necessary protection although, of course, officers had such safeguards. And there was the question of how far you could go in someone's garden unless you had strong enough suspicions.

Willie learned that Rose Cottage and its environs has been covered about one in the afternoon and it was much later that the occupants left for Ospringe. Eric and Gerald departed for their walk about eleven, just before Audrey and Rosemary made their grim discovery.

All four of them came to the cottage about midday and there was a police presence until they vacated about three.

Did nobody see the knife? Was it there to be seen?

If the latter then either the killer or an accomplice returned, a very brazen action indeed but, naturally, that return could've been overnight.

The forensic team inspected the site and then gradually withdrew a fearsome appearing object from the bush, a double sided knife, the stained blade over a foot long. A more detailed examination of the garden and the lane outside was now under way, and DCI Mehedren was coming out hot-foot.

Eric, being the first point of contact for the property, had received a call from the Detective Sergeant to appraise him of developments, and with the agreement of his employers had abandoned his day's work, departing his last port of call near Folkestone to drive home.

Mehedren screeched to a halt outside causing Willie to make some caustic remark about Starsky and Hutch. She scowled at him, a withering look that might've reduced him to a pile of ashes.

"We don't know for sure it's the weapon, but it fits the bill, especially being about an inch and a half wide, and by God I know a blood stain when I see it. Any theories Willie?"

"A guess at the mo, but I think it's been put there since yesterday afternoon, possibly overnight. And that would mean one cool cookie. You see, ma-am, the occupants walked past it when they went out, and we had at least one officer outside here once Audrey Modlum et al reached the cottage. The garden was searched about one o'clock. Mr Furness took Mr Samuels to

64

work about seven thirty this morning and they walked past it again. Unless, of course, it wasn't there even then."

"Frighten me some more, Willie. And what's et al mean when it's at home?"
"And all, and all others, ma-am."
"Well, why not say so? We don't all speak French."
"It's Latin, ma-am."

If Sheelagh's previous glare could've added another corpse to the picture her eyes now bored deep into Willie's and fried his mind, shrivelling up his senses.

"Sorry, ma-am," he whimpered with all the meek deference he could muster in the vain hope he would be instantly forgiven, and knowing it would be remembered forever and hurled at him from time to time together with expanded mention of other transgressions. There was no escape.

"If it's been there all the time someone will have questions to answer. But I agree with you, Willie. We could indeed be looking at more than one person, but the fact remains it seems the knife has been brought back almost to the scene of the crime, and that beggars belief.

"It's almost as if the killer stayed to watch developments, perhaps to laugh at us. What's the news with Lucy and Mrs Modlum?"
"They're at the Oast now, we have Audrey's prints, and she's going through the house, slowly, carefully, apparently with a notebook in hand. Lucy doesn't think she'll miss anything, she's in control alright, and appears very clear-headed and methodical. Doing it alone. Lucy is keeping Mrs Wandon company in the lounge, so I'm told, and Mrs Wandon don't like it much!"

***

Audrey had picked up a large holdall and was filling it with various bits and pieces as she went. Her clothes she laid out on the bed, for Rosemary had brought a suitcase and Rosemary could damn well pack it later.

Alone at last.

She studied the bedroom from two aspects. Was anything missing, anything tampered with, anything out of place, whatever? Secondly, she gave herself time to grieve, time to look at the bed she had shared with her beloved, time to experience the anguish of knowing they would share this room no more, time to cherish fond memories, time to recall his body left where it fell.

Slipping down to her knees at the end of the bed as tears swept down her cheeks she prayed to a God she didn't believe in and once more pleaded with Gareth to come back to her. Within minutes she had conquered the pain sufficiently to rise, wipe her face, and set off for another room, her notebook untouched.

And that was the way her notebook remained. She reported back to Lucy that nothing had been touched, nothing was missing, and she could see nothing out of the ordinary at all. It was exactly as she would've expected to find it had the tragedy not arisen. Rosemary was sent with her suitcase to collect the clothes, giving Audrey the chance to thank Lucy and speak her mind.

"Mostly I've coped with this Lucy, but I know there will be times, as there have been here today. I loved my husband and I openly admit I've no idea how much I will miss him. We were so very happy here. Right now I regret going to play golf. I had a hole in one, you know, when I should've been here by his side, playing my part in what happened. That's going to be my greatest sorrow.

"I know, I know, that regret will only eat me up, devour me and destroy me if I let it, and I won't Lucy. It won't win. I'm strong enough. And do you know, in a way I can't describe, I've been happy here today. You can't believe that, can you? But I'm

66

at peace, maybe that's what I mean. I'll have no qualms about coming home and living here again in due course." And the slightest smile spread on her face as Lucy nodded, knowing that Audrey would pull through, and knowing she admired her for her resilience.

This lady would not be beaten by anything. Not even a bloody good fussing by Rosemary who now re-appeared and wanted to do nothing but hug her friend. Audrey condescendingly allowed her to do so, and then the three set off for Ospringe.

***

At The Dahlias Cedric had agreed to spend the following morning with Molly, and come armed with all his equipment apropos his proposed artistic endeavours with the witness. He and Ernest set sail for Whodunit and a refreshing break from the aftermath of the murder.

"There still seem to be plenty of police up here, Cedric old chap, and much coming and going. I suppose they're still looking for clues and I wouldn't be surprised if their enquiries aren't already leading them towards the killer."

"It's a shame about Molly's car and shifty driver, Ernest, but maybe we'll turn up something ourselves." Ernest smiled inwardly to himself. If they want to believe that, it may provide some comfort as true horror of events sink in over time.

"Cedric, don't raise Molly's hopes too much," he said as soothingly as he could, "because I'm certain the police are sure of their facts."

"I understand that, Ernest, my dear fellow, but it's worth a try. You obviously think so, and besides it's about time you turned your talents, of which you are overly reticent, towards theorising about the case. You've hardly put forward any ideas and I know you better than that."

"That's because there is so little to go on. But I tell you what. If you and Molly come up with something, a starting point for

67

me, I promise I will give it all necessary consideration. How does that sound?"

Both laughed, Cedric because he appreciated the humour behind the suggestion, Ernest because he knew his friend did. Clapping each other on the back they entered Whodunit in good spirits, no doubt to participate in drinking some.

***

In due course, and following a most successful site meeting, Ananya Ghatik was on her way from Brighton, elated by her achievements and the fact they were recognised by those who mattered in this scheme. Bathed in glory she motored north-eastwards surrounded by the throbbing, thumping music she loved and which filled the car to capacity, little knowing her partner was lying virtually comatose having filled himself to capacity with whisky.

It was difficult to imagine which one faced the greatest shock.

Eric Furness, his working day cut short, arrived home and was briefed by DS Broughton. He was visibly shaking and Willie escorted him to the comfort of his lounge lightly holding his right arm lest he should stumble, for he seemed unsure of his step.

Willie's colleague Dira Graham, being a warm-hearted and caring officer, offered to make tea and slipped out to the kitchen while Willie, being a good detective but a typical male, watched the curves of her uniform trousers as she swung seductively out of the lounge.

The resultant tea brought Eric back to life and the realisation he needed to contact Gerald. This exercise having been concluded with Gerald knowing he now had an unexpected lift home (Eric would collect him later), Willie was able to ask him for more detail about his Sunday morning.

"I know you're both keen walkers and you were off Sunday morning when you came upon events at Hop Pickers Oast. Can you tell me a bit more about your day up to that point, you know, say from the time you opened your eyes, so to speak?"

"Well, we don't get up early Sundays, Sergeant, and this was no different. It's the only day we have papers delivered. So we have a relaxing breakfast, take it very easy and, if we're going for a walk Mr Samuels prepares the food we'll take. We're a bit old fashioned, and like a home-made picnic rather than a pub lunch. I'm good at map-reading so I tend to plan the journeys.

"Yesterday was the same. Being a lovely day we took breakfast out the back, sitting around our garden table flicking through the papers...."
"Can you give me any times, Mr Furness?"
"Oh yes, yes I see. Well, I suppose we got up about eight thirty and retired to the lawn around nine-thirty. It must've been well after ten that we came inside, cleared up after breakfast and got ready for our walk. I'm afraid I've no idea what time we set off, but the officer who took our statement worked out it was possibly ten forty-five-ish."

"So you wouldn't necessarily have been conscious of anything going on at the front of the house?"
"Not at all. I can show you, if you like, but we are completely enclosed at the back. We also sleep at the rear so even though we have our windows open in good summer weather, again we wouldn't see or hear anything at the front."
"Given your map-reading skills, sir, and your local knowledge, I wondered if I could put an idea to you, something you could help me with perhaps?"
"I'd be delighted to help, Sergeant, especially if it helps bring the killer to justice. The Modlums were good friends and neighbours and we haven't come to terms with this horrible situation."

Willie produced his own maps, mainly taken from the County Council's website and now adorned with the marks of felt-tip pens of various colours, and asked Eric about his theory. Could someone park on a nearby road and reach the Hop Pickers Oast on foot easily and quickly?

"Oh yes, definitely, Sergeant. You've done some excellent research here if you don't mind me saying so." Willie blushed. "I could point you to two spots which in any case have green marks on them suggesting you've done your homework well." Willie's embarrassment rose to the next level.

"Just a minor correction to this one. I assume the orange lines are the related footpaths?" Willie nodded. "This one wouldn't be easy or quick. Allow me, if I may borrow your pen?" And Eric drew a longer course using three paths. "I'm counting on the fact which you no doubt appreciate, Sergeant, that the killer would either need this local knowledge and/or had carried out some research, visiting the area before yesterday."

Yes, thought Willie, and that would point to a premeditated attack, which was precisely what he had suspected. He thanked Eric and took advantage of his host's offer to view the back garden where both men and PC Graham sampled the peace, a place secluded and not overlooked, and the loveliness of the burst of May colour amongst the many plants. Above them blue sky and the sounds of birds singing in their airborne travels.

It did not seem possible to any of the three humans that a murder had taken place about a mile along the road, a hideous, violent and repulsive killing, so out of place amidst this pastoral setting, this earthly paradise in the Garden of England, now so disgustingly sullied.

Meanwhile the initial post mortem results had confirmed the cause of death, and pointed at an instrument such as the one just discovered at Rose Cottage as the means. A single blow, straight through the heart, delivered almost horizontally in front of Gareth Modlum. He stood no chance.

Time of death narrowed to around seven-thirty to nine-thirty. Now the knife would be examined.

Chapter Eight

Monday Evening

Monday evening at the Ospringe home of the Wandons was clouded with a strained atmosphere.

Upon their return from Hop Pickers Oast Audrey had more or less gone straight to her bedroom to unpack, relax and avoid being fussed over. Rosemary was determined to fuss at whatever cost and was frustrated when her guest would not permit such indulgence.

So Mrs Wandon had to content herself by loading her burdens onto Mr Wandon, bewailing the issue of being kept downstairs at the Oast while Audrey went through the house, and bemoaning the fact the widow wanted to be alone. Desmond, whilst agreeing with much of this nonsense, and feeling put out that neither of them could fuss adequately, did manage to placate his wife by the simple expedient of fussing over her instead.

"Darling, of course she wants some time alone, and she'll want us alright, just you wait and see, and we'll be there for her, won't we? Now why don't you prepare our dinner? I'm sure Audrey would love another of your meals, and it might help her as well." This statement ignored the truth that Mrs Modlum had not yet enjoyed *any* meals at Ospringe, having merely picked at them or left them altogether.

But Rosemary was not to be so easily won over.

"We're her friends, Desmond, and we should be by her side at all times, just in case we're needed."
"Dearest darling, you are an angel, an absolute angel, so thoughtful and considerate, gosh I love you, y'know. I appreciate you're right, but we must give her time and space, my pet."

"Oh, I suppose so, but don't think you can get round me with words of love and fulsome praise. I'm too old for that sort of thing. But I will go and get dinner on. Pour me a sherry will you please, love?"

***

Ernest and Cedric, having enjoyed a wee dram or three, parted company for the night, Cedric to return to The Vines for his dinner and a quiet evening with *Daniel Deronda* accompanied by Mendelssohn's third symphony amongst other musical works. Ernest felt that another episode of *Foyle's War* was in order once he had prepared a modest supper. After that he felt he might make a start on Ian Rankin's latest book.

But as he toiled happily in his kitchen his mind wandered involuntarily to the murder and then to his late wife. Mrs Modlum was not merely faced with the pain of loss, he reasoned, but the agony of how her husband met his end, and he concluded he knew nothing of the awfulness of such feelings.

Edna's death had hit him hard; his life partner, his best friend, his soul mate. That was bad enough. But when the one you loved had been killed and so brutally? Well, the pain must be indescribable, unimaginable. In that brief interlude he resolved that he would play the detective, for he knew Cedric, assuming he had retained his craftsmanship, would work patiently with the ever-eager Molly until he actually got somewhere.

However, what was the point? The police had eliminated Molly's shifty driver, yet suppose she and Cedric produced something rather different? Might the police look again? With that he decided he would go to see Eric and Gerald at Rose Cottage the following evening and try to gather any pieces that might assist him. After all, they had been directly involved, so he understood. What he didn't know was that a knife had been found in their garden.

***

Eric had collected Gerald and gone home to Rose Cottage now unspeakably aware that one of their beloved rose bushes had been hiding a guilty and rather morbid secret. They didn't fancy any dinner as such, so Gerald prepared a kind of buffet that they could pick at as the evening progressed. To this they added a bottle of *Soave,* an inexpensive number, but a tipple they could both savour.

Tonight, welcome though the wine was as a pleasant additive, its consumption lacked the usual level of pleasure they might have expected, for they were too shocked by the dreadful discovery coming so soon after the crime itself. They had barely gathered their emotions following the departure of Audrey, Rosemary and the police on Sunday afternoon, having been first upon the scene when the ladies made their gruesome discovery, and then having to cope with poor Mrs Modlum and the over-reacting Mrs Wandon, and then the police enquiries.

And now this.

During their buffet, which Eric had to admit was delicious, he mentioned how he had assisted DS Broughton with local footpaths allied to the Sergeant's theory, producing a map to show his partner what it was all about. And Gerald became intrigued.

Gradually, their enjoyment of both buffet and wine improved as they became engrossed in the latest developments, this enjoyment leading to the unscrewing of a second bottle of Soave. The more wine they had the more interesting the whole case appeared until they were in about the same state of excitement as Molly and Cedric.

They started discussing all manner of theories, some too fantastic to warrant consideration. Nonetheless, it did help them overcome their emotional tangles and they soon found they were coping with the situation far better than had been hoped.

73

Half a mile along the lane, at Earth Cottage, someone else was about to have to cope with an unexpected arising.

***

It had gone ten and Ananya Ghatik was looking down at the dishevelled figure of the man she loved who was snoring loudly in an armchair. Her eyes took in the half-empty glass of whisky on the adjacent table and the bottle nearby which supported, in her estimation, less than two thirds of its original content.

Disbelief was her companion.

She did not know what to do apart from wanting to throw a bucket of water over the idiot. First she took the remaining drink, disgusted by its smell, and poured it down the sink. In a second or two of compassion she deliberated if anything might have driven him to such lengths, but eradicated any such kindly thoughts from her mind instantly, electing to believe her generosity of two bottles of beer had ruined him.

What a weak man! Giving in to temptation so easily the moment her back was turned. And then a nasty feeling struck her; did he behave like this when he was away? Suddenly she felt nothing but contempt and sickness, her whole understanding of love being brought into question.

Was he just another bastard? And she shuddered as coldness fell upon her. Yes, a weak man. But wait, she could save him! She could.

Surely that was her purpose for she had brought him so far, surely she could rescue him and provide salvation, surely she could bring him out from his darkness into the light.

One thing for sure, he was going to pay for his debauchery! Oh boy, was he ever going to pay!

***

Not far away another person was snoring, well, that is, breathing heavily in a sound sleep, a peaceful sleep devoid of guilt, untroubled by conscience or worry.

Molly Penderman had fed Tom and seen him amble off into the twilight for his unseen, unknown nocturnal escapades, then had retired to bed in the company of Felicity who probably had no idea what fellow cats might get up to at night, with even less desire to find out.

Felicity had purred on top of the duvet as Molly's hand had reached out to stroke her and tickle her ears, possibly as much excitement as this cat ever required. Lights out, the two were in the arms of Morpheus without a care in the world, a situation Molly was inadvertently about to change thanks to Cedric and Ernest, a condition that would add personal danger to their well-ordered and innocent lives.

If sleep beckoned for most residents of this rustic idyll it did not do so for the police who had been working hard on the murder case. Confirmation they had found the murder weapon was awaited.

The life and times of Gareth Modlum, gas engineer retired, were laid bare and spread amongst them.

Basically an insignificant life from the point of view of a murder enquiry. His work record appeared to be exemplary but his extra-marital pursuits had not yet come to light. There didn't seem anything at present to suggest he was killed for any personal reason, and it looked unlikely this was a robbery gone wrong.

Against that was the new theory the killer may have been planning the crime to the point where he, she or they had parked away from the lane and travelled on foot cross-country to carry out the deed. Less chance of being seen, of course. But returning to the scene to discard the knife? That just didn't make sense.

There was always the possibility, and an extremely slender one, that the knife had been missed on the searches, but Willie Broughton had spotted it when he wasn't looking for it. First option then for the officers was the concept the weapon had been brought back and planted at Rose Cottage. Was there any significance in that, maybe? Everything had to be considered.

Audrey Modlum had confirmed nothing missing. Taken into account was the chance that in her bemused state she had overlooked something, but it was a less likely scenario.

No prints that shouldn't be there, no forensic evidence worthy of note.

They were left with the impression Mr Modlum opened the door to his killer, either somebody he knew or a stranger, and was slain almost immediately, the assassin making good their escape taking care to leave no evidence.

Was this a professional hit? If so, why Gareth Modlum? Mistaken identity? Given the element of planning that was rearing its ugly head it was perceived unlikely such an error would occur. The general view was that the chance of this being a random slaughter was receding into the distance although you never discounted anything you couldn't prove.

Another theory was that the assailant wanted something, something material maybe, some information perhaps, and Gareth wouldn't part with it. The problem with this idea was its one weak point. If the victim said nothing doing why kill him outright? Surely you'd want to try and "persuade" him first?

If the intruder was after a material object (such as a valuable antique) you would search the house once you had eliminated the custodian. If you wanted access to Gareth's bank account and other financial wherewithal you'd keep him alive with dire threats and maybe some violence to make your point quite clear.

If you wanted access to his computer you'd need any relevant passwords and presumably you'd still want to steal it.

Again, if they wanted information surely they would have tortured him or at least threatened him first. But maybe not, who knows? The post mortem revealed no other injuries.

Another drawback to the theft hypothesis was that, if the new idea of the murderer arriving on foot was correct, without a vehicle outside they would've had to carry whatever they took back to wherever their car was parked. Unless what they wanted was small and light, of course.

Audrey had told them they had nothing of any worth other than personal items that were of sentimental value. The most expensive possessions were common things like the computer, laptop, television and so on. She also gave them a brief resume of her recent life.

Her last job had been with a telecommunications firm but she had been able to leave that ten years ago, effectively retiring with Gareth's blessing to the role, as she put it, of a kept woman.

"It was our little joke," she'd revealed with a tender and short-lived chuckle, "but Gareth had always said that as soon as we could afford it I could give up work and start to enjoy my autumn years. He knew how much I loved gardening and when we moved to the Oast I had a patch large enough to really make my mark. He'd done very well as an engineer and retired with a handsome pension. You'll appreciate my own pension income is small, but welcome extra money for all that."

In truth, they were an ordinary sort of couple, proceeding down life's highway in their own way and as their income permitted. There wasn't any obvious reason why either of them should attract enemies. Audrey had, for a while, been a very active member of a Womens' Institute until she fell out with other members over refreshment preparing duties. Hardly a dispute that might end with her husband's death, but you never know!

For the time being the whole business was an enigma but Sheelagh Mehedren had a good record at fetching out all the pieces of a jigsaw and making them fit together in a clear picture, and it was a clear picture, the result of Cedric's skill (and patience) that was going to add a new dimension.

Chapter Nine

Tuesday

Social media, with its tendency to be anything but social on occasions, provided the channel for an unpleasant and insensitive, and largely anonymous comment on Gareth Modlum's death. For the police it lifted the lid on the victim's otherwise equally anonymous and uninteresting past.

It read:

'Got what he deserved. Serviced my boiler once then serviced me many times. Dumped me like the rubbish when he tired of me despite telling me I was his everything, his one and only. Said I was the pilot light in his sex boiler. Never knew he was married. Blokes, they're all the same.'

So, there was another side to his life. Did Audrey know about it, and how to ask? Could it be a tenuous excuse for murder? Was it just a piece of malicious mischief making? Well, it represented another line of enquiry.

***

For the eagle eyes in news media circles a post like that was seized upon very quickly and by Tuesday morning the murder had been moved forward a page or two in the dailies.

Now the papers wanted to get in touch with Mrs Modlum, and an event that was sadly becoming all too commonplace to warrant extensive coverage was in danger of being landed with all too much publicity.

Rosemary Wandon stared at the paper unable to grasp what she was reading, knowing she must shield it from Audrey yet make Desmond aware of the article. Ultimately she failed in both measures as her husband could not follow what was going on and made sure Audrey was handed the offending paper when she asked for it. Audrey flicked through the pages and swiftly fell on the item while Rosemary stood trembling and threw in a diversionary tactic also doomed to failure.

"Would you like another slice of toast, my dear, and do you think we should go for a walk this morning? It's such a lovely day. Do have another piece of toast. Yes, I think the sun's going to shine soon....."

"Be a love, Rosemary, and fetch me a cup of tea. I've found an article, which I'm surprised you didn't see, and as it's about Gareth I want to read it. Undisturbed, if you don't think I'm being rude." Rosemary thought precisely that but retreated to the kitchen mumbling unintelligibly.

Belatedly Desmond took up his wife's gauntlet without actually realising why and made matters worse.

"Is it a good idea to be reading that, sweetheart, you'll probably end up upsetting yourself."

Audrey treated him to a scowl so black that he sunk back into his shell without further comment.

She was more than upset as she read on. Here was someone, hiding behind anonymity, claiming Gareth had wooed her, made love to her, and abandoned her, with the paper hinting the writer, or a person acting on the writer's behalf, might have arranged the killing. Her Gareth, her husband, her beloved man. How dare they!

It was nonsense, of course, and Audrey dismissed it as such, hurling the paper to the floor and shaking with rage. How dare they!

"How dare they!" she finally screamed, sitting bolt upright, shaking and causing Rosemary to squeal and throw the cup and saucer into the air. The tea went everywhere but it muted the situation and the three instantly set about the clearing up operation, Desmond muttering 'oh dear' at frequent intervals, Rosemary crying and whimpering, their guest becoming the calmest of all.

No harm was done to anything, other than a good cup of tea being lost. Good order was restored with Audrey taking charge, an action which led her to believe that such a role was the best way of coping with life at Ospringe, and she elected to adopt that attitude forthwith.

Now, how to deal with the story and prevent its proliferation?

***

There being a fair amount of paraphernalia relating to Cedric's past professional life, Ernest kindly fetched his friend and his equipment the short distance to The Dahlias by car, but declined to stay saying he wanted to work quietly on some theories. This wasn't untrue but was less true than Cedric and Molly believed it to be.

Molly, as ever, was the perfect host, offering Cedric refreshments which were accepted quite gleefully, and making her guest very much at home while Felicity wandered about in a displaced way as if sensing she was being supplanted.

Cedric was full of ideas with which he enthusiastically regaled Molly over French Fancies and coffee, none of which she truly followed to any great degree. Food and drink taken he then set up a large easel which he adorned with a large pad of white paper and asked her if she had a kitchen stool or some such that he could use. Aforesaid stool was produced post-haste.

"Actually, I think it best if you sit here Molly so you can see clearly what I'm doing. I'm used to working standing up," he lied, continuing, "so I'll just get my pencils and we'll begin. First of all we're going to work on the car...."

"Oh Cedric, is that wise? The officer showed me so many photos and I couldn't be sure, I really couldn't."

"My dear Molly, this is different, very different. Just watch this."

And he drew what could best be described as a small child's sketch of a car, basic in that it had an upright body, a bonnet and boot, four wheels and the head of a driver. Molly chuckled. Cedric didn't mind one bit and chuckled himself.

"Dark blue?" he queried.

"Yes, but Cedric I know it was daylight, it should've been clear but I'm having self doubts on the colour."

"That's nothing to worry about, Molly. What is important is what you saw through the window, and that's why I'm using large paper. As we progress I shall take my work outside and you can look through the window, just as you did Sunday morning, and see what I've produced. We keep adjusting it until you're satisfied."

"Oh Cedric, it's so good of you to humour me like this. I'm just a silly old girl...."

"Perish the thought, neither silly nor old, as we shall demonstrate with this exercise."

She went all coy and Felicity wrapped herself around Molly's legs as if to emphasise she agreed with Cedric's assessment, or at least to make the point the cat didn't want to be left out.

"And we may yet come up with a vital clue for the police, and that, dear lady, is our priority," he added and decorated his face with an utterly disarming smile that flustered her even more, but in a way she found she rather liked being flustered.

The work took over two hours, and involved the devouring of more French Fancies, chocolate digestives and coffee, and occasional moments of humour such as when Cedric fell over Felicity, collapsing in laughter in an armchair while a much amused Molly soothed the cat's hurt feelings. Fortunately neither man nor beast suffered any injury other than dented pride.

82

Finally, Mr Pugh-Calford stood outside holding up a picture and Molly shouted at him from inside the lounge.

"Cedric, Cedric, that's it, that's really it. Oh that's brilliant. What a clever man you are. That's the car I saw." He returned indoors with a triumphant look about him. He had done this assignment several times and made countless tweaks, patiently chivvying his host along, encouraging her to ask for changes no matter how small or unimportant they might appear.

"Well Molly, I shall now show you this car on my i-pad." His fingers roamed around the screen with all the dexterity of a younger person fiddling with their mobile phone, tablet or whatever, as seen on the streets of Britain everywhere. "There," he said, "is that it?"

"Yes, yes, yes," squealed Molly, clapping her hands and jumping up and down, "Oh Cedric, you are just so clever, so very clever, so very talented."

They were looking at a photo of a blue Kia Rio.

***

It had been impossible for Clayton Mainstreet to go to Bristol.

He was nursing the mother of all hangovers, was not in a fit state to drive, and phoned in sick citing the murder and his resultant distress. And all was of nought compared to the wrath of his partner which had been laid firmly at his door from the moment he first opened an eye to find Nemesis standing in front of him, arms folded, with eyes that might have sliced him in two.

In fact, he felt as if he had indeed been cut in two, and that was exactly how Ananya wanted him to feel. She wasn't done with him, and there was little chance of her ever being done with him over his latest fiasco. Having the headache from hell was one thing, having a living nightmare rattling on at him ceaselessly was a yoke too much to bear. Except there was no escape from either headache or nightmare.

Finally came relief. Ananya had to go to work and set off for Ramsgate but not without issuing warnings of a frightening nature with the added ingredient of threats of physical violence should he go off the rails again. He knew she meant every word.

He passed the time in a painful daze, flitting between a viciously disturbed sleep and bouts of waking unrest until the morning slipped away and his head recovered, whereupon he was sick. But he felt better, fresher and more comfortable, and it was in such state that he opened the door to Ernest Pawden early afternoon.

***

DCI Sheelagh Mehedren looked around the kitchen at Hop Pickers Oast.

It all seemed eerily quiet, as every other room had done. She'd wanted this visit, just her, nobody else, and the chance to explore every nook and cranny. Drawers, cupboards, all examined with care being taken to disturb nothing. Down in the hall where murder most foul had been committed it all appeared surreal, as if it was hard to imagine such violence had taken place there, as if by removing the body, carpet and cleaning up it might be easily forgotten.

The bedroom had a ghostly ambience, but not because Gareth Modlum was haunting it. There was something else. How did Audrey feel, Sheelagh wondered, coming here, notebook in hand, perhaps overcome by heartbreak and grief, and facing it all alone even if by choice?

Visiting the lounge once more the DCI sat on the sofa for a few minutes while her brain whirred and her eyes darted about, and inspiration was sought. Then it came to her.

This house is trying to tell me something, she comprehended at last. There's a clue here I can't yet see, or can't recognise for what it is. I've seen all the photos but it is physically being here that makes it so real. You can't stir your intuition with photos. And my intuition says there's something to find, probably not a material item hiding from view, possibly something took place here that we need to know and only the house itself will tell us.

Frustrated, she turned to leave, knowing the answer would not come today, and picked up the host of letters on the mat. Might as well take them to Mrs Modlum as it would give Sheelagh the opportunity to ask discreetly about Gareth's alleged wanderings. She looked through. Most appeared to be cards, of course, some maybe brief notes (the envelopes were handwritten), and there were several other routine items such as catalogue communiqués.

A last look up the hall. Being a police officer did not divorce her from human suffering and she knew tears had welled up in her eyes. She wanted to hold them back, be professional, but her sadness was too strong, and in her solitary circumstances alone in the hall she wept, for the shocking tragedy, for widowed Audrey, then went out, closed the door, locked up, blew her nose and got on with being a good detective.

Another good detective, DS Willie Broughton was chewing the cud watching the sheep doing the same, and waiting for the DCI. He was the Chief Inspector's chauffeur for this trip and having parked outside the Oast wandered along to the footpath, meandered some yards along it, strolled back looking all around him and asked himself by what act of sacrilege could such a romantic, bucolic and delightful spot be defiled by an atrocious inhuman feat.

From the other side of the lane the sheep eyed him with a hint of suspicion lest he should suddenly fall upon them and they be required to dash away as sheep are apt to do. It did not stop them chewing and it did not prevent Willie mentally debating if the killer came by car or foot. He opted for his speculation that it was on foot. From there it was short jump to the next point.

Did the thug know the area because he or she lived locally? Did they live even closer? Was the murderer here, right in their midst? A neighbour perhaps? It was worth considering.

There was Miss Penderman. With a coarse giggle Willie thought that in a crime novel it would be her because she was the least likely candidate. So what of Mr Pawden, crime novel reader supreme? He might think he'd know how to carry out the perfect crime! Mr Mainstreet – now there was a suspect alright. Full of remorse, driven to drink, his grief a manifestation of contrition as the sheer repulsion of what he'd done sunk in.

His partner – Ms Ghatik – the self-proclaimed strong one. No sign of conscience there. Maybe she did it and Mr Mainstreet was going to pieces because he knew and couldn't betray her! Then there was Mr Samuels and Mr Furness, first on the scene. Was one of them having an affair with Mr Modlum and the other took offence?

In Willie's mind Mr Pugh-Calford must be guilty solely because he had a double-barrelled name!

Reason told him that not one of the immediate neighbours actually had any obvious grudge against Gareth, or any clear motive, and certainly not one that might lead to death. But that didn't rule them out, of course.

And after all that supposing it was a pro coming by car? Driving from the west early morning they would've gone past both Rose Cottage and Earth Cottage where all the occupants were asleep.

"Willie, I think they're called sheep out here in the country and they make lovely meat and thick woolly jumpers. Stop staring at them like you fancy them and come and drive me away from here." Strong sarcasm and only a hint of wit tinted the DCI's words, and they brought the DS out of his reverie with a start.

"Sorry, ma-am. I was actually thinking about the case....."

"Of course you were. Which of those sheep did it, Willie, and are all the others going to cover for him?"

"Her. They're all ewes, ma-am, and I think they're innocent."

"Have you questioned them? It goes without saying they must've seen the killer."

"No, I haven't. They won't answer questions without a solicitor present."

"Get in the car Willie, before they witness another murder."

***

Ernest Pawden was taken aback at the familiarity.

He had quite naturally introduced himself as Ernest Pawden but did not expect Clayton Mainstreet to address him as Ernest at this early stage of their association.

"Hi Ernest, I'm Clayton, come on in and sit y'self down wherever. So you've come about the murder. Loved Gareth, y'know, and I love Audrey. Real people, like. It's done my head in. I'm off work I'm so hurt by it all, really cut up."

His visitor took this all in, tried to make some sense of the disjointed dialogue, and sat down convinced the young man opposite was so discomposed by events that he was beyond normal conversation.

"It's good to meet you Mr Mainstreet ... um ... Clayton, and I'm sorry we haven't talked before although I believe we may have waved upon passing along the lane. I was well acquainted with the Modlums and I understand they helped extensively with your garden."

"Sure did, fella. Without them we wouldn't have a single veg out there and it's very important for us as vegetarians, like, to grow our own."

Being called by his first name was bad enough, but now he was 'fella' and Ernest's heart sank. Is this what it's all coming to, he mused. Clayton continued.

"So what brings you up the road? I know, I expect you've left some flowers at the Oast. I took some along there today myself. My partner, Ananya, brought them home yesterday."

Ernest did not agree with the trend for public grieving and had most certainly not placed flowers at the Oast although he did notice, with some irritation, a stack of them along the front of the property. He couldn't for the life of him figure out why people did that. Probably imported the idea from America, he reckoned, an idea that added to his irritation. He chose not to pursue his thoughts with this over-sensitive young man.

"I'm very sorry, er ... Clayton, but I have no idea what you do."
"No of course not. I'm an architect, Ernest, and my partner's a builder. That is, she's not often found up a ladder laying bricks, like, she's more sort of middle management. But believe me she can lay bricks alright. She's a real girl, my Ananya. Can do all sorts of things connected with building work, but she's in her niche, like, running projects. Got a degree y'know, so she's knows what it's all about. What did you do Ernest?"
"I was an accountant. Probably sounds a boring profession but it taught me to pay great attention to detail. Tell me Clayton, what sort of things do you design, if that's the right word?"

Clayton was becoming absorbed in the conversation and forgetting to be grief stricken, a point Ernest did not overlook. He was in danger of appearing quite cheerful as he slipped into his stride.

"Yay, design is good for me, Ernest. I get involved in commercial design mainly, y'know, drawing up plans for shopping centres, larger developments like that. Not houses like. Although nowadays some of these town centre regeneration deals include apartments and so on, helps keep everyone's nose clean in this day and age, if you follow me." Ernest felt he followed only too well. Add some private homes in and a project could more easily be sold to a planning authority or a cynical public. Clayton was still talking.

"Working on one such at present. Should've been somewhere near Bristol today. Brownfield site. Developers got it through by including a mini-arcade of shops, which I've been helping design, along with their application for 870 homes, inclusive of a kind of village hall, y'know, community centre. All looks good on paper. Whether anyone will take a shop there, well, who knows. But it gets the houses built."

Ernest was slightly concerned at the way Clayton ran down those he worked for. Not very good public relations, biting the hand that feeds you. Possibly not very good for his own employment prospects!

"Do you and your partner ever work together?"
"How we met, how we met. But we've avoided it since. Work and pleasure not mixing, eh? We just hit it off from the get-go. Ananya helped me see the light. That's why we're vegetarians, soon to be vegans. Climate change is real, Ernest, and we've got to look to the future."
"Please forgive me being intrusive and personal but will you be having a family, do you think?"
"Yeah, I should say so. Ananya wants millions of kids. No seriously, she says she'd like four or five. And we gotta give them that future, we gotta do all we can to combat climate change for their sake."

Ernest would've liked to ask where over-populating the world benefited climate change but desisted, not being one to cause offence. So he changed the subject and moved on to the murder which Clayton was more than ready to discuss. His distress had vanished completely to be replaced with eagerness and an arrogant desire to get his opinions across, forcefully if necessary. Ernest proved a good if bored listener.

89

Clayton became a little excited projecting all kinds of outlandish concepts which stopped just short of death by alien invader from outer space. But Ernest did now learn all he needed to know about the extent of this couple's involvement which was basically talking to the police after the killing. They'd seen nobody, seen nothing, being either asleep or utterly immersed in each other to the exclusion of everything else. That was Ernest's reading of the situation which Clayton thankfully did not explain in great detail, especially with regard to the latter occupation.

Ernest left shortly afterwards leaving Clayton to his non-existent grief and forthcoming veganism, and headed towards Molly's.

***

Originally today had been set aside for Rosemary to service her husband's car.

Their garage had an inspection pit and the walls were adorned with cupboards full of tools, and all the objects you might associate with a commercial garage. Rosemary was a petrol-head, an ardent fan of motor racing, and a mechanical tinkerer.

Her Mini Cooper was only her current pride and joy. She would move on once the novelty had worn off. Desmond called her his Kwik Flit Fixer and left her to her own devices. She was never happier than when covered in dirt and grease and grime buried in the workings of a motor car.

They had met at Brands Hatch but Mr Wandon never had quite the same attachment to motor racing as his wife.

Unfortunately the servicing was going to have to wait. Mrs Modlum needed to be fussed over.

So Mrs Modlum was somewhat relieved when DCI Mehedren arrived on the doorstep.

Once in the lounge Sheelagh handed over the post which Audrey flicked through, pausing once to withdraw a handwritten envelope. This was ripped open, a brief observation of the letter inside was made, the letter being returned to its envelope which was replaced in the pile, the entire episode witnessed by the DCI whose curiosity was roused.

"Chief Inspector, you may have seen in today's papers a scurrilous accusation made on social media by an anonymous person." Sheelagh nodded, pleased a difficulty had been removed from her visit. "It's utter nonsense. Can people really post such claptrap and get away with it?" Sheelagh nodded again, this time with sadness knowing it was all too true. "Well, it's disgusting and I shall ask my solicitor to look into this and see if there's anything to be done."

"And it is nonsense, Audrey? Sorry I have to ask....."
"I've said it is. Of course it is. I was his wife and I'd have known, believe me, I would have known as most wives would. He wasn't the type."
"Would you have any objection to us checking out the computer, laptop and his mobile phone? It's just a formality so we can write off the idea of a revenge attack. It might even give us some clues as to where to look next, things we can investigate."
"I take it then that you are short of ... what are they called? ... oh yes, leads, and do not think it was a robbery or anything like that?"

The DCI gave this careful consideration. If her pen had been handy she would most surely have tapped her teeth with it.

"We've eliminated nothing. We are short of leads, yes, but we do need to start digging below the surface, and I can assure you we're good at it." Audrey gave the impression she herself was having a ponder before finally coming to a decision.

"Yes, alright. Please search anything you wish. You have the keys. I'm prepared to assist in any way I can because I want them caught and dealt with, whoever it is. Our password was 'all4oneand14all'. I'll write it down. Rosemary, pen and paper please." Mrs Wandon, deprived of a day messing about with a car, found fetching a pen and some paper a poor second but executed her duty well and with alacrity.

Mr Wandon had been banished to the kitchen but without instructions to provide refreshments thought it preferable not to prepare them unless asked. This was a poor appreciation of the situation, for which he was roundly upbraided when Rosemary burst in to ask where the tea was.

Lunch was being served at The Dahlias where Miss Penderman had a good appreciation of the situation. After his sterling efforts creating the mystery car Cedric was now working on the shifty man and looking tired and hungry. To fortify him Molly had put together 'a little number' as she called it, salmon and salad followed by homemade ginger cake, both elements devoured with gusto by her visitor.

The pair were getting on famously.

"I hope you don't mind me asking, Cedric, but have you ever been married?"
"No dear lady, but I have been in love. When I was young I wooed a very wonderful lady in Gillingham where I lived and worked. She would've married me but her father objected in view of my perceived poor prospects, and in those days a father's word could be law. So she had to give me up. It was a beautiful love, Molly. Not like today where, if I have the expression right, you chat someone up and then, well, go to bed with them to see if you like them.

"We adored each others' company, shared so many interests and so on, and I would have dedicated my life to her, making her happy every day of her own life. As our friendship evolved just holding hands was an exciting pleasure, and it was ages before we shared our first kiss and, do you know, it felt as if we'd been very naughty going that far! How times have changed. There's been nobody else so here I am, a confirmed old age bachelor. May I ask about you, Molly?"

"Of course you may. There have been no men in my life. I think my parents may have discouraged me. As you say, a different age. I've never had any interest, Cedric, and feel the better for it. I love my cats and I've had a few in my time, and that's all the close company I've required. Does that make me a sad old spinster, Cedric?"

"Certainly not. An honest lady, an honourable lady. Your cats are very lucky. By the way, do you know why we refer to unmarried ladies as spinsters?" Molly shook her head. "Well, centuries ago, before the industrial revolution, when wool came to mean wealth the spinning was done by the young unmarried girls who became known as spin-sters." "Oh Cedric, you're such a wheeze, so full of knowledge. Now do you fancy tea or coffee?"

Cedric fancied coffee.

And in time they put the car aside to proceed to the shifty man.

Chapter Ten

Together Now Together

During the mild summer evening Ernest Pawden made his way up to Rose Cottage, humming a pleasant tune, the name of which escaped him, and watching all around him, birds, sheep, a handful of harmless fluffy white clouds, a rabbit darting across the lane.

He didn't let the dark, unhappy and dread feelings engulf him as he passed Hop Pickers Oast, the feelings he had given in to when walking to Earth Cottage earlier, but he did once more scorn the plethora of flowers at the roadside. Nonetheless, he stopped to read some of the labels, finding the bunch from Clayton and Ananya and, in his opinion, the soppy words they had written, but also coming across one colourful collection without any name on its tag.

Three words scrawled untidily: 'Together now together'. What did *that* mean? An odd thing to say, really, the sort of thing you might write if, for example, a widow had just passed away and was at last re-united with her late husband. Ernest puzzled it while he looked at others but then moved away, still baffled, and duly strolled past Earth Cottage en route to Rose Cottage.

It had been an interesting and revealing day, Cedric working a minor miracle with Molly and coming up with the Kia Rio, but the shifty man had proved a step too far, the final outcome being none too clear with poor Molly unable to add anything to the completed item.

Not so much shifty as simply unrecognisable. The resultant 'face' suggested full cheeks, possibly a sign of the man's portliness, and an age nearer the top end of Molly's first thoughts which had been anything from twenty to forty. Cedric and Ernest agreed that, as far as could be ascertained from vagueness, a revised figure of forty to fifty might be more in order, but then again even Molly felt the 'face' could easily be sixty, now she came to think about it.

Eric opened the door and invited him in, insisting it wasn't at all inconvenient, was no trouble whatsoever, saying he was delighted he'd called. This overcame all Ernest's apologies for turning up out of the blue. Further, he was taken to the back garden where Gerald was reclining in a lounger, and offered a glass of fresh orange juice he couldn't refuse.

The murder was inevitably the topic of conversation from the outset which enabled Ernest to relax and tackle his subjects of interest without concern.

This lovely May evening, so warm and intoxicating to the senses, so peaceful, the surroundings so very Kentish with the sound of sheep and the vision of hops and apples growing around him, gave Ernest a strange awareness of the oddity of the situation. Discussing the cold-blooded killing of a neighbour they knew well was more than out of place, it was indecent.

But discuss it they did. Eric and Gerald told their visitor about the knife and he, in his turn, explained the work Cedric and Molly had carried out today, work marked by success and failure. They listened to each other intently. Ernest wanted to ask about their newsagent.

"Do you know what sort of car your newsagent has?"
"No idea," admitted Eric, "but I'll give you his number and you can ring him."
"But you have no idea what time he came Sunday?"
"Not a clue, Ernest, but ask him. Usually our Sunday papers are delivered by a member of staff. We understand it was the first time the owner had to bring them and having never been this way relied on Satnav which is one step up from useless out here. Apparently he stopped at each house in turn till he located Rose Cottage."

After more general chit-chat, especially relating to over-reliance on Satnav, Ernest asked about the knife.

"Obviously you didn't know it was there, and the police couldn't have seen it even when they searched. So my guess is it was planted here more recently. Please tell me more about the footpath theory." Eric produced his ordnance survey map and demonstrated the routes and parking places he'd agreed with DS Broughton.

Ernest was sharing their intensity of interest and becoming quite excited by the prospect he was doing exactly what the police were doing, and that allied itself comfortably to his knowledge of murder investigations as carried out in his novels and TV series. Suddenly, he felt a warm glow of a much deeper interest and knew at once he was truly getting hooked, as he believed the word to be.

He was dying to get home to write up his notes and analyse his work.

**

The knife found at Rose Cottage was indeed the murder weapon.

Enquiries of the search team exonerated those present, for it was agreed there was no way they could've missed it had they been as painstaking as they claimed they were, and there was nothing to contradict that view.

By coincidence DS Lucy Panshaw had been struck by the same label on the flowers that had baffled Ernest and now brought it to DCI Mehedren's notice.

"People do odd things, Lucy, but we shouldn't write anything off at this stage. Tell you what, shall we send someone up there to note all the names and messages? Not been unknown for killers to leave flowers at the scene, the bastards." Lucy was pleased her information appealed to the boss and was thrilled it was to lead to further research.

Gareth's computer, laptop and phone were being checked out. Audrey said there was nothing private therein from her point of view other than her bank account and other similar data all of which they were welcome to check. This made a pleasant change from dealing with someone who wanted such personal matters kept private even from the police. She obviously had nothing to hide.

Audrey was taking control of her own destiny at Ospringe and learned that the best way of avoiding kerfuffle was to be in charge so that the dispensing of fuss was limited to when she wanted to be in receipt of it. Desmond, being used to a role of relative subservience, resigned himself to the new hierarchy more easily than Rosemary who would still insist on trying to help and comfort her guest. Audrey was working on her. Friend or not, Rosemary would be brought to heel.

Molly felt quite exhausted after her efforts with Cedric, and settled down to a quiet tea of cheese and tomato sandwiches and some lemon cake, interrupted by the necessity of feeding Tom prior to his departure.

Relaxing afterwards, her favourite mug filled with tea to hand, Molly looked at the large picture Cedric had draped over the fireplace, awestruck by the sheer brilliance of the man. Her mind took her back to his sad tale of love gained, love lost, and how heartbreaking it must have been for the two young lovers to be torn apart because of a protective father. Yes, things were different in those days and you did accept such situations, employed a stiff upper lip and got on with life.

At least Cedric had known the love of a woman. For the first time in her life Molly speculated if she had missed out. What exactly did it feel like when you loved a man and he returned your love? Were the feelings worth having? Her mother had done her best to put Molly off men, marriage and giving in to any strange sensations relating to either or both.

Too late now, she sighed to herself as thoughts of Cedric's amazing skills wafted unasked through her active mind and played tricks on her heart. If you've never been in love, she considered, how do you know when love comes calling? The issue of love was already entangling itself with the name Cedric in that questioning mind of hers. How funny that had been when he fell over Felicity!

My, he did make me laugh so very much, she fondly reflected.

She chuckled out loud as she recalled some of the things he'd said that had amused her. He made me feel so happy, she decided, I've really enjoyed myself today. And didn't he adore the refreshments I provided. And he loves Felicity. And he seems the perfect gentleman.

But it was the last thought that stopped her in her tracks.

Mama said there was no such thing, she reprimanded herself, and with that returned to being a contented spinster. Fancy him knowing where the word came from! Must be a very learned man.

However, her mother's teachings wrested control once and for all at that point, and she obliterated further feelings about Cedric, bar one or two seconds when she took down and rolled up his artwork, an action that briefly reminded her of her respect and admiration for him.

That night, Felicity wrapped up in the duvet next to her own body, Molly discovered Cedric was not be so easily removed from her mind as he made his way back to her foremost thoughts. He'd been so kind and understanding, so thoughtful. Not once had he shown any impatience. Not once had he demonstrated despair. He was gentle, wonderful with his words taking care not to offend her in any way, and he was amusing. What a lovely gentleman .....

And so sleep overtook her.

Nearby someone else had been overtaken, but not yet by sleep.

Clayton Mainstreet had been overtaken by one angry partner, home from Ramsgate and ready to rock and roll achieving his salvation. So he was enduring a nasty mixture of forgiveness, condemnation and damnation while realising that, unless he abandoned Ananya and their relationship, he was doomed to this existence forever, with no time off for good behaviour.

There was only one way back into her good books and even then he knew the passage was laden with terror and sacrifice. Goodbye meat and alcohol. Total commitment to the cause. He'd had his last drink.

But how he loved her. He loved her for her beauty and sexuality, her strength of character, her passion and verve. He loved her for her anger, her stubbornness, her determination, he even loved her when she was in a bad mood. He loved her body and he loved the ways she used it to beguile him and utterly satisfy him, exhausting him in the process. No way would he sacrifice all that. But if there was just one act that might restore her faith in him? What might it be?

He could not possibly imagine what it would turn out to be and how much courage he would need to accomplish it, but his day was coming, his opportunity would soon arrive.

**

For the police the day had mainly been about delving into Gareth Modlum and trying to find an enemy, probably not a spurned lover, but nothing was discounted this early.

The phones and computer had thrown up little. In truth there wasn't a lot there. The Modlums seemed so ordinary if there was such a thing in this day and age, if indeed there had ever been.

Apart from a domestic finance spreadsheet that showed nothing untoward whatsoever, there were emails mostly relating to online purchases interspersed with an occasional communication with a friend or two, such as one of Gareth's former workmates, and their photograph collection which was being analysed.

Two officers had been detailed to go through the data with a fine tooth comb, and another had the task of following up the handful of numbers located in the mobile phone. No texts and no voicemail messages. Saved numbers included Green Flag motoring assistance, insurance company contacts, an ICE number which was Audrey's mobile, a local electrician and a local plumber and so on.

Boring in the context of a murder enquiry unless he'd upset the plumber too much .....

Willie couldn't help himself. If a plumber was after him surely it would've been death by drowning? And the electrician? Well, he'd wire up Gareth to the mains, wouldn't he?

Did Audrey want him dead? According to his will Audrey got the house. There were four small specific charity donations, the rest to his wife, along with all his worldy goods. No sign of a massive piece of insurance cover. Nothing out of the ordinary.

They had a joint bank account, with a pleasant enough amount in it, ideal as the main bills went out by direct debit, and he had a few Premium Bonds of his own. There were a couple of small long term bonds. Audrey had explained they had little in the way of savings as yet because they spent all they had buying the Oast. The spreadsheet demonstrated that as it went back a full nine years. Every penny in and every penny out accounted for.

Did Audrey want him dead to be free, or to join a lover? She had little to gain bumping him off just for the lolly, and the house was as good as hers anyway. They seemed a 'happy' and 'ordinary' couple, Willie decided, but there was the outside chance Mrs Modlum was not so happy in the marriage and wanted out for whatever reason. But to arrange a spouse killing?

Did she know about Mr Modlum's wanderings and was that sufficient excuse? People had been slain for less. Willie knew they had to examine every aspect, especially in a case with absolutely no suspects and no leads.

Apart from, that is, the one lead they didn't know about yet that Ernest Pawden was about to present them with.

***

Cedric Pugh-Calford went to sleep unencumbered by memories of Molly or the time they'd spent together. He'd spent the evening with Daniel Deronda and Brahms and that was good enough for him.

There was one moment when another memory caught him off guard however.

He'd just changed CDs and was sitting with his eyes closed, the book open in his lap, the first strains of the third symphony wafting up from the speakers, when he remembered Antionette Pelham, his one and only love. Molly's enquiry had stirred up matters he believed he'd buried years ago, many years ago.

He opened his eyes to try and stamp out the developing recollections but realised he could not do so. He picked up his book and started reading but by the end of the page found he had read nothing. So he put it down and let dreams of Antoinette swamp his very being for a few minutes in the hope he would then be able to dispose of her.

Gradually he forced her out of the picture and resumed his evening, Miss Pelham vanishing as quickly as she'd arrived.

Sheelagh Mehedren's picture was as gloomy as ever but always the optimist she knew something would turn up, but not necessarily out of the blue. That's what an investigation was all about; digging out ideas, seeking information that wasn't at once obvious, testing every conceivable avenue of enquiry, and her team was busy in all respects. She knew them all well, trusted them, appreciated them as dedicated professionals, the masters against the criminals.

They'd proved themselves before, many a time. They would solve this one, puzzling though it appeared to be. Her team was capable of handling the most monotonous of investigations with the proverbial fine tooth comb often finding a criminal's weakness or unearthing the weak point in a criminal's scheme. And many fine tooth combs were currently employed on this one.

It looked more and more like a premeditated act with Gareth the intended victim. The knife was a horror story all by itself and they were working on where it might have come from. Too easy to come by these days. It was an instrument of death, there being no other obvious and valid reason for its existence.

They were diligently working their way through a maze that was shrouded in fog but the DCI knew a better picture would emerge, hopefully sooner rather than later.

From this point of view tomorrow would give them the opportunity to consider they had already made a slip-up.

Chapter Eleven

Wednesday

DS Willie Broughton was examining the prospect of Gareth Modlum being into a more serious pursuit than fishing. He didn't belong to a fishing club but it appeared he took his hobby earnestly judging by the equipment stored in the garage, and they were able to piece together an idea of where he might have enjoyed his efforts.

Not a sea angler, but not tied to one type of catch by any means. He'd visited Wall End Carp Fishery on Sheppey, and Chilham Lakes, suggesting carp could be his favourite, but other locations he used in Kent showed he was given to diversity.

But imagine if he'd been in some way involved in the drug trade, or even people-trafficking, and you could see any number of reasons why he met his end, doing so at the hands of a professional. Willie was making enquiries, just in case, not that it was particularly easy for if Gareth had been playing a role in such activities he had covered his tracks well.

Another man making enquiries was Ernest Pawden. The newsagent had no intention of talking to him about his car or business so Ernest had called Eric Furness, who was at home first thing, and asked him to oblige. He duly did so, clearly entering into the spirit that had captivated most of them along the lane. The newsagent wasn't one for entering into any sort of spirit when it came to revealing what he considered to be private matters, but eventually he yielded up the information he had a blue Ford Fiesta and had delivered the papers after seven Sunday morning, probably no later than, say, seven twenty.

Just what Ernest was hoping to hear.

He joined Cedric at Molly's and tried to ring DS Broughton who was unavailable. DS Lucy Panshaw took the call and passed him to DCI Mehedren, advising her boss this was the elderly gentleman Willie had spoken about.

And that was just what Sheelagh did *not* want to hear.

She listened with a patience she didn't feel. Willie had described Molly Penderman as a lovely old duck who probably didn't know what day it was, a kind of maiden aunt as he'd previously termed her, who spoke of a car driver as shifty and when challenged identified the car itself as being virtually any size. An unreliable witness, his conclusion.

And here was a lover of fictional crime drama, a man in his eighties, trying to tell her that he and his friend had managed to tie the maiden aunt down to the type of car, and to placing the man in a different age group entirely from the one she first named. More than that, he was claiming that Miss Penderman saw the car about eight and the newsagent had delivered the papers a good three-quarters of an hour earlier.

What on earth made him think he could do the job better than her?

"Mr Pawden, I am running a murder enquiry. I have an excellent team, we've had successes because we're rather good at it, and you're telling me we're doing it all wrong. DS Broughton tells me you live in a house called Whodunit and are an avid fan of TV crime as well as murder mysteries in books. Sorry to sound rude, Mr Pawden, but I think I'm too busy for this. Thank you for your kind assistance, which is appreciated, of course it is, but you may be mixing fact with your fiction and getting carried away. I really am sorry if this seems rude and offensive, it's not intended to be, I'm just explaining our position."

"Chief Inspector, I know you're doing your job and doing it rather well, and I am a great supporter of our police force. I am not offended by your words and can understand why you think an old duffer like me, who loves fictional crime stories, should be interfering. But I really do think it is worth somebody's while coming to see what I am talking about and to learn how we arrived at it."

"Mr Pawden, I do not think you an old duffer, but the fact is that Miss Penderman almost certainly saw the newsagent's car and was mistaken about the time." Mr Pawden took a deep breath and chose to disagree.

"No she did not." This conversation had no destination and was wasting Sheelagh's time.

"Right. I will do this. I will send DS Broughton to you. You're at the Dahlias, aren't you, but if he decides not to pursue your information then not only will the matter be closed but we will not want to hear from you again unless you have cast-iron evidence. Once again, I am not being rude. I regard you as a true gentleman, Mr Pawden, who is naturally concerned about a dreadful murder along your road, the killing of a good friend. But please understand we are working on it, a whole team is working on it, and we will do our best to bring the perpetrator to justice."

"Thank you. Yes, we are at the Dahlias. I understand you, Chief Inspector, only too well, but accept your kind offer to send us DS Broughton, and also accept what you have said about his decision. However, I have absolute faith that we will convince him." The call ended and Ernest passed on the news. It had been a fight and Molly instantly offered him a drink, this time something stronger as he looked as if he needed it.

On this occasion he accepted and the three of them partook of sherry.

"She said she wasn't being rude but gave me an excellent demonstration of rudeness. I know they are all busy but this is so important and as a member of the public I should be entitled to more courtesy. That woman was really quite unpleasant, quite

105

unpleasant. And I *am* offended even if she thinks I ought not to be. Wretched woman."

"Ernest, you did so well, and it's all my fault...."

"No Molly, it isn't your fault. We have vital evidence and that woman isn't interested."

They grumbled some more, drank their sherry, and sat back to wait for Willie's arrival.

***

If Eric and Gerald had been collected and carried along by the tidal wave of interest being generated along the lane, once they had conquered their initial sorrow and revulsion of course, then they were about to be joined on this excursion by another neighbour.

As it happened Clayton Mainstreet's visit to the Bristol area would have been wasted primarily because a protest group was staging a sit-down on site and doing their best to disrupt progress. Video conferencing aided the state of affairs for Clayton and he was able to remain at home, doing the homework he should've done much earlier.

But once again the murder played on his mind and made nonsense of his efforts. Giving up the unfair struggle he rang Ernest for an update and became positively excited by developments. Thinking he was safe and his invitation wouldn't be accepted Ernest, with Molly's agreement, asked him along to the Dahlias on the off-chance he'd be there for Willie Broughton's visit. Clayton came, and at speed, as befitting a fit young man.

"Oh Ernest, what's that man's name again? Mainspring or something?"

"It's Mainstreet, Molly, but I think he'll expect you to call him Clayton, don't worry!"

"Do you know, Ernest, I don't think I could ever be a vegetarian or whatever it is."

"I get the impression, Molly, he's none too keen either. But he's in thrall to his partner and I believe he does what he's told."

Also about to do as he was told Willie received the news he was bound for the Dahlias with a shudder and a look of mock-horror, especially when told the reason why.

"I knew it, ma-am, soon as I saw the sign saying Whodunit. That guy fooled me. I really took to him, thought he was level-headed, didn't take that crap seriously, and, well, I just got to liking him. Now he does this to me."

"Oh there, there Willie. Come and rest your head on my shoulder and have a good cry, just like every weak man I've ever known." Her smile disarmed him as cackles from other officers filled the room, already noisy with phone calls and the sound of computer keyboards being tapped. "Take Lucy with you. Look good, two detectives turning up, and between you shoot him and his cohorts down in flames. There's good children. Now run along and play."

The two detective sergeants, sporting broad grins, for no offence had been taken, set off on their mission, in a funny sort of way quite looking forward to the encounter.

***

Taking a shine to her role as top dog Audrey Modlum had been laying the law down and her hosts, only too willing to humour her thinking they were comforting her, fell in with her demands. A reporter had arrived unannounced on the doorstep and was given short shrift, Audrey barging her way past an apologising Desmond to send the interloper packing.

She'd insisted they all have a healthy breakfast, much to Desmond's annoyance as he loved his full English, and she'd sat at the table thoroughly enjoying her own and taking great delight in their obvious dislike of the fare, and she'd chatted about her round of golf and her hole-in-one. Such talk made Rosemary feel

107

ill and she abandoned her meagre meal, making an excuse to go to the bathroom, leaving her husband to listen with equal distaste.

Now she'd retired to her bedroom. Sitting on the bed she remembered the letter, the one she had pulled from the pile and only briefly glanced at. She opened it again, read it right through then screwed in into a ball, throwing it into the wastebin. First that shocking post on social media, now this. Were people really so insensitive and inconsiderate? Gareth hadn't simply passed away, he'd been slaughtered at their dream home, and nasty little worms, as she thought them, said such unpleasant things that hurt so badly.

Was this what society was coming to? It left her with little hope for the future. But what future she faced she had to make the most of, with Gareth by her side in spirit to guide her and be a staff to lean on in times of woe. That would have to do. Soon she would return to the Oast and start her new life knowing her wonderful husband would always be there for her.

In the early part of their marriage Gareth hadn't always been there for her, and as social media can become a torrent of like-minded outpourings, the perfect channel for gossip, rumour and tittle-tattle, regardless of truth, it was inevitable that another of his conquests should gallop into the field to add her two-pennies-worth, and do so anonymously.

'Yay – Gareth Modlum – husband, bastard, heartbreaker. Stabbed was he? Waste of a knife. Should've cut bits off. At least he's safe from me now. To think I let him do all kinds of things to me. Yuk'

And the news media grabbed it with both hands. Life was going to start getting difficult for the widow any time soon, even worse when a 'victim' actually came forward and sold her story to a paper.

***

Gerald thought he had a cold coming.

He'd risen with a sore throat, his nose was running, he felt proper poorly. Eric was no reassurance at all, offering tablets, a nasal spray and a cough lozenge, Gerald accepting two of the three. He would have preferred a little sympathy but all his partner suggested was that, with fresh air and exercise, cycling to work as usual it would soon pass off.

Eric was then off to Pett Level, his first port of call, leaving Gerald to his misery. He wondered if it was nothing more than a reaction to the morbid events of the last few days. A packed lunch duly prepared he climbed on to his cycle and set off towards Faversham, declining to look at the rose bush and sending the merest glance in the direction of Hop Pickers Oast as he rode by and at an unusually high speed.

The lane had been open some time, the police attendance departed, and the blue and white tape removed from the Modlum's lovely looking home. How sad he felt that it would no longer be a happy retirement place for Audrey to share with her husband. She deserved better than that, poor woman.

As he pedalled on his way, detached and morose, he felt a pang as he suddenly tried to consider what life without Eric would be like. They were two peas in a pod. They had a holiday cottage booked for a week in June, travelling to Northumberland and a remote spot near Allendale Town, where they would walk to their hearts content. Back in March they'd had a cottage in Suffolk near Southwold and had loved every moment.

Come September they would be off to Scotland for a fortnight, self-catering again as ever, this time to Plockton. They had visited Skye and the Applecross peninsula before, and looked forward to seeing them again, but they had heard so much about Plockton it was just too desirable to miss. The photos of the area had excited them further.

Although Gerald had a licence Eric's car belonged to his firm so he had to do all the driving, and did so without any complaint. Gerald knew he wouldn't miss him for that reason, he would miss him for so many others. His presence, his cheerfulness, his kindness. His just *being* there. They were one person and he hoped he brought as much into the relationship as Eric. If Eric had been there he would've confirmed that, yes, Gerald did. And Eric would've praised him for doing the packing for their holidays as well as preparing all the meals.

And it was thus that his preoccupation overtook him, leaving him racing down a slight incline with a sharp bend at the bottom. All might yet have been well for Gerald woke up to the impending danger and applied the brakes, but a van coming towards him prevented him from swinging across the road.

With a resigned cry of 'Oh bugger' he disappeared into the hedgerow, man and bike in perfect disharmony. The van driver saw the accident in his mirror, stopped and dashed to the scene, where Gerald was extricating himself from a collection of vegetation including sharp brambles.

"You right?" asked the van driver. "You right? You hurt? You have accident?" No, thought Gerald rudely, I've just had one. But he relented realising the driver had a limited knowledge of English to call upon.

"Thank you, thank you, but I think I'm okay," Gerald decided, completely forgetting he was supposed to be starting a cold, but conscious he did not seem injured. His back pack was crushed and that probably meant lunch was too. With the driver's help he steadily withdrew the bike from the greenery. It didn't look damaged but it was sporting odd bits of twig extending from all parts.

"You not ride, it ... it ... it .... d-d-d-dangerous," the man said triumphantly, having remembered what he believed to be the right word. "Where go?" he asked.

110

Gerald knew he had to return home and explained this to the driver.

"Ah, not far, not far, right?"
"Yes, not far."
"You show me. You put it in back and I take you home, right?"
"Well, that's very kind. If it's not out of your way."
"Only take a ... a ... a ... what do you say? ... ah yes, only take a mo."

And a mo later, with the bike in the back, they were underway, running at the sort of speed you would expect delivery drivers to undertake, even on country lanes. Gerald learned his new companion was Jokubas and he came from Lithuania, had a wife called Ausra who, as far as Gerald could make out, worked somewhere near Sittingbourne, and that they both loved England.

"Nice place, nice people," Jokubas observed, leaving Gerald with many relevant thoughts on the subject, none disclosed to his chauffeur. Within minutes they were at Rose Cottage, Jokubas declining to come in for tea saying he had many deliveries to make.

"Do you know where you're going, do you need directions?" enquired Gerald.
"No, no, have Satnav, it take me anywhere." He checked his notes. "I go to Rin-goals-tone," he pronounced Ringlestone. "See, I put in code and it tell me. I off now, must .... fly, is that it? Nice meet you, Gerr-rall-ed. You take more care." And they waved to each other as Jokubas set off like Lewis Hamilton away from the grid. Gerald winced.

He took the bike to the garage to check it over later, phoned to advise his delay to his employers, and rang for a taxi. With that he made a nice cup of tea and repaired his packed lunch, which wasn't as badly damaged as he'd thought, and waited for the car.

It gave him time to think more about the murder. Must get in touch with Ernest, he decided. He didn't want to be left out, any more than Eric did, if Ernest was putting clues together. He would call him that evening.

***

Audrey wanted an outing. Rosemary had said she needed to get a little shopping which provided her guest with all the impetus necessary.

"We'll go to Faversham, Rosemary. We can park in Morrison's, you can get what you need, and we can have a stroll round the town.

"I usually go to Sainsbury's.... "
"Well today you're going to Morrison's."
"I don't have a Morrison's card...."
"Happily I do, and they'll give you one anyway."
"Do you think it's a good idea....?"
"Yes, that's why I suggested it. Surely you want to keep me company, Rosemary, and surely you don't expect me to walk all the way into town from here do you?"
"People do, y'know. It's not far."
"We can have a lovely walk in town, and along the creek. The Brents, Crab Isle. Do us both the power of good."

Little did Audrey realise it wasn't going to do her any good at all.

Reluctantly Rosemary agreed to the trip. Desmond thought it a splendid idea, but mainly because he'd have some peace and quiet. And they set off about the time Willie Broughton was arriving at the Dahlias.

***

Willie and Lucy were ever-so-slightly surprised by their reception at Molly's.

It was almost like party time. Almost.

Four of 'em, Lucy thought, doing this mob-handed! Willie was pleased he had company.

Cakes and biscuits at the ready, plates, cup and saucers, napkins, and an eager Cedric off to make the tea. Willie thought it best to go straight in at the deep end.

"Thanks, but we're okay. We really are tight for time and if you could explain succinctly what this is all about we can get back to our other enquiries asap. Know you'll understand." Cedric was recalled and asked to bring the drawing in. Ernest took up the mantle.

"Mr Pugh-Calford was employed as an illustrator for a magazine and spent some time with Miss Penderman working on this." Cedric unrolled the artwork which Ernest held at the opposite corner. "The important thing, officers, is not just this drawing but the experiment that went with it. If you'd be so kind, Miss Penderman, to stand by the window." She did and Ernest and Cedric took the thing outside and held it up.

The detectives stood and moved across to the window as Molly explained how she knew immediately it was the right car. Willie looked at Lucy and Lucy looked at Willie. It was Lucy who spoke.

"Thank you, Miss Penderman, that's most interesting." She sounded as if she'd just had a bit of a shock. The two men returned to the lounge with Ernest ready to take up the story.

"The driver we are still not sure of, but we think we're closer. Miss Penderman is more confident she would recognise him if she saw him again, and is prepared to admit her earlier assessment of age might be inaccurate. Mr Pugh-Calford understands, and I concur, that he may be somewhat full of face, chubby-cheeked if you like, and older than thought, possibly fifties or more. All this was gleaned by working on sketches like this until Miss Penderman believed Mr Pugh-Calford was as close as could be.

"Now. Second point. The newsagent has a blue Ford Fiesta and was delivering papers to Rose Cottage around seven in the morning, definitely no later than seven-twenty, and did not return by this direction. Miss Penderman knows she saw this car, the Kia Rio, about eight. Is that succinct enough for you, officers?"

Willie sat without realising he had done so. If he looked dumbstruck it may have been because he was. This blew an unpleasant hole in their investigations. Lucy came to the rescue, noting the signs and realising the implications.

"On second thoughts, perhaps a cup of tea would be quite welcome after all." Cedric slipped out quietly and quickly to oblige. "Mr Mainstreet, what's your role in this?"

"Me? Oh, well, I'm a neighbour, Earth Cottage. Sergeant Broughton interviewed me. The Modlums did our garden for us. We're vegetarians, soon to be vegans, like, and they helped transform the garden into a mega veggie patch. I loved Gareth and I'm grieving for Audrey. I just want the killer behind bars, and I'm a supporter of Ernest here, he's great at this sort of thing. And as for Cedric and Molly, wow, what craftsmanship. Have you seen anything like that?"

Lucy shook her head. Willie was weighing up the prospect that the whole road was engaged in doing their job for them, and he was suitably embarrassed that they might actually be one step ahead. And all because he thought Molly Penderman an unreliable witness. Due to that they'd easily dismissed the car and lost track of a vital clue. But had they? This was all still conjecture.

114

It might even be nonsense, an unintentional red-herring, but he knew he was clutching at straws.

Lucy was awed by the effort that had gone into the exercise, and said so, adding that it was astonishing the way they thought of doing a large colour sketch and holding it up outside the window for Miss Penderman's perusal. Willie just wished she'd keep quiet. This wasn't going to look good if it proved to be correct. His colleague was reading all the signs, had a pretty good idea what was going through his mind, the mental turbulence he was suffering and, like a typical man he wasn't going to admit he was wrong any time soon.

She'd work on him.

Tea was served, cakes and biscuits accepted. Lucy's phone rang.

"Yes, ma-am, still at the Dahlias, and this is interesting, believe me."
"I don't like the sound of that. Get your rear-quarters back here, pronto, and explain."
"Will do, ma-am." And the call was ended by the DCI. "Looks like we're recalled Willie."

Nevertheless, they finished their refreshments, thanked their hosts, advised them full statements might be needed, and fled to their car, Lucy taking the wheel.

"Well, well, well. Anything in it Willie, do you think?"
"Sadly yes. But the worst part is going to be explaining this to Sheelagh Mehedren and standing clear of the fallout."
"Just do it succinctly, Willie. I think that was the word, wasn't it?"

***

Being to the manner born Ananya Ghatik shot up the ladders, twisting past the scaffolding poles, the planks, the fittings, doing

115

so with great athleticism and agility, and within seconds was standing watching two young men fixing roof tiles.

They were carrying out their work to her complete satisfaction despite an earlier concern that their minds could be wandering, and not in a way to achieve perfection in their task.

She turned and looked at the distant sea. Despite being well inland, from up here she could see over Ramsgate's rooftops to the water beyond. Hundreds and hundreds of rooftops, all higgledy-piggledy, all shapes and sizes, a wide variety of buildings of all ages. And it occurred to her that she was reminded of the road to salvation, the path being rough and rocky, but the destination being as calm and beautiful as the clear blue sea.

It was worth reaching.

Clayton had been gifted to her so she could prove her worthiness. Seducing him had been the easy part. Keeping him safely with her on the journey to salvation and paradise was the challenge, and she must succeed. She took a deep breath. She knew she could do it, for her own sake and his. They would play their part in trying to save the planet so that their own children should have it to enjoy.

Her partner had just demonstrated why alcohol was a bad thing. It was like a drug; it could be mind altering and depressing, and her Clayton was not going to plunge down that route to purgatory, not if she could help it.

Some gulls flew by noisily, chasing one that had a lump of bread in its mouth, trying to encourage it to drop its food. Nature at work, she mused. Gradually she became aware of someone shouting at her from below, and realised she was needed in another theatre of her operations. As she descended Gareth's premature death clouded her optimistic thoughts, but she knew the best respects they could pay to his memory was to keep the

116

vegetable garden thriving, and it was just possible Audrey might come back to them for much the same reason.

It was a straightforward case of keeping Clayton off the proscribed script he had started to follow and redirect him to all good things, and doing good in the world, and doing good *for* the world. He would have to prove himself but in so doing she would be victorious.

Little did she realise he was to have the opportunity quite soon.

***

Audrey had privately considered Faversham to be the dowager duchess of small Kent towns, displaying stateliness and breeding and being worshipped for it.

Aged as the old girl was she adapted to certain changes and successfully repulsed others, and stood magnificent at the heart of her estate, unchallenged and in complete control. Audrey had come to love the quaint, quirkiness of the town, old and rambling at its centre with an array of truly local shops, the brewery standing guard close by.

The Creek she could take or leave. A thick, glutinous mud-squelch at low tide, transformed into the core of a picturesque riverside at high tide. New housing developments had sprung up here, tasteful additions to some, hideous eye-sores to others.

After following Rosemary around Morrison's, an eye-opening and eye-watering experience being with such a ditherer who could waste time for England, they wandered along West Street to Middle Row, Court Street and on to Abbey Street. She marvelled at the varied architecture whereas Rosemary was bored once they left the shopping areas. Giving in all too easily Audrey led her friend back to the shops and waited outside while Mrs Wandon invaded one.

Approaching from Court Street was Gerald Samuels on a brief lunch break.

He noticed Audrey talking to a man who moved away quickly, so he made his way over to say hello. God, he thought, she's as pale as a sheet.

"Hello Audrey," he called out when less than ten paces away, and she turned looking startled and horribly wan. "I didn't want to come and interrupt. How are you, love?"

"Oh ... oh ... he just wanted directions," she stammered, clearly shaken, "you wouldn't have been interrupting. Gerald it's lovely to see you again. Thank you and Eric so much for what you did Sunday. You're two of the best. I'm so grateful."

"I'm pleased we were there. Are you alone?"

"No, I'm with Rosemary who is busy annoying a shopkeeper somewhere." The colour was returning to her cheeks and she looked better, much to Gerald's pleasure.

The said lady emerged.

"Why Gerald, hello, how are you? What are you doing here? I don't know, these shops Audrey, I can never find what I'm looking for, dear me. Thank you for all you did Gerald, you and Eric, I don't know what I'd have done without you, and Audrey really appreciates your help, don't you dear? Audrey's looking a bit brighter now, don't you think? Good to get out in the fresh air. Anyway, I suppose we mustn't keep you, Gerald. Great to see you. You and Eric must drop by some time."

Gerald blew air out of inflated cheeks as Rosemary turned her back, and he saw the faintest glimpse of a smile on Audrey's face as she looked at him and shared his despondency over the breathless, pointless drivel her companion had just spewed.

"Yes, my lunch break is nearly over and I must be going. Pleased to see you both once more and I wish you all the best Audrey. Our condolences."

118

"Thank you Gerald. Thank you for your kindness and understanding." They stared warmly at each other, somehow kindred spirits after a fashion, he knowing only too well, having listened to Mrs Wandon in full flow, the depressing time Audrey must be going through.

After a few steps he looked back. He was haunted by his own thoughts. He knew deep down that Audrey had a closer acquaintance with the man she was speaking to than she'd suggested, and the meeting had left her white and drawn. She'd recovered almost at once as soon as he came to her.

And he was bothered without really knowing why.

Chapter Twelve

A reluctant newsagent, Thomas Becket, and wi-fi

In the incident room which was their command centre for the murder investigation Willie Broughton appended Cedric's sketch to the wall. He explained (succinctly) how it was achieved as Lucy Panshaw showed the picture on her mobile around the waiting fellow officers.

"Holding this up outside enabled Molly Penderman to identify the car. *At last.* They were also able, by similar means, to narrow the shifty driver down to age forty-sixty, with chubby cheeks." There really was no disguising the mockery in his voice, or his incredulity, and Lucy was quite disappointed with him.

"Right," boomed Sheelagh Mehedren, "the words wild-goose-chase spring to mind. First of all, Willie, you tried every means at your disposal, without success, to learn what sort of car it might have been and now two doddery old fools spend their time with a confused old lady to make an idiot of you. What about auto-suggestion? Literally *auto*-suggestion in this case. Hugh-Pulford takes the cat woman down the road he wants and finally draws a Ria Kio and bingo."

"It's Pugh-Calford ma-am, and the car's a Kia Rio."
"So bloody what? He's led her on and now they've stuffed you and Lucy."
"What about the times ma-am? The newsagent's car ..."
"Give me strength, Willie, for pities sake. She saw the newsagent's car about seven not eight, and has now identified it as a Rio not a Siesta."
"Fiesta ma-am..."
"Don't interrupt when I'm tearing you to pieces. And to wrap it all up nicely the age of the chubby shifty man is anything from twenty to sixty or even older. That vastly narrows it down,

eliminating a huge portion of the male population, doesn't it Willie?"

He looked crestfallen. He should've thought all that through. He'd concentrated on his own feelings and the possibility a mistake had been made to the exclusion of examining the evidence properly. Lucy spoke up.

"Supposing, just supposing ma-am, this new information is correct? Surely we shouldn't discount it?" It was being a woman that probably saved her, for the DCI glared so forcefully Lucy thought her eyeballs might explode, and probably would have done had Lucy been male.

"Surprised you were taken in, Lucy, but I forgive you. No doubt you were carried along by this size ten clown swallowing a pile of rubbish. Willie, you and me is going to have a private chat in my office, so decide which instrument of torture you fancy most." Gentle laughter drifted across the incident room.

Humiliated, regretting he hadn't gone with his first impression, he slunk off behind his boss to a mild sniggering and a round of applause from his colleagues.

"Back to work," screeched the DCI from the corridor, which only served to increase their humour. Lucy felt so sad, and far from certain she'd been taken in. In fact, she still wanted to believe in it, conscious that if it proved accurate they would all look rather foolish. But there was nowt she could do. Or was there?

***

Audrey had returned to Ospringe and retreated into her shell which enabled the Wandon's to fuss at leisure. She was all but silent and stared ahead at nothing in particular. And things were about to get worse.

A reporter and cameraman reached the doorstep and advised Desmond their paper had an exclusive story for the morning regarding one of Gareth's girlfriends, and did Audrey want to comment? Desmond received little response from Gareth's widow but his immediate indecision was washed away by Rosemary who stormed out to tell them to get lost, promptly slamming the door.

"Desmond, please get me a solicitor," came the soft, resigned and saddened voice of a defeated woman. "I need someone to act on my behalf. I don't know why these people are doing this to me. Gareth never strayed. He was a loyal husband. Whatever have I done to deserve being held up to ridicule like this?" Rosemary took control.

"Desmond, you've used a local solicitor. Ring her now. Go on." He slowly extricated himself from his chair only to be encouraged to act with more speed. "Oh for heaven's sake, Desmond, do get a move on, can't you see how desperate Audrey is?"

Audrey wasn't desperate at all, but she wasn't going to argue. The fight had gone out of her but she was already gaining strength, still looking at a bare wall as if it was an artistic masterpiece, quietly determining to rise above anything anyone could do to her. Desmond was back.

"We've got an appointment tomorrow morning at ten, with a Ms Rowhedge."
"We?" she queried, without changing her expression one iota.
"Well, I can come with you, or Rosemary can, if you'd like support." Audrey relented and lowered her gaze to the floor, now studying the patterned carpet.
"Yes, Desmond, if you'd come as well please." And she closed her eyes as little tears fell from them bringing Rosemary to her side to comfort and fuss.

***

Ernest Pawden was waiting patiently, and that made him unique, for his companions were like cats on a hot tin roof, except Felicity the cat who was curled up on a footstall fast asleep.

Willie Broughton rang.

"Mr Pawden, for the time being we've decided to take no further action pending any developments that may come to hand. I'm sorry, for I know what it means to you, but we've had a detailed conference here and the general feeling amongst the team is that Miss Penderman may be mistaken about the time, and may have been accidently and unintentionally guided to identify the car. We believe she saw the newsagent's car earlier than she thinks. Sorry, but keep in touch if anything concrete comes up."

The news was relayed to a disbelieving audience who muttered their irritation all at the same time. Clayton spoke.

"Molly, why not go see the newsagent, actually see him in the flesh? Whaddya say Ernest?"
"A brilliant idea Clayton. Are you up for it Molly?" Molly was.
"Can we go now?" she pleaded.
"Yes, no time like the present. Let's get a move on. Coming Cedric?" Cedric nodded.
"Well, I must get back to the grind," Clayton ventured, "but please keep me in the loop."

It was agreed the loop would include Mr Mainstreet, and within minutes Ernest, Molly and Cedric were bound for Eric and Gerald's newsagent.

Once there, and having explained their purpose, the owner put in an appearance and did so with great reluctance, clearly angry with their impertinence, a matter he briefly took them to task over.

Now they were staring at him. How dare they!

The reason they were staring was that the man in front of them was thin, tall, about thirty-five, and had a beard and moustache.

"I am so sorry to trouble you, Mr Peffry, but can you please confirm you took the papers to Rose Cottage Sunday morning in a blue Fiesta. The situation is this: Miss Penderman here saw a blue car, which we believe was a Kia Rio, about eight o'clock, and the police don't believe her."

Mr Peffry felt his anger subside to be replaced with interest and curiosity.

"Yes, I took the papers, and about seven, maybe a bit later. Tell me more."

"Miss Penderman saw the other car through her window. It stopped outside and she had a second or two to observe the driver. He didn't have a beard."

"I've made a statement to the police." Despite his interest levels rising Mr Peffry wasn't too keen on any further involvement. "But I tell you what. Come out the back and I'll sit in my car and Miss Penderman can see for herself. I just don't want any trouble and I don't want to end up in the papers myself."

"Understood Mr Peffry. Very kind of you to co-operate. Neither we or the police are looking for you. We're all after another car and driver and we simply need to convince the police Miss Penderman wasn't mistaken." The newsagent nodded, deep in thought, then led the way through the storeroom to the parking area beyond.

"That's not the car," Molly said at once, but as soon as Mr Peffry climbed into the driver's seat she was convinced past reasonable doubt. "No, definitely not this car, not Mr Peffry."

The trio set sail for the country with Mr Peffry being sufficiently interested now to ask to be kept in the loop. An ever-widening loop mused Ernest.

124

Cedric and Molly gabbled endlessly all the way to the Dahlias with Ernest concentrating on his driving and finding it difficult to do so.

It was Lucy Panshaw who took the call and the details and felt her heart leap. Surely the DCI must listen now. Surely.

***

"Have you got wi-fi?" Audrey suddenly asked.

"Well, y-y-yes we have. Do you want to use our computer for something, you'd be most welcome," Rosemary offered.
"Thanks. I've got my laptop in my room. Just need the passcode or whatever."

This was the first Mrs Wandon had heard of a laptop in her guest's possession.

"Yes, I'll get Desmond to write it down. Are you sure you don't want to use our computer, dear? Is it anything important?" The answer was yes but Audrey wasn't going to tell her that.
"No, I'd just like some time to myself, do some ordinary things, start getting my life back to normal, well, as normal as it's ever going to be now."
"Yes of course dear. I understand. I'll go and find Desmond for you now."

Desmond was fetched, the required data handed over, and Audrey went to her bedroom closing the door tightly behind her.

***

Gerald Samuels sat in the back of the taxi by choice and enjoyed a peaceful journey home.

Try as he might he couldn't get his encounter with Audrey Modlum, or hers with the mystery man, out of his mind, and he

125

convinced himself it was worrying, though for what reason he couldn't imagine.

The Modlums had lived at the Oast for three years and Faversham was their nearest town. It now boasted three of the main supermarkets and a host of smaller shops, so it would be quite likely that Audrey was a frequent visitor. She may have friends there. But that being the case why pretend the man was a stranger?

Take it at face value, he argued with himself. The man was asking directions just as Audrey said. Why should she lie? He gave up fathoming it out and turned his mind over to the evening's dinner which, as usual, he would be preparing. Eric would be home about seven where, waiting for him, would be a delicious meal, one of Gerald's special creations.

He loved cooking as much as Eric loved eating, a perfect combination, except that Eric was starting to put weight on. Should do some cycling, he reflected. In its turn that reminded him that he had to check the bike out, plus give Ernest a call for an eagerly awaited update.

Gosh, he thought as the taxi reached Rose Cottage, it's all happening!

It was certainly all happening at the incident room where DS Panshaw had been anticipating the DCI eating humble pie rather than a delicious meal. The latest revelation was, however, met with scepticism.

"Lucy, they are getting on my nerves. These TV shows and books make everyone into Sherlock Holmes or Vera, depending on their sex, and they bloody well think they know it all, and we don't know what we're doing. This old guy is up to his neck in this nonsense so he's creating a story worthy of his beloved works of fiction, of course he is.

"To misquote Henry the doo-dah speaking about Thomas Becket, will nobody rid me of this turbulent sleuth? Have him taken down the road to Canterbury Cathedral and dealt with. Look, ladies and gentleman, the mad cat woman is mistaken, how many more times? Now let's concentrate on finding an enemy for Gareth Modlum."

Lucy spoke without thinking, a dangerous venture and an unusual one for the Detective Sergeant.

"Sorry ma-am, but I think you're wrong. I think we ought to confirm the newsagent's story, perhaps take his photo and compare it with Mr Pugh-Calford's drawing." The room fell into a silence in which two ringing phones were temporarily ignored. They all waited for an explosion that didn't come.

"Right. That's put me in my place. To put this to bed once and for all I will go and see Ernest bloody Pawden right now. Does that satisfy all my well-meaning underlings?" Sheelagh Mehedren treated Lucy to the look of death then suddenly smiled. "Okay, okay, you've made yer point, and I will go and see him. I don't think you're right but I will do as you suggest then we can get on with this investigation. Fair enough?" Lucy looked sheepish but smiled and nodded in reply.

She'd won. For now.

***

Eric Furness was leaving a business in Rye where he'd been working and heading along the road past Camber Sands, an area springing into life as the new summer and holiday season arrived, the new beginning heralded by the apparent number of visitors wandering about. It was a good day for the beach.

The road took him on a jumble of straight stretches and tight corners as it drew across the flat marshes towards Lydd, his next port of call. There was nothing in his mirror and as he was not the sort of person to treat this road as a race-track (too many did) he let his mind drift back to the murder. A dreadful thing, the sort of thing that never happens to you, always someone else.

Not this time. It happened where they lived and to a neighbour they knew and liked. Poor Gareth. It wasn't the first occasion Gareth's loss had upset him today, for if truth be told he couldn't push it into a corner of his mind the pain being so real. He felt for Audrey, and for the umpteenth time since Sunday he shed a tear for her anguish and heartbreak.

Yes, of course the police would catch the villain, of course they would. Then there was dear Ernest Pawden, fighting Audrey's corner as it were, determined to help the police! The horror of events had at least brought them all that much closer together. Even Clayton and Ananya! They were no longer people who lived here and there along a country lane, people who waved to each other and spoke on occasions, they were a community united by adversity.

They would look after Audrey. And they would become a hamlet of friendly souls, not a disjointed group of disparate individuals, who merely happened to live close to each other. This would be a new start for all of them. And with renewed spirits he looked forward to hearing from Ernest. It wasn't real excitement, the situation had been too sorrowful and unpleasant, too evil and nasty, but the adrenalin was flowing and they all wanted the killer in custody.

Meanwhile it had fallen to DS Lucy Panshaw to go and see Mr Peffry and as soon he emerged into her line of vision all doubts were expunged. By now he had become totally swamped by inquisitiveness and with great enthusiasm invited the Detective Sergeant to come and see him in his car. She took photos. Of course it wasn't what Miss Penderman saw. Nobody could be that mistaken.

She subsequently showed him her earlier pictures of Cedric's drawing. The pair showed the pictures to the two assistants in the shop, they showed them to two customers, and all were agreed.

128

There was no resemblance between the two other than the colour of the car. Needless to say the two assistants and two customers wanted to know what it was all about so Lucy left Mr Peffry to enlighten them and made good her escape.

The photos were sent to Willie back at base, he printing them off and adding them to a wallboard, side by side with Cedric's original masterpiece, and he had to admit it was persuasive.

Fresh from his light-hearted verbal flagellation at the hands of the DCI, and knowing you couldn't be hanged twice for the same offence, he summoned Sheelagh to the incident room and showed her his work with pride.

"Okay Willie. I've rung Pawden and I'm going to see him tonight. He asked if he could invite his neighbours round and I suggested he widen the field if space permits and invite all the local villagers and half of Faversham. What do I care? No I didn't say any of that, but this is getting silly. One way or another it ends tonight, and the way I feel it could end in murder.

"He's managing to make it look like a Poirot-esque summing up! You know, they all sit round while he tells them and a grateful Inspector Japp whodunit in some long drawn out dialogue full of red herrings. Gawd save us from fiction. Fancy coming for moral support Willie, and for the sheer fun of it?" Willie did. In fact he couldn't wait.

Chapter Thirteen

Wednesday Evening at the Dahlias

The investigation into Gareth Modlum's past was proving fruitless.

Regardless of whether he had been a naughty boy, which wasn't against the law, there was no evidence yet that he'd put a foot out of line. His widow might come to think differently. The police were talking to workmates, his employers, friends, fellow anglers, and coming up with precisely nothing, a big zero.

Short of believing he was slain by a jealous or spurned lover they still had so little to go on.

In fact, admitting that Molly might, just *might* be right after all, would give them a lead on the killer himself, even assuming Molly's shifty driver was the assassin. It could be another dead end. Publicise the blue Kia Rio and a genuinely innocent person might come forward, and that would be that.

Of course it stood to reason that if Gareth was involved in criminal activities such involvement would not be sticking out like a sore thumb. It would be buried in a world of darkness and fog.

Over at Ospringe Audrey Modlum was back in control.

She'd bathed and come down to dinner, an uninteresting and uninviting meal described by Rosemary as lightly-dusted cod, chipped potatoes and seasonal vegetables, with home-made tartare sauce, which Audrey knew was fish and chips by any other name.

Desmond had uncorked a pleasing enough Frascati, a mite too dry for Audrey, but welcome all the same, and the widow decided she might as well get drunk or at least merry.

"Delicious wine Desmond. Do you have another bottle ready?"

"Um ... um ... well ... yes, but it's not chilling."

"Well, it's not doing the right thing, is it? Chill it, dear Desmond. Chill it."

"Er ... yes ... okay ... yes, I'll just put it in the fridge."

"Well done Desmond, there's a good host."

Rosemary remained silent, silenced by the new Audrey's approach to life.

"Do you think drinking's a good idea, my dear?" she queried.

"Absolutely first class, Rosie. Nowt better." Rosemary slipped into another period of silence as she tackled her fish and chips, stunned by her guest's reaction. She'd never been called Rosie before. Right now she found she actually liked the concept. Rosie sounded rather splendid, rather open and colourful, fresh and young, full of life. Yes, she liked being called Rosie, and with that decision came another.

"Desmond dearest, please make sure we do not run out of wine." Audrey looked up startled, smiled at her friend who smiled back, and knew they were in for a most pleasurable evening regardless of whether Desmond approved or not. He could join in or clear off for all she cared.

***

At the Dahlias Molly had arranged refreshments as you might expect of such a lady.

There were cakes and biscuits, home-baked cheese straws, sausage rolls, egg and cress sandwiches. She knew how to entertain.

131

At her behest Ernest had advised all concerned that food and drink would be available but that had not prevented Gerald preparing a culinary delight for his partner. Eric had been pleased to hear they were invited to Molly's to meet Sheelagh again as he hoped a great deal of news would be forthcoming. There was no dessert tonight as Gerald explained it might appear rude to turn up and not partake of Molly's fare.

Cedric had arrived and placed himself in charge of teas and coffees, which suited his host admirably.

Next in were Ananya and Clayton followed by Ernest.

They waited impatiently for the police officers and eventually temptation overcame them all and they set about the spread, this coinciding with the arrival of Eric and Gerald. Cedric busied himself with beverages.

Sheelagh Mehedren could scarcely believe her eyes as Molly brought her into the lounge, now a cramped venue of people, chairs of all shapes and sizes, and food galore. Willie simply smiled to himself. Just how he would've expected it.

Sitting and accepting a steaming hot black coffee as ordered she decided she might as well enjoy herself and duly set about gathering a plate of sausage rolls, sandwiches and a piece of Battenberg cake, demolishing her choices with gusto.

Entering into the spirit of the occasion she called to Ernest unfortunately spraying cake crumbs in all directions as she spoke, a misdemeanour she swiftly recognised and sought to correct.

"Oh, excuse me, sorry everyone. Mr Pawden, who did it then? You must have some ideas?" It was, of course, a sarcastic question but Ernest played a straight bat to it.

"Chief Inspector, if poor Mr Modlum was sent to his maker by a professional assassin then that is something I have no knowledge of, and which is very much in your realm. Otherwise, if you will forgive the chestnut I think it could be a case of cherchez la femme."

"*What?*"

"Cherchez la femme. Look for the lady."

"Mr Pawden, why do English people talk to me, an English woman, in French?"

"It's just an expression, Chief Inspector."

"Okay. Go on."

"I just happen to think that, excepting a professional killing, there has got to be a woman in it somewhere, even if the woman in question didn't carry out the shocking deed. Now may I please ask if you accept Miss Penderman's view of the car and driver?" This took their guest by surprise, and did so just as she was refilling her plate.

"Miss Penderman, assuming you to be compos mentis, please don't be offended, are you absolutely one hundred percent sure of your facts here? It really is vitally important." Ernest interrupted.

"Chief Inspector, you complain about me using French and then use Latin. How strange."

This was not lost on the DCI, who felt Ernest was in any case speaking up in defence of Molly.

"Touché. Oh God, I'm doing it myself. Okay, let's call it a draw. Sorry Mr Pawden, sorry Miss Penderman, but please, are you certain?"

"Completely. And I am not mad, as you've implied rather rudely, if I may say so Chief Inspector. I am completely certain. I accept it may not be the killer but it was not the newsagent."

Sheelagh chewed through a sandwich which she found delicious, munched into a cheese straw and weighed up the balance of probabilities.

133

"Okay, I'll buy it. Miss Penderman, would you be able to identify the driver if he stood in front of you?"

"To be honest I've no idea. But I would like to be given the chance." Ernest silently applauded Molly's confidence and the fact she'd given the right answer in his view.

"Right, well we'll say we are looking for this blue car, a Kia Rio, which was seen near the victim's house Sunday morning, and wish to eliminate the vehicle from our enquiries. How does that sound?" There appeared to be approval all round, and the DCI picked up another sandwich and cake and polished them off as if she hadn't eaten for days. Willie was amazed.

"Okay, listen up peoples. We will catch this killer. We want him or her as much as you do, but please don't get in our way. Mr Pawden, are you happy to be the point of contact for your neighbours?" Ernest nodded once. "Good. Then let me ask you all to direct any information or queries through Mr Pawden. I'm appointing DS Broughton here as liaison." Willie looked horrified at this unexpected arrangement. "He and Mr Pawden will be the medium through which this will operate. Let's all keep this simple. It'll save time and keep unnecessary distractions away from my officers. Are we agreed?"

Those present glanced at each other, then at Ernest who was still nodding, and Sheelagh despatched two biscuits while she waited. Yes, agreement seemed to be the order of the day, with Willie unable to look his boss in the face. Seething was probably a good word to describe his position at that moment, but he knew he'd been set up and that he'd get over it. Sheelagh continued.

"Obviously Mrs Modlum is not here tonight, but I'd be grateful if Mr Pawden would speak to her when the time is right, perhaps on her return to the Oast, just to keep her in the picture. Any questions?" While awaiting queries she nibbled away another cake. There were no questions. Ernest spoke.

"Thank you Chief Inspector, that's very kind of you, and I'm sure none of us wishes to waste valuable police time. You have

134

come up with a highly commendable idea and I think I speak for us all when I say it is much appreciated, wouldn't you agree Sergeant?"

"Um ... yes, I'm happy with that and delighted to be appointed, thank you ma-am." He sounded anything but happy and nowhere near delighted, but wore a resigned look that brought a smile to the DCI's face. Gotcha she was thinking!

"Right, back to the coalface then. Thanks for the refreshments Miss Penderman. Nice to have met you all, and please rest assured we have an extensive team working on this. We can't tell you about all the things we're doing, as I'm sure you'll understand, but we are working twenty four seven on every aspect. And, Mr Pawden, we shall be cherchezing la femme." Laughter all round.

***

Ananya and Clayton went back along the road in the company of Eric and Gerald who found they were quite taking to the young couple. The four stopped for a final chat at the edge of Earth Cottage's vegetable patch whereupon Ananya took her partner inside their home with every intention of ripping his clothes off and doing interesting things to him.

Eric and Gerald strolled home to Rose Cottage nattering about the meeting but mainly condemning the eating habits of the DCI.

"Built like a brick out-house," was Gerald's rude and offensive comment.

"Did you see how much she scoffed? No wonder she's well built. Wouldn't want to meet her on a dark night Gerald!"

"Nope. Mind you, I was impressed with her performance, and I like the idea of Ernest and that Sergeant as liaison. At least she's taking us seriously and recognises Ernest could be the main man here."

"I liked his idea of search for the lady. My money's on a woman, not that I think a woman killed Gareth, but who knows."

"Quite. But it does seem we will be kept in the picture and I suppose that's the best we could hope for."

"Mmm ... and slightly changing the subject, when do you reckon Audrey will be back?"

"I would hazard a guess at after the funeral sometime."

They'd reached home and both stood for a second or two to gaze at the rose bush.

"Not the rose's fault," Eric commented rather over-dramatically, "just wish the knife hadn't been put there. Don't suppose there's any significance in that do you?"

"Who knows, but suggest that to Ernest. I think he's desperately keen, don't you?" They shared a wry grin and went indoors to see what was on the telly.

Ernest finished writing his notes while Cedric and Molly cleared up and tried to avoid treading on Felicity who was obviously short of care and attention, ambling around their feet as they tried to make progress. Eventually Molly took hold of her cat and stroked and cuddled her before returning to the kitchen where Cedric was washing up. Tom arrived from his day-long siesta upstairs and wanted feeding so Molly gave herself over to her duties with her feline friends leaving Cedric to his domestic employment, a task he was more than happy with.

Back in the lounge Ernest was pondering a number of things and by curious coincidence was on the same lines as Eric, wondering if there was actually anything noteworthy about the place where the weapon was discarded. He knew the police would be looking into both Gareth and Audrey anyway, but felt he would like to chat to the widow. His intuition was telling him there was something to be found, but he couldn't imagine what.

And with that he packed his things away, pausing to glance at the heading on his folder 'G Modlum Investigation' and then prepared for his departure. Molly wanted him to stay but he said he needed to get back home, whereas Cedric gleefully accepted her invitation for a further chat, and they set about that most pleasant of occupations once Tom had set off for the countryside.

Once again Molly acknowledged her sadness at Cedric's lost love even though his heartbreak had been decades before and was all but forgotten. They talked about the murder, about the evening's meeting, about Cedric's friendship with Ernest, about Ernest himself. They talked about Sheelagh Mehedren and Willie Broughton, they talked about Brexit, they talked about life in the country and all the time Molly was conscious of her despondency over Cedric and his beloved Antoinette.

During a pause in conversation she recollected her devastation when her father and mother died, the utter desolation that tore her apart, and wondered if you underwent the same pain when you lost the love of your life. Presumably so.

Suffering pain had been Willie's lot that evening. First being assigned to role of liaison officer and then seeing the DCI grinning with the smile of the shark as she rejoiced in the mental chaos she had wreaked upon him. Satisfaction was hers, dismay was his.

"Willie, my boy," she remarked mockingly on the way back to base, "I bet you wanted to kiss me when I promoted you back there. Coveted post, that," and she burst into laughter. Willie had never coveted such a position and certainly not the desire to ever kiss his DCI. "You'll be the envy of the team. Don't worry mate, it won't last. There'll be a little flourish and then it'll all die a death, you wait and see. And in the meantime you get to keep Ernest 'Colombo' Pawden off my back." More raucous laughter.

There was raucous laughter at the Ospringe home of Mr and Mrs Wandon. Rosemary and Audrey were tackling their third bottle of wine, were rather like newts as might be said, and the pair of them were, in Desmond's opinion, behaving like teenage schoolgirls. The topics of conversation had deteriorated in direct proportion to the increase in wine intake, and they were now engaged in the subject of sexual pleasure which both demonstrated they had little experience of.

"Not sure how I got preg ... preg ... pregn't," Rosemary guffawed, "but a year after Cecilia was born it happened again!"

"N-n-n-n-n-not been pregnant," Audrey drawled, "no miss ... no miss ... no ... *mystery*." Both women whooped with hilarity.

Wine waiter Desmond, whose services were no longer required, had gone off to his study to watch a DVD and enjoy a gin and tonic, rather more gin than tonic, but returned in time to overhear about his wife's knowledge of procreation. They had two grown-up children, Cecilia and Robert, both married but without children, a matter that had left Desmond a saddened creature for he felt bereft without grandchildren to fuss over.

It was almost inevitable that after the humour misery should follow. Alcohol can have that effect. Having exhausted what they judged to be a very funny assessment of intimacy they sank into a wine-induced depression about Audrey's loss, while Desmond listened intently from the hall.

"Sorreeee, Audreeee. Sh-sh-sh-shame. Nice man, Gar ... Gar ... Gra'th," Rosemary slurred.

"Izz ... izz ... izz alright Roseeeeee. Not had sex with Grith for ... for ... *yares*. He not thart nice," Audrey gave in reply, sounding like a replica of her inebriated friend.

"No, 'tually Des he not that nice eye ... eye .... eye-vor. No sex. I don't like sex, Audreeeee, seeee."

"Izzzz alright with right man, Grith not right man," Audrey revealed.

After that they both drifted into a trance like state prior to passing out altogether, observed by Desmond who had appeared in the doorway and caught the last part of their drunken discourse. He wasn't so much concerned about his wife's confession as Audrey's closing statement.

Chapter Fourteen

Thursday

DCI Sheelagh Mehedren placed the paper down on the desk.

"Right. We've got a lead. Let's nail it."

DC Hassana Achebe piped up. "Already on it ma-am." The DCI looked impressed. "Single mum in Dover, we have name and address. Very co-operative paper! We can see her asap."

They had been reading the newspaper expose about Gareth Modlum's one time girlfriend Jackie, the lass who had sold her story and unintentionally given them a break.

"Lucy. Go girl go. Take Hassana. We want the truth. If this story is basically a fabrication we want to know what's behind it. You can't promise any immunity but tell her we'll try and keep her out of it. You don't have to mean it! Just get to the bottom of this pronto."

DS Lucy Panshaw gathered up her things and led Hassana out of the building to her car, thence in the general direction of the M20.

Audrey Modlum's head was in no fit state for her appointment with Ms Rowhedge let alone for reading about Jackie and her Gareth, but she made a bold start on the article before being overcome with the shakes.

"Why are they doing this to me, why, why, *why*? I just need to see that solicitor, but in the meantime I want to speak to that police officer, the Chief whatever." And with that her headache, which had come with her awakening, grew unpleasantly worse as her heart was filled with pain.

Desmond was far from convinced the solicitor would be able to do much to stem the tide, knowing only too well the general attitude to this type of revelation was that there was no smoke without fire. The paper's page three exclusive was producing exactly that reaction certainly throughout Kent and their part of it, probably titillating a much wider audience across the nation.

Gerald usually bought a paper in town so he and Eric started the day in ignorance of developments, Eric leaving early morning for Herne Bay. Ananya and Clayton never bothered with newspapers as a rule, getting all they needed from their tablets and the television, but with Clayton working from home he did pick up on the story online long after his partner had headed for Ramsgate.

Every now and then Molly's friend Agatha Polimpton from nearby Sheldwich would pick her up for a shopping trip to ASDA in Sittingbourne, and that is what happened today. So as yet they had no knowledge of the expose, continuing their journey westwards and looking forward to brunch at the store.

Ernest took Cedric to Teynham for their papers not knowing what lay in wait for them.

Thus it was that the extra-marital behaviour of Gareth Modlum deceased was laid open to scrutiny not just in Kent but throughout the kingdom, with interest levels in the murder rising especially in the immediate vicinity of the dastardly deed.

There were those who felt that maybe, if he was such a philanderer, he got his just desserts, whereas others simply realised how sorry they felt for the mistreated widow. A few no doubt raised a glass to the gas man's exploits, some found it disgusting, others dismissed it as another detrimental example of the age in which we live. The story produced wide ranging discussion particularly within about a thirty mile radius of Faversham.

Even Erica Rowhedge taking breakfast with her barrister partner read it. That was unusual as she did not take any pleasure

140

in scandal and rarely read such trivia as she would've described it. Today, however, she knew she was meeting the widow in a professional consultation and thought she'd gen up on the late Mr Modlum.

The one aspect that added fruit and sauce to the whole saga was the fact that the woman involved claimed to be in her 'early thirties' and had been romanced, if that is the right word, over about three years, indeed three fairly recent years. If her tale was true it would show that Gareth had been enjoying himself well into retirement, and doing so with a girl half his age.

Scandal indeed.

**

Despite taking tablets Audrey's headache had far from abated, but even with such a screaming pain in the foreground she finally picked up the article and read it through, slowly but surely. It did not calm her.

There was a photo of Jackie cuddling a baby which Audrey hoped wasn't Gareth's, not that anything like that was suggested. The story followed the same pattern as the social media posts but was a great deal longer and very much more detailed.

He'd carried out some work on her central heating and then carried out some work on Jackie. There were two specific dates mentioned, these being core to the tale as they related to sessions of servicing that were spelled out in minute detail for the benefit of readers. A man of wide ranging skills was Gareth, handy with all his tools if everything written was to be believed.

Audrey checked the diary she kept on her laptop and found both dates coincided with all-day fishing trips. Aaaarrrggghhhh!!! With an ear-splitting scream she tore the paper into shreds much to Desmond's chagrin as he hadn't read it yet. There was a crash in the kitchen as Rosemary once again dropped cups and saucers.

It was much more peaceful at The Vines where Ernest and Cedric had been perusing the papers quietly until the latter chanced on the exclusive. Now he was reading to his guest as they had only one copy.

'Gareth was so tender. I knew he was a real gentleman. Didn't think they made them like that anymore. He was such a lovely change from younger men who are just so macho, got to prove themselves, making it all about them. Gareth made it all about me. He said his greatest pleasure was giving pleasure and I thought, Oh my God, does he give pleasure! That's the benefit of an older guy – so much experience and knows how to use it well. He was brilliant. Five gold stars every time.'

Ernest interrupted.

"Sorry old chap, but I think that's quite enough. I do believe we get the picture."
"There's much more...."
"I don't doubt it. But I don't like that sort of thing, and the section you've read actually says it all. Is there anything about where this woman lives, how the relationship ended? No need to read it all out, Cedric, a précis will do." Both men chuckled. Cedric scanned through quickly, assessed the relevant points and answered his friend.

"Says East Kent here, that's all. Apparently he just packed her in, last year it says, because he'd found someone better! That's the way to finish with your girlfriend. Sounds an absolute bounder."
"If it's all true, Cedric. And I've got my doubts. Wonder if Audrey's seen it? Hope not."

But Audrey had seen it and sadly she was filled with doubts for the first time. The two brief posts on social media were meaningless, presumably untraceable, the work of mischief makers.

However Jackie had mentioned two dates when Gareth was indeed away from home all day. Could there be any truth in it?

Yes, he'd been firing on all cylinders when they first married, far too active, far too much for her to bear. He soon went off intimacy, but was that a sign he was helping himself to pleasures of the flesh elsewhere, and couldn't abandon it when they moved to their dream retirement home?

She'd assumed that he had simply calmed down, much more to her liking, and she believed that was quite normal for couples. It wouldn't have occurred to her that he was playing the field, if she had the right expression. Now she was devastated.

It was time to set off to the solicitor, and Audrey went with a blinder of a headache, a heavy heart, and a mind in havoc. Sheelagh Mehedren had been unavailable. She was offered Willie Broughton but she wanted to speak to a woman, preferably the one in charge. Even Lucy Panshaw wasn't there, so she left it for the time being.

***

Lucy and Hassana had trouble parking in the outskirts of Dover, for there was none available where Jackie lived. Settling for a roadside spot some distance away the two women set a brisk and determined pace, chatting as they went, checking the map on Hassana's mobile phone periodically, and finally arriving at the flat.

Waiting for them was a surprise.

Jackie was accompanied by a representative of the paper and a solicitor, in Lucy's unspoken view trebling the difficulty rating for this interview. She even thought about ringing the DCI but decided that might create another barrier.

Meanwhile Audrey and Desmond had been shown into the solicitor's office and introduced to Erica Rowhedge who came

143

as something of a shock to the system, even to Desmond who had met her before a couple of years back. She'd changed and not in his opinion for the better.

Her long red hair fell about her face where it was constantly being brushed aside. Parts of it were braided, most of it loose. Her lipstick was bright red and there was a ring through her nose and a stud above her upper lip. None of this bothered Audrey who was prepared to accept modern fashion remembering that when she was young she shocked her parents with her clothes and make-up, but it had an adverse effect on Desmond that was sadly all too apparent from his facial expression.

Erica, perhaps sensing his disapproval, chose to look at and talk with Audrey exclusively, even on the odd occasion she was listening to Mr Wandon, and definitely when addressing him.

Over in Sittingbourne Molly and Agatha were upstairs in ASDA enjoying refreshments, their papers yet to be purchased. Their conversation, normally covering all manner of subject matter, was this time largely associated with the murder, Molly explaining excitedly her role in the police investigation and how her friend Mr Pugh-Calford had come up with an ingenious way of identifying the car.

It was precisely that issue that was occupying Ernest. His paper did not have Jackie's exclusive which had so captured Cedric's attention. But it did have an update on the killing, located around page sixteen, in which the police stated they were looking for a blue Kia Rio, seen in the immediate area by a neighbour of the victim. The witness, the police report suggested according to the article, might be able to identify the driver. Ernest mentioned this.

"I'm a trifle worried, Cedric. The DCI has gone further than she said. What bothers me is that the police are also alerting the killer to the fact his car was noticed and that he could be identified. My goodness, Cedric, we could be talking about a

144

ruthless, merciless assassin, and this item could put Molly in danger."

"Good grief, you could be right my dear chap. What should we do?"

"Let's contact our liaison officer for a start. I'm disappointed with that DCI. She's gone too far in my opinion. I'll ring now."

***

DS Panshaw was having a torrid time. Of course Jackie wasn't going back on her story when in the presence of a woman from the newspaper who had paid her and the paper's solicitor. The latter kept interrupting every time he thought Lucy's questioning was leading in the direction that fibs might've been told. Heaven forbid! DC Achebe had been watching and listening and making mental notes, hoping to find a weakness somewhere. It was almost like a verbal game of chess for them all.

Simple questions received simple answers.

"Did you know Gareth was married?"
"Yes."

Anything more complex or off the beaten track encouraged interruption before Jackie could respond.

"Did he tell you what his wife thought he was doing when he was in fact with you?"

"Jackie does not wish to answer. He spent his time here in her company," the solicitor intervened.

"Sir, it is important to a murder enquiry."

"Yes, we know that, but consider it irrelevant unless you can show otherwise, Sergeant."

How Lucy wished Sheelagh had been there. She had keys to these unlockable doors! Lucy couldn't show otherwise, for in truth it wasn't vitally important, but other matters were and they just could not for the life of them break down these dams and ask

145

outright. It was becoming pointless continuing. Then Hassana spoke and everything changed.

"It's all a pack of lies Jackie, isn't it? We need to hunt down a merciless killer who may well have you in his or her sights now you've revealed yourself. Your life could be in danger."

The newspaper lady and the solicitor both leaped to their feet in protest. Lucy ordered her colleague out before a row could erupt and followed her having surreptitiously left her card where Jackie could see it but the others couldn't.

Walking back to the car Lucy smiled at Hassana who was ready to apologise.

"Hassana, it was hopeless back there. Hopeless. But you did it right. Spot on babes. Perfect timing, perfect approach. She'll be scared stiff. Bet you she contacts us as soon as she's free of those two nannies. I was despairing you know, completely wasted trip, and they were getting on my nerves, then you come up with the ideal solution!"

DC Achebe felt the warm glow of happiness that comes with fulsome praise.

Now it was just a question of time. Hassana was convinced, having studied Jackie throughout the meeting, that the girl had another story to tell. Just a question of time.

***

Erica Rowhedge could promise absolutely nothing as far as any outcomes were concerned but did say she would pursue every angle in the hope that pressure might be applied. She said she would challenge the paper to produce evidence or at least confirm they had verified Jackie's version of events, but knew there was no obligation, not even through the courts.

"So people can just libel each other," Audrey remarked in fed up kind of way, "and there's nothing anybody can do anymore? Is this what our country's coming to?"

"Mrs Modlum, you can sue for libel but you still need to produce the evidence to contradict the story. By the time someone publishes this sort of rubbish you'd be bolting the stable door, wouldn't you? I'm sorry, but it is, after all, your late husband who has actually been libelled. My suggestion is to talk to the police. It may be that they will want to talk to this Jackie in case it gives them leads. They may be doing it already."

A very dissatisfied Audrey left the solicitor's still nursing a headache and now a grievance. Once in the car she said to Desmond:

"Take me to the Oast please Desmond. I want to be alone in my home. I shall be perfectly alright, tell Rosemary not to worry, and I shall phone later for a lift back if that's okay with you." Desmond reluctantly agreed that it was and that he'd drive straight there, thinking to himself that it was him that had to explain this to his wife, not a task he relished.

Back at base Sheelagh had been appraised by Lucy and Hassana.

"Well done Hassana. As you say, just a question of time. Small wonder the paper was so co-operative. This was a set-up. A warning shot across the bows to keep us at a respectful distance and to prevent us challenging this wretched girl's tale."
"That's it ma-am, and if I've read her aright I've put the wind up her, and she'll expect the police to protect her, not those two spare farts."
"Try to avoid using the words wind and fart in the same sentence, Constable, otherwise you'll sound full of hot air......" Chuckles all round.

Earlier Willie had taken a call from Ernest. He was astonished to hear what he had to say and was quick to reply.

147

"Mr Pawden, that is simply not correct. Our media statement mentioned the car and the fact we wanted to eliminate it from our enquiries. That's all. We said the car had been identified by a neighbour. Full stop. If the paper has intimated that the witness might be able to identify the driver then it has taken it on its own back to do so. We didn't suggest that. Besides, we speak of a witness, not a lady. There's no obvious danger to any of you. The witness could be anyone."

Ernest had to leave it at that but was far from satisfied.

He turned his attention to writing his condolence card having passed the news to Cedric. He was to take both their cards and drop them through the letter-box at the Audrey's. No time like the present Ernest decided, and set off on foot for the Oast.

Chapter Fifteen

Audrey

Ernest made his way along the lane he had walked so many times, but never had it seemed so devoid of rustic charm, so lacking in loveliness, so empty of character, its beauty lost for the moment hopefully to return in the fullness of time.

For this was a lane of desolation and deprivation.

A lane that was so very Kentish was now a track of tragedy. He looked at the orchard, the branches deliberately trained to hang downwards to make fruit picking easier, and felt they were bending their heads in blessed memory of the victim. He saw wreaths where the hops were growing, and the sheep grazing he saw as sad mourners. And then he saw Audrey.

She was tending the front garden. All the floral tributes had disappeared.

"Hello Mrs Modlum," his greeting voiced with genuine melancholy, "I was just bringing a couple of cards, from me and Mr Pugh-Calford and didn't expect to see you."
"Oh hello Mr Pawden. Bless you, that's such a nice gesture. If you have the time do please come and have a cup of tea and a chat. So good to see you." Ernest was taken by surprise.

"Well yes, I'd love to, and I have as much time as you require of me." He handed over the cards and was led indoors to the lounge and bade to sit while Audrey went and prepared their tea. There were plenty of cards dotted about including some of the labels from the flowers left outside. He guessed the flowers had been taken away for none adorned the parts of the house he'd seen. Audrey returned.

"Mr Pawden I'm not looking for a shoulder to cry on. I've always regarded you as a fine gentleman, as level-headed as I think I am, sensible and correct. May I say old-fashioned without offending you?" He nodded. "You are just the sort of sensible person I need to talk to and would appreciate the opportunity but I won't be upset if you'd prefer not to. I am not going to off-load my grief for I am not that sort of person. But I'd just love a natter with another rational human being!"

"Mrs Modlum, I'd be delighted. Far from being offended I am rather pleased when I'm called old-fashioned as I cling to qualities that I believe to be right at a time when they are no longer de rigueur, in fact often forgotten if they have ever been learned."

"Then we have something precious in common Mr Pawden. So will you forgive my familiarity if I ask you, as a dear old friend and neighbour, to call me Audrey? I should be so happy if you felt able to do so."

"Thank you Audrey. Please call me Ernest. I cannot imagine," he added with a grin, "anyone would think us forward! And I'm pleased to be of service. I can fully understand what you imply, as when my wife Edna passed away well-meaning people rather overdid the comforting although I was very grateful, of course. Happily Mr Pugh-Calford, Cedric, was just the tonic I needed, and if I can be *your* tonic, Audrey, that would be grand."

"Ernest that's lovely, thank you. You must miss your wife very much, I am so sorry for your loss."

"Oh Edna was my rock. Her death left me without a vital part of my whole being, but although I am not a religious man I do sense her about me all the time. But Audrey, tell me about you. I don't suppose any of this has sunk in yet."

"No of course it hasn't. Too recent, too raw. But when I came here with Sergeant Panshaw I found I could cope reasonably well. I was able to wander around the house alone, they wanted to know if anything was missing, disturbed, that sort of thing, and I actually found peace. Gareth was here in spirit as he is today and that's so warming. I shall be fine coming back here to live, I really will."

"I can follow that Audrey. Edna watches over me. I'm sure she's there, guiding, praising and admonishing as necessary." They shared friendly grins. "If it's not out of place to ask did you find anything missing?"

"No. Nothing had been touched. I had all the time I needed. At times I felt a sadness rising, such as when I went into our bedroom and when I looked out over the back garden where we shared our last evening. But I coped Ernest, I coped and I knew then I'd be alright. I think I was pleased nothing had been taken, if you can understand what I'm driving at, but it does make Gareth's death all the more puzzling."

"Did you know Miss Penderman saw a car along here early Sunday morning?"

"Yes but it was the newsagent wasn't it?"

"Apparently not. It has been established the newspapers were delivered around seven and Miss Penderman saw her car at eight. The newsagent has a Ford Fiesta, Miss Penderman saw a blue Kia Rio." He noticed the sudden look of horror on Audrey's face which vanished almost as soon as it had come.

"The police are appealing for the driver to come forward in order to eliminate him, but I have a feeling they are suspicious. It could turn out to be a vital lead."

They sipped at their tea. Ernest swiftly changed course.

"You've been staying with Mr and Mrs Wandon I believe." Audrey looked relieved.

"Yes I have and I mean this kindly but it has been an experience. To use your expression well-meaning people but a little over-bearing. Rosemary is a wonderful friend but I need a break now and then. They are doing their level best to look after me in difficult circumstances and it is truly appreciated, believe me. And there is so much to do and Desmond is very calm and practical; he'll be such a help with all the formalities, arranging the funeral and all that. I do need both of them but, if you'll forgive me and never mention this, in slightly smaller doses."

This time they both laughed and then drank more tea.

"If you would like to, Audrey, do please tell me about yourself. I only know that you came here from Allington when your husband retired."

"Ernest, it's a boring old story, but I'll tell you briefly if you'd really like me to?"

"I am sure it's nothing of the sort and I'd love to hear it. And I am certain you remember meeting your husband for the first time. When was that?"

"I was born and bred, to use an expression, in Sutton Valence, south of Maidstone. Do you know it?" Ernest did. "I had a good education, about eight O-levels if I recall, and three A-levels, but didn't want to go to university. I had this simple dream, Ernest. Be a secretary until Mr Right came along, hopefully wealthy Mr Right, marry and settle down in the country and eventually become, if you'll forgive my terminology, a kept woman with no need to work.

"I managed the latter as you know but I didn't marry a wealthy man or live in the country. I met Gareth when he came to do our annual gas service. I was still living at home, a spoilt brat of a single child, but he was handsome, very funny, and quite charming, and I was bowled over. Mum and dad weren't keen but we were soon a couple and I was very much in love. They gave in, against their better judgement, and we were married, buying a terraced house in Snodland.

"Gareth did well enough and was earning good money. I was now a top secretary at a telecommunications firm, that's where I met Mrs Wandon, and in due course we were able to move to a semi in Allington. She worked in personnel and we hit it off straight away. Our friendship blossomed and it was she who introduced me to golf.

"Funny, looking back now, my manager was an absolute bigot, thought that women existed for one purpose only, the sort of person I think is commonly described today as a misogynist,

152

not that he gave me any trouble. The other girls detested him. Thought him smarmy, too smooth by far. I don't think he ever touched any of them and he never tried anything on with me. To be honest we got on fairly well, understood each other at work, if you follow me. Rosemary didn't like him.

"Shortly after I left his wife died. He had no children or near relatives and he phoned me in desperation, unable to handle the loss. Gareth was always a kind, caring man, and he was more than happy to suggest I go and console him, which I did on several occasions as it turned out. He said I saved his life, because gradually he came to terms with his grief and starting rebuilding his world. That was the about the last time I saw him and over the years we lost touch.

"We came by the Hop Pickers Oast by chance. As Gareth approached retirement the last part of my dream was yet to be realised; living in the country. This place was not only an absolute gem Ernest, it was a gift from heaven. Sadly heaven didn't provide the money! It was too expensive. Then, out of sorrowfulness elsewhere a miracle happened. An aunt of mine, a remote relative, died and left me a sizeable legacy that more than made up the deficiency between the value of our property in Allington and our required funds. And here we are. Sorry, I should say here I am.

"It has been paradise and do you know what, Ernest, I am not going under. I am going to swim not sink, but I'll not forget my beloved Gareth and he will indeed be with me here always, still enjoying our retirement home in Kent's glorious countryside. Now, come on Ernest. Enough of me. Tell me about you. I insist."

"Only if you do insist. Your story was far from boring, Audrey, but mine is sadly a good cure for insomnia."
"I'm sure it isn't and I do insist, I assure you."
"May I first ask an impertinent question Audrey? What was the name of your manager? Just curious, that's all." Once again Ernest observed a slight seriousness slide across her face.

"I cannot imagine why you want to know, but it was Ray Boulchard or similar if I remember rightly. Why?"

"I found myself wondering what happened to him. Did he re-marry, that kind of thing? No, it isn't important and I probably asked without actually knowing why. Please forget it."

"I've no idea. I was pleased I was able to help but, as I say, we lost touch. As far as I know he didn't re-marry. But I will do as you suggest and forget you asked." Both laughed again.

Ernest related his life story bringing a smile to his host's lips in the light-hearted manner of its telling, more than once sharing laughter with the widow.

He explained he'd been born on a farm near Detling Aerodrome before the second world war and that he and his sister played their part in farm work, rising very early every day and putting in a full shift as it were before coming in for a hearty late breakfast. Thence to school!

A very different era to the present.

His father was a natural farmer, a beloved dad, who had his favourite armchair nobody else was allowed to sit in, and where he enjoyed a pipe of an evening when the day's toil was done.

"He could put his head out of the door," Ernest reminisced, "and correctly forecast the weather for the next twenty fours far more accurately than the Met Office can do today! He did have a habit of finding things before they were lost, if you understand me, but he was a well liked and much loved gentleman who would do anything for anyone.

"He'd give a starving man his last few pennies and he would occasionally give shelter and food to a passing tramp. He was just so genuine, Audrey, and such a kind, caring person."

On the farm there was, of necessity, more to do once the war began. As children, unaware of the danger so close, they had

154

stood in the doorway while the Battle of Britain raged overhead, and not always so far overhead either. Kent was very much the front line county.

He recalled the time Detling aerodrome was bombed, and talked of the two German prisoners-of-war who were assigned to work on the farm, and he chatted with ease in an entertaining way Audrey liked.

It was clear she was enjoying a new kind of freedom and a strong developing friendship with a man she'd always admired. He had put her at ease, made her comfortable and yes, he'd made her happy, she knew that now. He was a sound and natural conversationalist and she was having a lovely time of it.

After speaking and answering Audrey's questions about his life as those questions arose Ernest once again changed the subject, keen to get away from the topic of Ernest William Pawden.

"Audrey, I almost forgot, unforgiveable I know, but Miss Penderman, Cedric and I did not leave floral tributes outside as, being old-fashioned, we do not share the current passion for doing so where a life has been lost. We would not wish to offend....."

"Ernest, please forgive my own rudeness interrupting, but I can totally reassure you that I am like minded. I adore flowers as you know but agree with you entirely. I have collected them up, unwrapped them and found a quiet corner in my back garden where they can rest, and I can go and see them when I wish. I would not want flowers to be ignored. They are nature at work in the most enchanting and fabulous way.

"I couldn't have them outside or in the house but they are not thrown away. The tags I have kept and where I have addresses will write notes of thanks in due course."

"I hope you don't mind Audrey, but I took the liberty of reading some of them. One caught my eye. Sorry, it's my ridiculous curiosity again. It simply read 'Together Now

155

Together' – there was no name or address. Do you know the person concerned?" Ernest was struck, as he had been before, by the serious expression on his friend's face and the look of wariness about her. It soon passed as she replied.

"I've no idea. I destroyed it. Couldn't make head or tail of it. All very strange. Didn't recognise the writing. Now, would you like some more tea, Ernest?" She sounded rather sharp and agitated and Ernest moved at once to safer ground.

"If you would like a cup Audrey, I'd be honoured to have one with you. And needless to say you will always be most welcome at my house. You have my phone number anyway so don't hesitate to ring, even if you just want a chat down the old dog-and-bone."
"Thanks Ernest, that's so appreciated." And off she went to the kitchen.

Tea and biscuits taken (he was particular pleased to find a couple of custard creams, an old favourite) Audrey had a question of her own.

"What do you make of all this nonsense about my husband that the papers seem to be determined to create a malevolent brouhaha out of? I cannot understand all the fuss over social media anyway but now this confounded young person has come up with a cock and bull yarn which has been swallowed hook, line and sinker by the press. It cannot be true. Not my Gareth."

"Well, I think it caters for public taste as, rather sadly, I suppose scandal always has, right throughout the ages. My advice is to take no notice, but that's easier said than done, even when you know your husband was innocent."
"Oh, I know," she replied with an acquiescent and laconic sigh, "and you're correct. Easier said than done, especially when you do get an unpleasant shock. This awful person gave two dates and when I checked the diary I've kept on my laptop they were days Gareth was away fishing. It was just the initial surprise. The moment I stopped to think I knew it was pure

coincidence and as he had never strayed I quickly regained my senses and faith in him."

"I have a feeling she may have been put up to it Audrey, and I'm confident the police will pursue it. Whoever took your husband's life may have paid her to write such tripe. Rest assured the police will be more than interested. And if you think about it, not everyone keeps a diary at all. Choose a couple of dates at random, what does it matter? Few would be able to recall exactly what occurred in their lives on those dates. Once the story's gone to press that's the account that appeals to readers, not the denials and retractions."

But Ernest had noted the matter and Audrey's reaction. If Jackie had been paid to promote her account of an imaginary affair the person who paid must've known Gareth was fishing on those dates. Interesting.

As he wandered home, otherwise paying attention to very little at all, memories of the conversation untangled themselves in his mind. He recalled the three occasions when the colour appeared to drain from Audrey's face, when there was a look of surprise, when her unease then passed in the blink of an eye. Was he in danger of becoming too much of a sleuth, and suspecting everyone? He smiled inwardly, and wrote off the notion, but nearly walked right past Whodunit so absorbed was he in his thoughts.

Nonetheless, as was his current habit, he sat down at his desk and wrote up the principal themes of the chat while he remembered them. It had been an engaging time. Two friends cementing their relationship in a most pleasing way. He felt closer to her and hoped he had helped and not brought her further distress. They did have much in common, there was no shame being old-fashioned, and they shared many opinions as well as a desire to be genteel and down to earth.

While Ernest made his notes a good few miles to the east a young lady was coming down to earth with a bang.

***

"It's Lucy Panshaw speaking. How may I help?"

"Miss ... miss ... it's Jackie," a nervous voice echoed in her ear.

"Call me Lucy. What is it Jackie?"

"Miss ... I mean Lucy, I'm afraid. What the other girl said, is that true, I could, like, be in danger?"

"Are you on your mobile Jackie or is it just a bad line?"

"On me mobile, out walking Noah, in the pushchair like, just wanted to talk."

"Okay, go ahead Jackie."

"Can we meet in private? Away from y'know, them two, but without anyone, like, knowing?"

"Of course we can. But not a set up Jackie. Don't try taking us for a ride. If they've put you up to calling me forget it right now."

"No no no ... no Lucy. I'm scared. Really scared. Scared for Noah. I need help but I don't want anyone to know. Don't want it getting back to them. I'll tell you the truth but not if, like, it comes back on me, know what I mean."

"The truth," Lucy paused deliberately for effect, "as in correcting lies. I'm only interested in that kind of truth. I'll do my best to keep you out of it if you'll help us. Just can't make any promises. This is about murder, a guy stabbed with a fearsome knife, and a killer who may kill again." Lucy had decided to apply a little extra fright to provide the necessary impetus for Jackie's confession.

It worked. Jackie was almost squealing with fear.

"Lucy, you gotta help me, you gotta save me 'n' Noah. Please."

"I'll protect you Jackie. Let's start with a meeting where no walls have ears and I promise you we will look after you and little Noah."

158

"Okay, okay, okay. How about a shelter along Dover seafront? And can you, like, bring that other lady? She's nice, I liked her."

Well, thanks a bunch, thought Lucy. Here I am offering to help and you want Hassana who accused you of lying! Still, perhaps that was the reason. No matter.

Arrangements were made, Sheelagh agreeing to DC Achebe's involvement, with the two detectives ready to set off later. It was a hot summer's day, and an early evening meeting was fine for Jackie and even for Noah, apparently.

***

Clayton Mainstreet, working from home, was applying himself to the Bristol project when the phone rang and he was told the site meeting was re-arranged for next week. That gave him time to look at a new scheme for somewhere in Northamptonshire, he never could remember exactly where, and to contemplate the sum of his knowledge about the death of Gareth Modlum, gas engineer.

Bit of a lad, he mused. He instantly rendered himself serious and sympathetic. Mustn't think like that. Poor Audrey, and these stories might be inventions designed to hurt her more. But just suppose her husband had wandered. Not a good enough reason to slay him, surely?

His mind took him on a tour of various possibilities. One: Audrey paid a hit man to take him out.
Two: a spurned lover paid a hit man to deal with him. Three: a spurned lover, unable to take rejection, killed him. Four: husband, partner, boyfriend hired an assassin, or five: carried out the deed themselves. Six: none of the foregoing.

Perhaps his death had no connection with the revelations at all. Maybe the murderer was paying the authors, including this Jackie, to come up with this nonsense to distract the police. Now what was that expression Ernest used? Ah yes, look for the lady. And a new dimension was added to his ponderings. Was Audrey having an affair with another woman who decided she needed Gareth out of the way? That could be the lady they should search for.

And he resolved to ring Ernest later.

***

Theories were abounding all around and about.

Molly and Agatha had been positively captivated by it, taking care not to overstep the mark of decency and lose their pity and angst for Audrey and her bereavement. Gerald had left a message on Eric's voicemail having read Jackie's expose and was feeling pangs of unhappiness, worried her memoirs might be all too true which would only add to Audrey's grief.

Cedric had been disturbed to realise he had been aroused, in a salacious way, by the broad intimate information Jackie had given. He thought she must be quite desperate for money to sell her soul to the devil in such a public way. Her photo was there, not even pixelated, anymore than she'd used a false name, and so was her baby's photo, a baby who would grow up to discover things about mum he or she might be upset or embarrassed about.

A sad old world.

But was it in any way pertinent? Like Gerald, Clayton, Molly and Agatha he puzzled over a number of possibilities, hoping Ernest, or even the police might be getting nearer to solving this one.

Sheelagh Mehedren, always the optimist, still believed the answer lay in Gareth's more distant past, her copper's intuition telling her he wasn't into anything criminal. She had her fingers crossed that more might be unveiled by Jackie once she was speaking the truth, but still feared a media stitch-up.

160

Audrey's mind was frozen on the subject, her way of coping. She'd so benefited from her time with Ernest, he was so lovely and was proving a good friend. And she was almost dreading going back to Ospringe, not that she had anything against Ospringe itself. Roman remains had been found there, unsurprising as it straddled Watling Street, the Roman route from London to Dover. Not that the Romans called it Watling Street! Nowadays it's the A2. And right there is Maison Dieu, the remarkable and historic timber-framed building that always caught Audrey's attention.

But right now it was Maison Wandon that scratched her emotions. Still, as she'd learned, she just needed to remain in control.

And with that in mind she rang a flustered Rosemary for her lift home.

***

Lucy and Hassana located Jackie and a sleeping Noah in his pushchair in a deserted shelter overlooking the beach twixt the two harbour areas. The busy throbbing Eastern Docks, where the cross-channel ferries ply their trade, were away to the left as they looked out to sea. To their right the long-gone hoverport and beyond it the Western Docks, now primarily a berth for cruise ships. A few bathers were taking advantage of the pleasant May evening and, presumably, a sea that had been warmed in the sun all day.

Jackie looked worried. She was ready to talk and did so prior to the detectives taking a seat either side of her, a pre-arranged strategy.

"Look, straight up, I'm a working girl. Me benefits don't run to looking after meself and Noah an' besides I like a bit extra for the nice things in life." Lucy and Hassana didn't doubt the nice things included weed and perhaps something stronger along the same lines.

"Anyways, this punter books an evening with me. Old bloke, overweight, slobbered a bit when he got excited, like, an' he weren't much good. I had to smile, get 'im worked up, y'know, let 'im all over me body ... well, goes with the territory don't it?" Hassana could've cried. "Anyways, afterwards he gives me a f-f-f .... great big tip and, like, flashes all these notes at me. Tells me if I do a post online about this bloke who's been done in I can have plenty of the dosh.

"Well, be a fool to refuse. No harm done. He gives me the gen as he called it, name of the dead man, two dates I spent with him, all that stuff and I say I'll do it like. He gives me loads of cash and after he'd gone I thought to meself I might as well make a whole lot more. Gotta be a paper out there willing to pay for me story. Better than having some creep like him all over me body.

"An' this paper grabs it with both hands. Loads more money. Easier than earning it on me back. All I did was, like, make up things based on me experience of punters I've had. Dead easy. But you reckon this guy'll be after me now to, like, silence me? Just protect me, right, protect me baby, okay? All I ask. Cos I'm scared, an' scared you'll drop me in it." Lucy had a question.

"Does the paper know you lied?"
"Naw, 'course not."
"Okay, we'll do all we can to keep you out of it. Now can you describe this man?"
"Look love, no offence, but don't trust the police, never have." Hassana replied to this, her first comment.
"I won't let you down, Jackie. Look at your lovely boy. That's one good reason why I won't let you down and why I won't let anything happen to you." Her comment broke the spell.
"Okay, okay. I'll do me best, but don't let that paper know what I've said."

***

162

Thursday evening at Ospringe was, so she determined, going to go Audrey's way.

Rosemary was not happy at being excluded from the visit to the Oast, Rosemary was working herself into a lather of indignation, Rosemary was cross with everything from the oven to her husband that wouldn't do precisely her bidding, Rosemary was in a dither, not a good state of mind for preparing dinner which she was presently doing. Nothing would go right, least of all Desmond who was trying his best but finding his best was falling well short of the high standards demanded.

Mr Wandon had been given an account of all the bad things in Mrs Wandon's world this very minute, and given an account in nauseating detail. Audrey had been kept in ignorance. The couple's domestic arrangements and difficulties were not for the ears of their guest whom they thought should be wrapped in cotton wool and fussed over.

To this end Rosemary was trying to prepare an exciting offering, a dish she had not tried creating before, and the move was proving to be fraught with problems.

The widow, far from being fussed over, was locked in the bathroom revelling in one of her deep, deep fragrant baths, her eyes closed, her lips pursed in a gentle, relaxed smile, memories of a most agreeable afternoon spent with Ernest Pawden drifting through her mind.

All kinds of thoughts were drifting through Ernest's mind as he studied his notes and the various remarks he had added at times since he started out on this mission earlier in the week. Certain things bothered him, but there was something else he needed to do.

He believed Clayton was working at home and rang on the off-chance. The architect answered and immediately requested an update. Good, thought Ernest, he's enthusiastic. Ideal.

163

"Clayton, I know you're extremely busy but I wondered if I could ask a favour?"

"Ask away old buddy." Ernest winced.

"I expect you're well up with the internet, know your way around it and so on, and I am not. If I gave you a short list of things that I'd like researched in depth and as soon as possible, would it be at all likely you would have the time for a hunt round?"

"Yay, Ernest. Just give me your list, bit of background, what sort of digging you want me to do, y'know, the full SP, and I'll hit the ground running. Count on me brother." Ernest began to wonder if he was doing the right thing. "Take it this is to do with the murder?"

"It is Clayton. And I would appreciate you treating this as a private matter and not talk to anyone about it, other than your partner of course."

"Her name's Ananya, Ernest. Lovely girl. I love her to bits, I really do." Ernest considered the extra information unnecessary but assumed it was the way the young spoke these days. He passed over the data while Clayton said 'yep' about every four words, an intervention Ernest found rather annoying after a period.

"By the way, Ernest, got me a little theory. Can I run it past you?" Ernest agreed and Clayton spiritedly described his idea of Audrey having a jealous female lover, which Ernest said he would note.

They said their goodbyes and the call ended.

Another call had just ended in the DCI's office.

Sheelagh clapped with glee. "Stage one complete Willie. Jackie made it all up. How ... ever," she stretched the word out conspiratorially, "a customer paid her to do one of those social media thingies, gave her the two dates she mentioned, and she decided to make a splash of it by going to the paper. Oh dear, how sad, never mind. Not, I'm sure, what her customer had in

164

mind, but who's counting. She's given Lucy a description which might, and I'm only saying might match the mad cat woman's idea of a chubby cheeked shifty man."

"Mmm ... what do you mean by 'a customer' ma-am?"
"If I called him a punter would that help?"
"She works in a bookmakers?"
"Aw Willie, you are so young and innocent and, I take it, still a virgin. Come and join us in our adult world, it's so much more fun than your nursery..."
"Oh I see. Yes, I see now. Sorry. Don't think I'm that innocent and as I kissed a girl last week I don't think I'm a virgin anymore."
"Blimey you are innocent, mate!" And both detectives laughed heartily.

They understood each other and shared a sense of humour. It made a good working partnership.

"Any idea of name or address for Mr Shifty ma-am?"
"Not looking too good. Booked through an online outfit which Hassana has checked out and all you need is an email address and a mobile number to join. But we'll get both from the firm and try and trace. Apparently, according to Hassana, this business does sort of Tripadvisor reviews for the girls and the punters alike. Jackie with nine reviews has cleared four or five stars each time, some girl eh? Our punter joined recently, had two reviews both mentioning he was a really good tipper."
"So did he pay the two of them to dirty Gareth's name? Is he behind that ma-am?"

"More to the point is he the killer, or in the killer's employ?"

***

If Audrey was likely to suffer a meal to forget Eric was getting a dinner to remember. Gerald had dished up one of his favourites and they scoffed their food down while debating the latest news on the murder.

"Must ring Ernest," Gerald reminded himself and observed his partner nodding furiously. "You never know, he and the police might've moved a whole lot closer to solving this one, and frankly I want that murderer caught asap so poor Audrey can get some type of closure. At least she might learn why he was slaughtered. What a dreadful way to die Eric."

"Too much knife crime, and it makes you wonder how safe any of us are. Poor Gareth. I'm hoping that when we get the truth it'll put him in the clear. I'm bothered about these stories. Why malign someone who's been attacked so violently, killed in cold blood?"

"Yes, know what you mean. Maybe the killer has put them up to it."

"Possibly. You can ask Ernest. He may have considered that already. Now, shall we have some cheese and biscuits and perhaps a glass of port?"

"Excellent idea. Then I'll ring our sleuth!"

Meanwhile Audrey was smirking as she did her best with the awful meal Rosemary had invented. Tasteless, some parts hot, others cold, and Desmond smiling and praising his wife for a delicious repast!

Oh how she adored such a splendid performance. An Oscar for Mr Wandon please! Elimination from Bake Off for Mrs Wandon!

Audrey, full of joy and bursting with derision, decided to join in the fun, scarcely able to keep a smile off her face.

"Rosie darling, you are so kind to me in my time of misfortune and suffering. To go to all this trouble for me, a really appetizing treat, fancy you preparing such a wonderful dinner. I've so enjoyed it pet." She glanced at Desmond who looked up momentarily and who evidently did not know whether to laugh or cry. Rosie was uncomfortable and self-conscious and

166

consequently bewildered. Audrey found she quite liked bringing about such a state of affairs. This was the widow in control.

I am positively evil, she concluded. How could I be so appalling to two lovely friends who mean so much to me? Quite easily it would seem! Must resolve to be a better and more appreciative person. They don't deserve it. Well, perhaps they deserve a little bit. And it was all she could do to suppress laughter.

Then the phone rang.

DCI Mehedren was pleased to hear Audrey was in a reasonably good emotional state and cheerful.

"There was something I'd like to ask you, Mrs Modlum, if you feel up to it. First I must say that we have interviewed the girl featured in the paper and have reason to believe she may have created the story with assistance from her paymasters. Sadly they were represented at the meeting so we have, as yet, no clarification of the story, either way.

"I thought it might be a crumb of comfort to you as I'm aware you strongly believe your husband innocent. In fact, there is a possibility we are looking at an orchestrated smear campaign here. For what reason we have yet to learn. I would appreciate you keeping this to yourself for the time being as it could hamper our enquiries if it got out."

"Chief Inspector, thank you for this information and of course I do understand. You may rely on my discretion. I appreciate you taking me into your confidence and I shall not speak of it. Now, you said you had a question. Ask away, I'm quite settled now. I spent some time alone at my home without any problems today, and in fact had quite a long chat with my neighbour, Mr Pawden. Do you know him?" She thought she heard a sigh in the pause that followed.

"Yes I do, I have met him Mrs Modlum. Grand gentleman."

167

"Absolutely. He was a tonic I can tell you. We talked about ordinary things, about our lives, and he was so easy to get on with."

"I can imagine." Sheelagh was struggling to keep exasperation out of her voice. "Now, can you tell me this? The dire young woman who was responsible for that article mentioned two specific dates she was allegedly with Mr Modlum. We don't think she was but do those dates mean anything to you at all?" Now it was Sheelagh's turn to detect a slight sigh.

"No, I can't say they do, Chief Inspector. I really have no way of knowing. I don't think most people would recall what they were doing on actual dates, unless a major occurrence took place. No, they don't mean anything to me."

"Your husband enjoyed fishing. Might he have been fishing on those dates do you think?"

"I wouldn't have a clue, I'm sorry. Look, I want the murderer caught but if this lass has made her account up, embellished by a journalist, the dates were probably chosen at random."

"Yes, that's what we wondered, but I hope you can understand why I have asked you. Sorry to have been a bit of a nuisance, Mrs Modlum. I will just say this: we are making progress in a number of directions but I cannot provide you with detailed information at present."

"I'm delighted to hear it and I never doubted you would."

The conversation ended soon after and Audrey returned to the table for her dessert having completely lost her appetite.

There were no lost appetites at Rose Cottage where Eric and Gerald discussed the case over their own dessert and re-filled glasses of port. This was a diversion from their usual sort of evening where the television reigned supreme as a rule. Gameshows, reality TV, the soaps, they loved them all.

And Gerald was to ring Ernest.

Along the lane Cedric, knowing his friend was occupied, popped to Molly's on the pretence of seeing if she was alright. He was welcomed and, as he hadn't eaten and had nothing prepared for himself, she quickly rose to the occasion and provided her guest with a round of toasted cheese and ham sandwiches which he devoured with great happiness. She had the same and then took him by surprise.

"Cedric, I was going to have a few chips afterwards. I don't suppose you'd like to join me?"
"Goodness me, well yes, if I'm not depriving you. Shall I put the kettle on while you get them ready?"
"Yes please Cedric. A nice pot of tea, always a firm favourite."

Over the Indian takeaway Ananya had brought in Clayton disclosed and outlined his task and she had leaped at the opportunity to help.

"Two searchers better than one, Clay. Wonder why he wants to know? Some guy that. Wouldn't mind betting he's closer than the police, whaddya say?"
"My gut feeling babes is that he's quite capable of pulling this off, and wouldn't it be great if we helped him do it?"
"Yay, let's go to it detective Mainstreet."

And so Thursday moved on its way taking the residents of this isolated country lane along with it.

Friday was peeping round the corner and on this fine summer evening as the sun slipped below the horizon few of those residents could've realised what the next day or two would bring.

Chapter Sixteen

Friday Morning

Clayton ate his poached egg on toast and poured a little milk into his fair trade coffee.

He'd loved poached eggs since childhood, and eggs and milk were permitted under their form of vegetarianism providing they were confident no animal had suffered in their provision. But they would be banned when they were committed vegans.

There was a sigh as he studied his empty plate and sipped his drink.

Christmas had, for him, been a disaster. They'd spent it with his parents in Bexleyheath. With their guests' approval Mr and Mrs Mainstreet had addressed a traditional roast turkey dinner on Christmas Day, washed down with glasses of *Sancerre,* while he and Ananya had tackled a curious meal of roasted nuts and vegetables and a glass of fruit juice.

The evening buffet, also attended by Clayton's sisters and their partners, featured hot sausage rolls and other meat-related snack bites, as well as bountiful quantities of beer, wine and spirits, none of which he was able to touch. They played charades, his mother instantly guessing the film title he was miming, George Clooney's *Up in the Air.* They'd all laughed at how easy he made it.

He didn't think it was funny.

"Bullocks!" he exclaimed out loud to himself, illustrating an unnecessary politeness given he was alone. "And I did it all for my love of Ananya. So what am I going to give up? Ananya or poached eggs on toast? I know, I know, what good's a poached egg when you want sex." And with that observation he returned

170

to researching Ernest's info, a project he and his partner had both enjoyed and which had been revealing.

He paused for a moment while washing up. Expect someone's used a poached egg in some sort of sexual activity he felt. Way things are today. After all he and Ananya had discovered some entertaining things you could do with a large cucumber which was one of the upsides of being a vegetarian. No animals had been ill-treated and they'd eaten the cucumber, thoroughly washed of course.

Back to the murder.

***

The murder was the topic in the incident room where Sheelagh Mehedren was holding court as befitting her rank.

They had learned much about both Modlums, their history and their recent lives. The DCI was bothered by one factor: Hop Pickers Oast. There was something rattling around in her fertile mind and she couldn't place what it was. Her earlier opinion was that the house itself was trying to tell her something, but what was it? More vitally, was it actually important?

"Okay Willie, run Gareth Modlum past me again."

"Born Chatham, tried various jobs eventually qualifying as a gas engineer. British Gas, his last employer, say he was very good, very good indeed. Sorry to see him retire. Worked mainly in Kent but occasionally East Sussex and south-east London. Parents long gone, no close relatives. Always been keen on fishing. No close friends as far as we know but we have spoken to a couple of acquaintances and three people he worked with at British Gas, all say number one guy. Well-liked, caring sort of bloke, heart of gold blah-blah-blah.

"Appears to have been a loner where fishing was concerned. We've taken the dates Jackie mentioned and we're hiking them around angling clubs, fishing lakes, that sort of thing, but if he'd been fishing it could've been anywhere, so not too hopeful. Other interests, according to his wife, included TV sport and watching old black and white films, which they both enjoyed. Not a great reader, not much attention given to music and didn't care about politics.

"Just Mr Ordinary ma-am. Helped Audrey in the garden and, of course, they worked in the garden of that right-on pair at Earth Cottage. Bit of a DIY man apparently."

"Yep. Now take me on a tour of Audrey Modlum."

"Right ma-am. Born and bred Maidstone, no great ambition beyond marrying a wealthy man, giving up work and living in the country. Met Gareth when he came to provide an annual service at her parents' home. They married, lived in Snodland then Allington. She gave up work ten years ago, so obviously Gareth was coining it, but they needed a substantial bequest to fund their purchase of the Oast. Aunt Phoebe provided it by dying right on cue.

"She was a distant relative in every sense. Again, like her husband Audrey had no close relatives, both parents deceased, no siblings. Became a secretary in the Medway Towns, telecom firm, which is where she met Rosemary Wandon who encouraged her to take up golf.

"All year round gardening fanatic. Enjoys romantic fiction. Did have a crack at a local WI but there was a fall out. Again, no really close friends apart from Mr and Mrs Wandon. Seemed quite happy and settled at the Oast especially, so she said, with Gareth in tow.

"Holidays pretty rare. Occasional nights away, mainly in Kent. In the early days of the marriage they tended to save their pennies, so she says, and only took a proper break now and then. And the habit stayed with them as the years advanced. Not been

172

away since her husband's retirement, other than those odd nights now and then.

"Goes shopping with Rosemary at least once a month. Bluewater, Hempstead Valley, Canterbury and so on as a rule. Groceries mostly bought online from Tesco and delivered. Plays golf, always with Rosemary, two or three times a month. They both belong to the same club but Audrey shuns the social side."

"Thanks Willie. The one stand-out thing is that neither of them appear to have been sociable. Not mixers. No close friends. Does that have any relevance I wonder?"

"It could be said Gareth was all too sociable with women ma-am, but then we could just be looking at a smear campaign, maybe orchestrated by the killer."

"Mmm .... there's nothing pointing at any obvious enemies, is there? So is the mostly likely scenario a spurned or jealous lover, someone acting on their behalf, or an angry partner of a lover?"

Sheelagh tapped her teeth with her pen as her usual accompaniment to deep thought.

"Something comes back to me Willie. Remember that floral tribute outside, the one with the anonymous label 'together now together'? Perhaps that's more of a clue than we realise. Get Lucy to chat to Audrey some more. And I tell you what, why don't you get Mr Wandon on one side for a private natter? We have a full statement from Mrs Wandon but her husband might be worth tackling. Just be hyper-friendly if you know what I mean, Willie. He might know something and he may not realise he does! You know the form. Tease summat out of him!"

"My intuition has constantly led me to believe this is related to something in Gareth's past a long time ago. But why would the killer wait until now? My nose is twitching in another direction Willie, and I'm beginning to think the truth is closer to home and more recent."

Had he been the sort of person to use the expression Ernest's nose would've been twitching and in an intriguing direction as he dissected the data he now had.

There was extra input from Eric and Gerald, but it was the work the young couple at Earth Cottage had begun that was producing results that threw a series of question marks into Mr Pawden's deliberations.

Not being strictly computer literate but having an accountant's brain he had arranged things neatly on pages of graph paper and in his notebook using good old pen and ink, precisely biros of different colours plus a number of highlight pens. The words and figures were clear, immaculately written with a delicate evenness. Just how he'd been taught at school, despite the best efforts of the Germans to disrupt his education.

His analytical mind was busy working its patient way through what was now a mass of intelligence gathered from many sources principally, it had to be said, his own. There were rays of light appearing. And he duly wondered if Cedric and Molly might like a trip to Kemsley, Sittingbourne.

Cedric had strolled along to Molly's more out of concern than anything else, but prompted no doubt by feelings he hadn't had in a long time.

To this end he had dressed with extra attention to personal detail and stood in front of a full length mirror feeling quite satisfied.

A crisp freshly-ironed shirt, his National Trust tie, light alpaca jacket, cream slacks with a knife edge crease, highly polished brown shoes adorned his slender body. He was just under five feet five and drew himself to his full height for greater effect. Like a guardsman, he thought. He still possessed a full head of hair (unlike Ernest) and today it was neatly combed and parted to one side.

He had taken great care with his razor to ensure a smooth finish and had tidied up the back of his neck and made sure no strands of his hair fell about his ears. He was ready, and he was all man!

Molly welcomed him like a long lost friend although Felicity failed to match her enthusiasm and looked at him with disdain from a safe distance. All three went to the kitchen, the humans to make some tea, the cat to watch proceedings. Felicity might have been guarding Molly's honour such was her stance.

Cedric made a fuss of her which made a marginal improvement in the man/beast relationship.

Over in Ospringe Desmond was making a fuss of Audrey which was manufacturing a substantial deterioration in the beast/guest relationship. The widow came to a conclusion.

"Desmond, I'd like to collect my own car. I'm perfectly fit to drive. If you or Rosie would take me home I can bring myself back here later." Rosemary, who had just entered the lounge, bristled and piped up.

"Oh do you really need to, pet? We can ferry you wherever and whenever you want to go."

"My mind's made up Rosie. No offence. No words can describe how grateful I am to you both but I want my car and I'd like to have some more time at home. Start my rehabilitation if you like. I must do it. I'm determined not to go down." Desmond was more supportive than might've been expected.

"Yes, you're right sweetheart ....."

"Desmond!" Rosemary exclaimed with a cry, "that's not the best thing to say, I'm sure it isn't."

But Mr Wandon, for once in his life, was prepared to make a stand, even if it left him in eternal damnation as was most likely.

"No Rosemary. You're wrong, Audrey's right. Now, shall I take her or you?"

Mrs Wandon took exactly six seconds to burst into torrents of tears which, in peril of his life, Desmond chose to ignore. Audrey was unfeeling and stomped off upstairs throwing a few words over her shoulder.

"When you've sorted out who is taking me I'll meet whoever outside in five minutes if you please."

It was red-eyed, sniffling Rosemary she met there.

Meanwhile a grim faced Desmond had plopped down in an armchair. He had been mortified to learn what he considered to be beautiful love-making meant to his wife, and more importantly what sort of rating she had awarded him in the intimacy stakes. His response had been to cast aside years of compliant submission and turn himself into master in his own household.

How this might work out was anyone's guess, and he was trying to puzzle out an uncertain future sitting quietly alone when the phone rang.

***

Ananya was getting her message across by employing obscene verbs and adjectives in her grammar believing it was the only language they understood. This belief was based on the approach the building contractors had adopted when berating her methods. Initially she had been stunned although she had heard it all before, and she found herself thinking that dear Ernest Pawden would've been disgusted by their words directed at a young lady.

She didn't stop to think what Ernest would've thought of a young lady using such terminology.

The heated argument calmed down. Ananya said she was in charge and they'd do it her way and that was going to be that. She supervised and everything worked out fine as she knew it would. The contractors, five men, apologised and warmly congratulated her, one admitting the job had been completed quicker and more efficiently than doing it their way. They'd learned a lesson.

She couldn't help but think that learning such a lesson from a woman was painful and hideous for a man, and that in itself was a victory! Returning to the office for a coffee an extraordinary brain wave touched base in her mind. Ananya sat in the ragged old armchair with her drink in hand, looked around the Portakabin and let this new mental incursion flourish to the point where it lit a smile on her face.

Ernest was a lovely guy and he'd come up with some wicked ideas. She and Clayton had worked wonders. What a team they made! But wait a moment. Would Ernest actually solve this one? Surely the police were on the case? She, Ananya Ghatik, had brains. A university education, a brilliant mind (in her opinion), a track record to be proud of. She should be at the forefront of this investigation.

It was time to get the rest of the day off, fly home to Clayton, give him a good seeing-to, and go visit Mr Pawden, find out what was going on and take the lead. She could do it. Juggling her different roles was what she was all about. And it would be a positive step on the road to her partner's salvation.

And, she declared to herself, that would mean becoming vegans immediately.

***

"Thank you for seeing me, Mr Wandon."

"Please call me Desmond. I've no idea how I can be of any use to you, Sergeant, but I am only too willing to try. I want Gareth's murderer caught pronto."

"Thank you Desmond, and you're welcome to call me Willie. It's short for Willoughby."

"Would you like a drink ... er ... Willie?"

"No thank you Desmond." Willie was being hyper-friendly as decreed by she who must be obeyed.

"We have your wife's statement which is, naturally, a very formal matter and a vital one for us. But we thought we'd like to talk to everyone on the edge of this awful business and do so without formality. Almost off-the-record you might say. We're simply looking at creating a full picture which might help us find new leads."

"Anything I can do I will, I assure you."

"Thank you Desmond. Now, can you tell me anything about Mr Modlum's fishing habits? I expect Mrs Modlum has told you that Jackie, the girl in Dover, gave two specific dates. These could, of course, have been chosen at random. But supposing Mr Modlum had indeed been fishing and we could verify that it would put him in the clear and that would surely be a great relief to his widow."

"Ah Jackie is in Dover is she?" Whoops, thought Willie, dropped one there. "I'm so sorry Willie but I really have no idea where he went angling or when. Sorry. The only thing I know is that Audrey checked those two dates in her diary and he was fishing those days." Willie's ears pricked up.

"Her diary?" he queried.

"Yes, on her laptop," Desmond revealed innocently. Willie was enthused.

"Her laptop Desmond?"

"Yes, she keeps a diary going back years on her laptop."

"Was that the one we checked out at her home."

"No idea. She brought it back here when she collected her things with your DS Panshaw."

Willie decided to change tack, having noted all he needed to know about the laptop.

"Sorry to ask such a question Desmond, but were the Modlums a happy couple in the broadest sense of the expression?"

"Oh yes. I think Gareth, not that I knew him that well, might've liked a family but Audrey was none too keen." He was thinking back to the drunken revelations of Audrey and Rosemary and feeling the pain. "We have two children, Willie," and he paused as the distress overtook him, "but my wife doesn't seem too sure how." He was in a world of his own and Willie was keenly aware of the agony Desmond was suffering, aware he was an intruder in some sort of private grief.

"Audrey didn't think Gareth was that good at sex. Oh, I'm sorry Willie, I've wandered. I do apologise. May I please ask you not to repeat what I've just said?"

"No of course not Desmond," he lied.

But Willie was wide awake to this rather startling piece of information. Could it have some relevance? There was little more to the meeting and Willie soon set off for base, stopping to take a call en route. It was Ernest.

"Sergeant. I need an urgent meeting. It's important. I wouldn't trouble you otherwise."

Willie took a deep breath then advised he'd divert to Whodunit as he was only a few minutes away.

Chapter Seventeen

The Book of Revelations

Needless to say the sole topic of conversation at the Dahlias was the murder.

Felicity slunk off somewhere plainly fed up with the whole business and bemoaning the fact it seemed to be responsible for her being denied attention on an ongoing basis.

Cedric was giving Molly a great deal of attention and Molly was lapping it up just as a cat might well do. They were sitting together on the two-seater settee, a facility small enough to be barely deserving of its two-seater title. They talked freely, drank tea and the distance between them vanished into nothingness.

"I think Ernest is on to something," Cedric advised. "I think he's going to try and see that Sergeant Broughton today if he can. The couple at Earth Cottage have done some research in response to Ernest's request as they have exceptional skills with computers and something called tablets, and they are also on an outfit called Facebook I believe."

"Oh yes, I've heard of that. Doesn't always attract very good publicity."

"No Molly. Y'know what? I think we're better off out of it. I'm pleased we don't belong to the computer age. Ernest has been doing all his workings out with pen and paper, and that's the world we belong to."

"You're so right Cedric. Poor Audrey Modlum has been a victim of this so-called social media and I wouldn't give you a thank you to be on it."

The so-called social media had proved a solid hunting ground for Clayton and Ananya in their research. The former was turning up more information right now. He was aware most would be useless but Ernest would tell them if they hit on anything valuable.

He was gloriously unaware that his beloved was even now heading his way with the good news that he was to be intimately savaged and the bad news he was about to become an instant vegan.

Just down the road Rosemary Wandon's Mini pulled into the drive at the Hop Pickers Oast with the driver delighted she was going to be invited in for coffee. She had no idea DS Broughton was having a private chat with Mr Wandon and even less idea what Desmond was revealing. The drunken talk between her and Audrey was long forgotten if it had ever been remembered. Both women were sozzled at the time ignorant of the fact Desmond had heard hurtful words.

Of course Rosemary wanted to stay as long as possible and Audrey was having none of it.

"Rosie, bless you for your kindness and for all you and Desmond are doing for me. I am not deserting two such true and trusted friends, without whom I could not have managed, just please understand I want to be alone so I can adjust to returning here to live." Rosie's red eyes managed a few more little tears, all wasted.

"Audrey, Audrey, I do understand, but don't you see, even Desmond has spoken sharply to me today, he's never done that before, and I'm in such a state."
"Rosie, Desmond loves you to bits, believe me. I think he's being strong for you and you should like that in a husband."
"Do you really believe that Audrey? He's never shown any signs of support. He just does as he's told....."
"Well Rosie, perhaps that's it. Maybe he's being strong when you are so upset. That's a good thing my dear, a very good thing."
Rosemary seemed to accept this, dried her eyes, drank her coffee and sat back in her chair much to Audrey's annoyance.

"Right Rosie, I'll be home in time for dinner. Drive safely."
Her guest took some while comprehending this overt hint but
eventually acknowledged the inevitable and departed. Audrey
flopped down exasperated but relieved. She had been the soul of
diplomacy, a wise counsellor and was fast becoming an
accomplished liar.

I don't think Desmond is being supportive, she debated with
herself once Rosemary had gone, and I think he's rebelling Rosie
dear and you had better be prepared for a shock. A worm could
be turning! I'm sorry my dear friend that I don't want you here
but I have things to do away from prying eyes and walls with
ears. This is my castle and I've pulled up the drawbridge and you
are persona non grata. That's the way it is, sweet little
overbearing Rosie.

***

DS Broughton pulled off the A2 and found a place to stop.

He switched off, sat back, closed his eyes and thought.

Audrey told the DCI she had no way of knowing what Gareth
was up to on those two dates and now we discover she knew all
along. And she has a diary, obviously going back a couple of
years or more, maybe even further back. And it's kept on a laptop
we don't know about.

Now is that suspicious he considered? Mr Pawden suggested,
what was it, ah yes search for the lady. Is Audrey that lady? I
wonder what else her laptop might surrender if interrogated by
our experts? Right, let's go and see what Poirot Pawden has to
say and try and keep an open mind and display a reasonable
degree of politeness and courtesy!

His final thought as he turned the ignition concerned sex. That
is, the words Desmond had spoken about sex relating to his wife
and to Audrey and Gareth. This is all getting spellbinding! And
with that he set off for Whodunit.

***

Also heading in that direction was DS Lucy Panshaw who had made an appointment to meet Audrey at the Oast, but who was now in possession of extra detail supplied by Willie.

Back at Ospringe Rosemary had suffered a double surprise and it was hard to tell which had upset her most. First she had to avoid a pile of dogs muck on the pavement at the end of the drive. That sent her near purple with apoplexy to use an expression.

"God," she raged at Desmond who was being despatched to clear the offending effluent, "to think that dirty, filthy people stand there and watch their dogs do it. God! This new vogue for having dogs, it's so typical of the arrogant, irresponsible morons we're breeding, idiots who cannot accept their duty to clear up after the animals. They want the dogs to show off but don't want the by-products. It's disgusting."

When her husband returned from his task an already angry Mrs Wandon was subjected to the news Desmond had been interviewed by DS Broughton.

"My God, what did you say to him?" she screamed. In fact she was in for a third shock as he moved closer to her and looked her right in the eyes before speaking.

"What are you afraid I might've said?" he challenged in soft but authoritative voice.
"What?" she replied, unmistakably startled.
"What are you afraid of Rosie? There's nothing I can tell the policeman that you don't know about, and being a good citizen I would tell him the truth, as I have done. I ask you again Rosie, what are you afraid of? What's there to be afraid of? Do you think I might've revealed what colour knickers you're wearing? Tough. You weren't here. We chatted, that's all. If you'd like more detail I'll tell you but only when you've calmed down and

183

are prepared to stop treating me like a dimbo, and have a decent conversation."

And with that he gathered up his newspaper and sat down to read it leaving Rosemary rooted to the spot, open-mouthed, white as a sheet, eyes bulging. Eventually the power of speech returned to her.

"How ... how ... how *dare* you speak to me like that!" she howled.

"Very easily," he responded quietly without taking his eyes from the paper, "and any more trouble from you, darling, and I'll put you over my knee and spank your bottom."

Thus was the blue touch paper lit.

He was given chapter and verse about his failings, current, recent and historical. His shortcomings as a man, husband and father were outlined at length in nauseating detail. The reasons why she treated him like a dimbo were given with enormous and unmistakable clarity. He turned a page and commented.

"That's nice dear. Now shall we have a cup of coffee?" She reached over and grabbed the paper tearing it to pieces which she threw over him.

"Oh that's a shame Rosie, as I haven't finished reading it. Before we go any further, as you have been so kind as to illustrate what an awful person I am, I may as well have my two-penneth. And it's simply this. I heard from your lips that you don't like sex, and don't know how you got pregnant. How do you think that makes a man feel? You're a spoilt child and I've been guilty of spoiling you silly. Well, Rosie, no more. This marriage is going to be a true partnership from now on. Equal stakes, do I make myself clear?"

He had, and he watched as his wife crumbled into a heap on the settee sobbing her heart out, then he stopped watching and left her to her desolation, going to make the coffee he wanted.

Things were much quieter at Hop Pickers Oast where Audrey and Lucy were having coffee on the patio in the sun. The Sergeant had been trying to find a way of approaching her next issue, the diary.

"When do you think you'll come back to live here, Audrey?"

"Oh I don't know exactly, but I'll know when I'm ready."

"I'm not so sure I'd be as strong as you....."

"I hope you never have to find out. Not this way. Not seeing your dead husband lying in a pool of blood in your own home."

"I'm so sorry Audrey, I really didn't mean to....."

"No, no Lucy. It's alright, I didn't mean to be so sharp with you. I'm sorry."

"Not a problem Audrey, I'm sorry if I said the wrong thing."

"Not at all. Perhaps I'm a bit on edge. To be honest my friends are getting on top of me at the mo. I love them and they've been kindness personified and I couldn't manage without them, but, well, you know, sometimes it's a bit too much. Desmond has been superb helping me with the formalities and arrangements. He's a darling. He seems to know exactly what to do and there's so much to be done."

"I can imagine. He must be rather like a diary for you. I'm sure you must be losing track of time, day of the week, that sort of thing."

"Yes, it's getting like that. He does keep an eye out for me though. Yes, I suppose you could say he's my diary." Both women laughed lightly.

"Do you keep a diary anyway Audrey? I do, but it's all electronic for me, y'know, on the computer. Can access the info anywhere, and I do add brief notes about what I've done each day. I don't think many people keep diaries these days, well not to reflect on what they've been doing."

"I've never kept a diary, written or electronic Lucy."

"I noticed you've left the laptop here Audrey, so nothing you need it for obviously. I take it you're not really into computers."

185

She studied the widow who was shifting uneasily in her seat. Any warmth of companionship in her face engendered so far had disappeared.

"No Lucy. They're not for me. You've checked ours out and no doubt you know almost everything on there was Gareth's. But I suppose I'll have to get at all the bank stuff and so on, but Desmond's offered to help, he's a little more clued up than me."

Lucy was between a rock and a hard place. But first and foremost she was a police officer. The time for pretence was over.

"Audrey, Desmond was visited by DS Broughton this morning and I have to tell you this. I don't wish to drive a wedge between you and your dearest friends, and maybe Desmond was muddled and used the wrong words. But he said you kept a diary on your laptop, obviously not the one here, and that you were able to check the dates Jackie gave. That isn't what you told DCI Mehedren is it?"

Mrs Modlum was looking directly ahead, her face frozen. Finally the words came, cold and emotionless.

"You deceitful little bitch. Backed me into a corner pretending to be friendly. What a nasty person you are. Get out of my house. Yes, I have a diary on my own laptop, and that's my business, nobody else's. I knew my husband had allegedly been fishing those two dates and it frightened the life out of me. I wondered if there was actually any truth in Jackie's words. I was shocked and in doubt and I didn't want to feel Jackie's account was going to be afforded any credence. That's why I kept it from your precious DCI. Now go."

Lucy went without a word. Her main unease surrounded the possibility they might need to check that laptop out. She also assumed it was at Ospringe. It was at the Oast and Audrey was getting ready to set about it fearing the police might examine it.

"Were you evacuated during the war Cedric?"

"Not really. I was sent to live with an aged aunt and uncle on the North Downs above Lenham. My parents, well my mother really, wanted me close at hand, for visits and so on, and reckoned I was a darned sight safer there than the Medway Towns, Chatham Docks being a target for the Germans of course."

"I expect you saw much of the Battle of Britain."
"I did indeed. Horrific. My father was in the RAF. Ground crew, based at Hornchurch much of the time. There's nothing romantic about killing the enemy Molly, or being maimed or killed by them."
"Oh I'm sorry Cedric, I wasn't speaking in the romantic sense. I knew it must've been unimaginably awful for our pilots and theirs.
"No apology necessary Molly. Goodness me, my dear Molly, perish the thought. At least my father survived the war. But here we are talking about the repulsion of killing when we've become so fascinated by Gareth Modlum's murder."

"Oh yes Cedric. That's very true. I wonder how Ernest is faring? Shall we give him a ring?"
"Good idea Molly. Will you or shall I?"

And so the repulsion of killing was easily expunged from their thoughts.

***

"Good to see you again Mr Pawden."

"Sergeant, the pleasure is all mine. Come in, come in and sit y'self down. Would you like a drink?"
"I could murd .... oh sorry, I meant to say I'd *love* a cup of tea Mr Pawden."

"Yes, our language throws up all kinds of awkward expressions, doesn't it? I'll get us both a cuppa. Kettle's just boiled so won't be a jiffy."

He was back within the twinkling of an eye.

"And, you know, we British use many sporting terms in our everyday conversation don't we? Especially cricket and golfing terms. We're '*on the back foot*' and something's '*par for the course*'.

And we do say we could murder a drink! So here's a tea you can quench your thirst with Sergeant." Both men enjoyed a hearty chuckle.

"Well, Mr Pawden, my time's yours. Do I need my notebook?"

"I think you will remember what I have to say but I have prepared some notes for you. I'll give those to you afterwards, if I may, as it will give me the opportunity in the meantime to add full dramatic effect to my presentation." Ernest looked at the crestfallen DS whose face was a picture of dismay and then roared with laughter.

"Oh Sergeant, I do apologise. I am only joking. I know you regard me as an amateur sleuth whereas I know I am nothing of the sort. As I explained from the outset I enjoy the entertainment value of crime novels and TV murder mysteries, but I accept them as fiction. I do not aspire to be a private eye and I am certain I am not capable of inventing a story. I'd be no good at it.

"So, what I have prepared is a resume of data collated from my own research and the thoughts and input, if I have the word right, of my neighbours including Mrs Modlum herself." Willie visibly relaxed, smiled a great deal, and sat back to savour his tea and Ernest's words.

Chapter Eighteen

Ernest rounds up a posse
Molly rounds up a pussy

"Sorry ma-am, thought I'd done it right, but I should've just asked outright. She really got the rats, called me a bitch. Guess I deserved it."

"No you didn't Lucy. The only reason I'm excusing her is the situation she's in, poor woman. We're all learning all the time, me too. It's called life isn't it?" The DCI was rather resigned and philosophical. "Call it on the job training Lucy. We don't always handle things the right way but we learn and we get there in the end. The main thing is we know she lied about those two dates and I'm not convinced her explanation holds water."

After a moments pause Sheelagh continued.

"Do we ask to see the laptop? Probably pointless, but she's an intelligent woman and will expect us to do it. I'll ask her."
"Trouble is she says that label 'Together now together' means nothing and we know now we can't trust her."
"True Lucy, and I share your suspicions over that. Wonder how Mr Liaison is getting on with Hercule Poirot?" They giggled together in a girlish sort of way.

Mr Liaison, aka Willie Broughton, was all ears, listening and drinking a delicious cup of tea. He had to hand it to Ernest, the guy made a mean cuppa. If truth be told he was hoping Ernest would be brief and his mind was already wandering.

It didn't take long for his host to gain his full concentration.

"Sergeant, I must first ask you to remember I am going to be talking about a good friend and neighbour who has been bereaved in the worst possible way. I honestly think she has no idea who committed the murder, but dreads the possibility she might do, if you follow me. I have no compunction in saying I do not believe she was in any way involved in the murder. But you have your job to do, I understand that, and I appreciate you may need to act on my information.

"Mrs Modlum has been a kind neighbour, often checking up on the gang-of-three as I call myself, Miss Penderman and Mr Pugh-Calford. We are not in the first flush of youth and it's quite lovely that someone cares that we are well and have all we need. A true friend indeed Sergeant. Her husband likewise. In fact, a delightful couple.

"I have the good fortune to have other good neighbours and I have been able to call upon the young couple at Earth Cottage to assist me in matters technological, as well as gain the thoughts of Mr Furness and Mr Samuels at Rose Cottage. They were distressed when the knife was discovered in one of their bushes and have puzzled its appearance there.

"I've cobbled together a few points having had a chat with Mrs Modlum. I'll explain. My expression was cherchez la femme. I have a feeling the lady in question was right in front of us all the time. Not that, as I've said, I think she had anything to do with the killing.

"Mrs Modlum always dreamed of being, in her words, a kept woman. She longed for a quiet country home shared with a husband who provided for her. She didn't have extravagant needs and was happy at work paying her way in the early days. Mr Modlum did very well and in time they were able to afford the move from Snodland to Allington. Financially, I would suggest, things went from good to better and Mrs Modlum was at long last able to give up work. She adores the garden you see Sergeant and I expect the one at Allington was a decent size. As I'm sure you're aware, when Mr Modlum retired they were able to buy the Oast thanks to a sizeable bequest from a distant relative, and Mrs Modlum was in her element having achieved all her dreams.

"I suspect the problems started earlier. You know about her career?" Willie nodded, hoping this saga was going to gather some pace soon. "Well, I understand she was a secretary to an absolute bigot of a man named Ray Boulchard. Although she says she got on well with him she knew he believed a woman's role in life was, shall we say, to look after her man, have and rear children and be subservient in all things. Most of the ladies working there loathed him.

"It was where she met Mrs Wandon who persuaded her to take up golf. Shortly after Mrs Modlum left the firm the wife of her former boss died. Mr Boulchard was distraught and unable to cope. There were no children, no close relatives and precious few friends. In desperation he contacted Mrs Modlum who, with her husband's agreement, went to see him, a gesture of compassion in the circumstances.

"Her comforting appears to have worked for eventually he found he could stand on his own two feet and, according to Mrs Modlum, they lost touch. Now it's my belief that far from losing touch the pair of them had begun an affair which continued until quite recently. Just intuition Sergeant. But it fits into place. Mr Modlum was, until three years ago, fully occupied at work for long hours each day, and he loved his fishing, a hobby that also occupied him for many hours at a time. Plenty of opportunity for an unfaithful wife to visit her paramour.

"But what I imagine happened when Mr Modlum retired is that his wife, having acquired a dream-come-true in all respects, found love again with her husband. She discovered that, now he was home much of the time and they had this beautiful house in the country, they were having a re-awoken marriage. Something had to give of course, and Mrs Modlum decided Mr Boulchard had to go.

"As I'm certain you realise Sergeant, Mrs Modlum is a very strong person, so she had little trouble giving Mr Boulchard his marching orders, painful though it may have been, for she'd enjoyed many happy and fulfilling times with him. We also know Mr Boulchard was quite different.

"He'd gone to pieces when his wife died and now he was being rejected by a living woman. I doubt he could cope. He may have continued pestering Mrs Modlum but she was capable of resisting. The affair was over and he couldn't accept it. I think it explains the mystery floral tribute, the label with its simple inscription 'Together now together'. He left it, or had it delivered most likely, and the note is a reference to the idea he and Mrs Modlum could now be together.

"By itself that doesn't make him a murderer. But we've been doing some research Sergeant. Mr Boulchard is on something called Facebook as are the couple at Earth Cottage, and we have reason to believe he lives at Kemsley and drives a Kia Rio. I was expecting to take a drive over there later in the company of Miss Penderman and Mr Pugh-Calford.

"The disposal of the knife might also make more sense. Mrs Modlum must've talked to him about her neighbours and it is quite conceivable that to a man who thought a woman's place is in the home, at her master's service, the thought of two men in a relationship was anathema. So the knife was semi-hidden there to cast suspicion on Mr Furness and Mr Samuels. That's my theory for what it's worth. And to wrap it up Sergeant, my guess is that Mr Boulchard paid prostitutes he'd visited to besmirch Mr Modlum's name.

"Mizzz Ghatik," he pronounced it, "and Mr Mainstreet located a website where such ladies may be booked and they found a young woman rejoicing in the pseudonym of Kissy-Katy-XXX in Dover. Her online photos looked incredibly similar to the one of Jackie in the papers.

"Of course I could be barking up the wrong tree."

Willie thought that barking wasn't a bad word. So that's how amateur sleuths work things out! But that blanket condemnation had to be counter-balanced by certain credible aspects, not least that they'd traced Jackie and knew Ray Boulchard lived at Kemsley and had a Kia Rio. Supposing it was a different colour? That'd blow that one out of the water.

Lucy had obtained a description from Jackie. Would it match his Facebook photo if he had one? Worth checking.

"Mr Pawden, you've done a great job, but we need a touch of evidence before we go wasting time." His words were liberally laced with ill-disguised patronising scorn.

"Well, as I mentioned, we are going to Kemsley for a drive round on the off-chance. I've no doubt you could trace his actual address and find out about his car much quicker and more efficiently than we can, but we don't want to get in your way Sergeant, and duplicate your efforts."

Ernest was as good at thinly-veiled sarcasm as Willie was.

"You won't be in our way, no problem. Please go ahead and let me know how you get on. Really appreciate that. I'll report back to DCI Mehedren and we'll institute enquiries straight away." His enthusiasm was undone, in Ernest's eyes, by the lack of commitment in his voice. Ernest handed over his written précis which Willie knew, just knew, would make the DCI's day. Still, serve her right for appointing him liaison officer. Gawd!

***

Clayton was amazed to see Ananya home early and hoped nothing was wrong.

Whereas he was tall, muscular, physically fit and of athletic build, his partner had a degree of plumpness and was relatively short with a round angelic face which made her all the more attractive. He hadn't fancied her at first but after being set upon in the wild on the forest floor amongst autumn's fallen leaves he'd lost his heart and knew he'd never desire another woman.

193

And here she was, hi-viz jacket flapping in the gentle summer breeze, with that look in her eyes as she strode purposefully into the house.

"Come 'ere," she bellowed, "I want you and I want you now. Come 'ere."

Afterwards as they rested peacefully and exhausted on their lover's cot she told him about the other reason she'd come home, and as a result their conversation quickly moved on to the murder and Ernest's work.

"Right," he said, "let's give him a call and take it from there."
"Give us a kiss first."
"You'd make a far better Kissy-Katy."
"Yeah, but could you afford me?"
"Get a second mortgage for an hour with you."
"We got a second mortgage Clay!"

And so they kissed, Clayton blissfully unaware there was another reason why she'd got the afternoon off. Veganism beckoned.

***

Rosemary had waited anything but patiently for Desmond to come and apologise and in this she was disappointed.

"Have you nothing to say to me?" she cried, making one more circuit of the lounge.
"Yes. What's for dinner darling?" With a subdued shriek she'd left the room slamming the door behind her and raced upstairs to the bedroom. She wanted to grab his clothes and rip them to shreds. She was boiling. She pulled all the bedclothes off and piled them up on the floor and then realised she had no obvious reason for so doing.

This calmed her and in due course she set about begrudgingly making the bed. The toil had barely ended when Desmond strolled in.

"You've come to apologise I take it. Well, you can have another......" Her voice trailed away as he moved ever closer exercising a glint in his eyes she'd never seen before. She backed away but only as far as the wardrobe which arrested her retreat. Suddenly he was right in front of her.

"Rosie, you have the right to refuse, but I'd like to put my arms around your waist and kiss you passionately. Will you let me?"

"I ... I ... I ... I ... I ...I ...," she stammered, stunned beyond sense.

"I think the ayes have it." he gloated as he slid his arms around her. "Say no now if you want to stop me." There was just enough time to shake her head, which Desmond took to mean she had no objection, before their lips met for the first time for years.

***

"I don't think he believes me but he's taken my notes away to show the DCI."

Ernest had arrived at the Dahlias to join Molly and Cedric, received a call from Earth Cottage which resulted in an invitation to Ananya and Clayton to come to Molly's, and he had just finished talking them all through the meeting with DS Broughton.

"Wow" exclaimed Clayton, "Brilliant Mr Holmes. What powers of deduction. Love it, love it. Now it's not so much cherchez la femme as cherchez la auto. Sorry, don't actually speak French."

"Bloody sounds like it Clay!" Ananya interjected. A chuckle escaped and ran around the cramped room.

"Kemsley's a large place to be looking for a car, the proverbial needle in a haystack, and he may not even be home" Ernest commented in a forlorn manner. Ananya, bursting with zeal, seized the moment.

"Best chance would be this evening guys, agreed? Hey look, between us we've three cars, and if we wait till tonight, like, maybe Eric and Gerald could come. Four sets of wheels. We've all got mobile phones, it'd be really wicked. We can keep in touch. We just need a plan of action with each car searching a set area. Kemsley ain't that big is it?"

"Won't the police get his address and car details?" Molly suggested. Ernest replied.
"I don't think they're going to bother. Sergeant Broughton said they needed more proof and spoke about them not wanting to waste time." Ananya took the reins.

"That's cool. We'll do it. Now Ernest, who can draw up a search plan for Kemsley?"
"Well I suppose I could do it, but the best person would be Mr Furness. He's a dab hand with maps and directions."
"Cool, cool. Wowee, I can hardly wait. Ernest babes you're the dream. I know, you can be the sheriff and we'll be your deputies. We're your posse!"

"Oh dear," whispered Molly, "I shan't be able to come. I must stay here and look after Felicity."
"No no," cried Ananya, "she'd love a trip to Kemsley, I know she would. We can have a pussy in our posse! Whaddya say Molly?"

Molly, rolling with gentle laughter, said yes.

***

Sheelagh Mehedren dropped the document on her desk.

"Gotta admit Willie, it ties in with some of our work. This old boy's done his homework. I know what you mean, there's a great deal of supposition, but we can examine some of it. Basically he's gone down the same road as us in his methodical way. He's made some good guesses and hit the right answers. And, let's be honest, that couple finding this Boulchard guy on Facebook and learning he has a Kia Rio is a step in the right direction. Plus they ID'd Jackie through that website. Behind all this are some facts. Can't ignore it boy.

"Let's get an address for Boulchard and check out his car. That'll give us a clear idea of how far we need to go. Get Hassana on it immediately. Appreciate all you've done Willie. Your reward will be in heaven....." Willie trusted it would be a long time before he found out, and in the meantime wished he could be rewarded on Earth, preferably in Kent, much sooner.

Elsewhere in the county a buoyed couple were making their merry way along a narrow country lane.

Ananya and Clayton were going almost at a trot as they made their way home. It had been agreed that Ernest's posse would have a meal break, await the arrival of Eric and Gerald, and meet up again at Molly's early evening. Ananya had suggested leaving the search till evening when there'd be more chance of Boulchard being home. Much to her joy she had been appointed co-ordinator for the trip, not that there had been any opposition when she'd proposed the notion, and she was going to take Molly as her 'secretary'.

Molly was delighted, excited, overwhelmed, warm and glowing with pleasure.

The young couple now passed the Oast, calming their revelry appropriately, unconscious of the fact Audrey was there and carrying out some essential gardening at the rear. Once past they livened their step and resumed their tête-à-tête about the forthcoming evening.

197

Being May there was so much to do in the garden and, of course, it had been woefully neglected for nearly a week. Audrey threw herself into it and was annoyed at the interruption when her phone rang and she saw it was Sheelagh Mehedren. She guessed what it would be about and allowed the call to go to voicemail. She'd ring back later.

As the sun continued its long post-noon descent towards the horizon Audrey took stock of the time, finished a few jobs, tidied up, put her tools away, washed and prepared to drive to Ospringe where a shock awaited her.

Desmond, she discovered with alarm, was cooking dinner under Rosemary's expert tuition. As far as Audrey knew Desmond had never tackled anything more complex than toasting bread and here he was preparing a meal of sausages, mash and vegetables. Not very challenging, she realised.

"It's the new us," declared Rosemary, full of herself, "as Desmond wants what he calls an equal partnership from now on. In my eyes that means he can learn to cook and do some more detailed housework than simply putting the Hoover round. He says I'm no longer in charge and in future we will discuss all issues and make joint decisions."

Audrey could not see this working out.

"What brought this on Rosie?"
"I've no idea. I suspect the male menopause. He's behaving very strangely. Of course he may get over it and status quo can be restored." She grabbed Audrey by the elbow and led her to the lounge, out of Desmond's earshot. "We did something very naughty this afternoon. He seized me and kissed me with great passion and do you know I thoroughly enjoyed it, sweetie. We haven't bothered kissing for years. Not seen any point in it. Anyway, after that we, ahem, found ourselves in bed."

Rosemary was winking at her which Audrey took to mean there would be no further discourse on their time in bed, which Audrey considered to be wise.

"And did you enjoy yourself there, Rosie dear?" she asked in a less than serious vein. Rosemary winked and smiled again. "I presume that means yes, Rosie. Well, I'm pleased for you. Now I think you'd better get back to supervising the chef as he's new to the job." Rosemary slipped away, her departure marked by the smoke alarm bursting into its noisy wail. Audrey decided to listen to Sheelagh's message when the alarm had been extinguished, but forgot.

***

Eric and Gerald were so enthusiastic about the next adventure they might have been ready to clap.

Eric set to planning the search areas and drawing up the appropriate maps together with crystal clear instructions. Gerald busied himself conjuring up a small meal for now and some sandwiches to take with them. His partner didn't think the latter would be necessary but Gerald was in his element.

In her own element was Ananya. She was writing down lists of call-signs which would be distributed essential, she felt, for a covert operation. Mustn't use real names.

Ernest was designated Sherlock after the great fictional sleuth and predictably Cedric was given the code name Watson. Molly was to be Pussy Galore and Clayton was down as Murtagh, named in honour of the detective in the *Lethal Weapon* series. Ananya chose Cool Sister for herself.

Eric, being an electrician by trade, was to be called Sparks, and for Gerald as a brewery worker it was Pint-pot. Molly insisted Felicity be given a pseudonym and Ananya chose Kitty-Kat.

**

Sheelagh and Willie stood together looking rather aghast.

Hassana Achebe wasn't sure if she should continue. They seemed to be staring at her. It didn't last. The DCI spoke.

"Thanks Hassana. An address in Kemsley and the guy is the registered keeper of a blue Kia Rio. Okay. Now what's the best strategy? This guy could be so innocent. Willie, you'd better go and take Hassana with you. Diplomacy, that's what you need. All we want to know is what he was up to Sunday morning and how it can be verified. If he's innocent it'll put his back up, you know how these things go.

"I'm still waiting to hear from the widow and I'm getting impatient. I might send Lucy to Ospringe anyway." She tapped her teeth with her pen as usual. "Yep, find me Lucy someone." The decision was made.

Chapter Nineteen

Kemsley

There was no car in the drive and no reply at the front door.

Willie waited there on the off-chance while Hassana made enquiries at the next property.

"Apparently he's retired and comes and goes," she reported to the DS. "Neighbour says he keeps himself to himself but there's often a woman there. As far as they know he's a widower. Few other visitors. Never sure when he's going to be there, but usually home most nights."

"Okay Hassana, I'll radio in and we'll probably have to pop back later."
"Yeah, and I'm due off in an hour. What are my chances Willie, cos I got a date tonight?"
"I think you know the answer, but it might depend how seriously the DCI is taking all this."

They regained their car.

"Tell you what, I'll tell the DCI we'll wait here half an hour and if there's no sign of him I'll bring you back to clock off. See what she says." Hassana nodded agreement, only too aware that her chosen career could damage her private life.

However, Sheelagh was happy with the arrangement so it looked to the DC that she might get her date as planned and that position filled her with good cheer.

However, Lucy Panshaw cut a cheerless figure as she made her way to her car. The last thing she needed was to be packed off to Ospringe to arrive unannounced and confront Audrey Modlum, the woman she had offended so sorely earlier. The DCI had argued that it was an officer's lot and the encounter would help 'toughen her up'. It was Lucy's turn to be offended.

Fuming inwardly she silently asked herself how toughened up she had to be having already reached the status of Detective Sergeant. Surely she was toughened up enough? Makes me sound like a lump of raw material that needs strengthening, she reflected. At the last minute, perhaps as a gesture of conciliation, Sheelagh Mehedren had provided company in the shape of a rookie detective, DC Sian Stramer.

This was a mixed blessing.

Company was always a good idea, but there were limits. Sian was young and possessed all the fervour and dedication of youth without yet acquiring wisdom and tact as essential additives.

She was also an astonishing beauty, facially exciting, well-proportioned and nearly six feet tall, the latter merely serving to enhance her loveliness. Lucy thought herself ordinary, certainly in comparison. She felt she was overweight, that any shapeliness was marred by the fact the shapes had not always appeared in quite the right places, that her bum was too big, and that she was featureless.

This overlooked the fact she had a bubbly personality, a ready wit, able to see the funny side of almost anything, and was a kind-hearted girl. It also ignored the matter of Sian having little personality whatsoever and zero sense of humour. Lucy's boyfriend said Lucy was gorgeous, sparkling company, that she lit up his life and made him feel alive, and he loved her to the moon and back.

The real reason the DCI sent Lucy was because she actually had the utmost faith in her and knew she was destined for greater things if she pursued her police career. Far from needing toughening up Sheelagh knew she had all the attributes to be a first class detective. But ongoing experience was vital.

About the time Willie and Hassana were leaving Kemsley empty-handed Lucy and Sian were drawing up outside the Wandons'. As they alighted from the car Lucy stepped in some fresh dog waste. Oh shit, she said, then laughed to herself realising how appropriate her exclamation was.

"What's wrong?" asked Sian from the other side of the car.

"Put my foot in some dog poo. I'll wipe it on the grass over there and then take a tissue to it."

"My nan says if you walk in dog mess it's lucky," ventured Sian thoughtlessly.

"This had better prove to be," came the ratty response.

***

The posse had gathered at the Dahlias.

Eric briefed everyone on the maps and Ananya asked for a dry run on communications.

They tried their best, managing to get the various call signs correct, but there some hazards to be found amongst the phonetic alphabet. Ananya was annoyed with herself. She'd overlooked the concept that the sheriff's deputies might not be familiar with it, and not able to grasp it quickly, and wished she'd printed out copies. Black mark Ananya, she reprimanded herself privately.

But she was taking command and everyone, Ernest included, was quite happy with that.

The other difficulty she was landed with was that, although they all had mobile phones, the golden-oldies were not into texting at all, let alone the art of sending texts simultaneously to several recipients. With their permission she programmed their mobiles and then gave them lessons in text-speak and text despatch. Fortunately good humour abounded, there was much laughter, plenty of joking, and Ananya aka Cool Sister discovered a patience she didn't know she had. She knew she was going to need it.

203

Basically, to save time, if the car was located an abbreviated address was to be texted at once to the other three cars that would then divert and converge on it.

Ananya pointed out they were the Magnificent Seven and Eric inanely regaled them with a piece of trivia.

"Did you know, in the film, y'know, the Magnificent Seven, Yul Brynner does actually take his hat off once. Most people think he doesn't what with being bald and that."
"I loved Yul Brynner in the King and I," Molly added.

There followed what can be best described as a pregnant pause. Nobody could think of anything to say so evidently the matter of Yul Brynner's hat was concluded, and it was time to go.

"Don't forget," Ananya advised, "there may be more than one blue Kia Rio in Kemsley. Report any findings to Pussy Galore," Molly blushed and went all coy, "and only send the main signal when you're sure it's the right one."

Not far away at Ospringe Lucy and Sian had received a surprisingly warm welcome. Mr and Mrs Wandon seemed almost festive in their good spirits and Audrey briefly embraced both detectives apologising profusely to Lucy for her earlier manners. Lucy could smell the drink and at once all was revealed.

Desmond's meal had been an absolute peach, according to Audrey, and a decent couple of bottles of wine were being demolished. He was very proud of his creation, his wife was excited with his success. The wine did the rest.

The girls declined a glass with Lucy anxious to press on and get the meeting over and done.

Audrey saved her a difficult job.

"Lucy, once again I'm sorry for my unforgiveable behaviour at the Oast. Here's my laptop which you can take away and examine. Please, please explain to your Detective Chief whatever she is my reasons for not saying that I knew what my husband was about on those two dates. You see, I really was so very worried that what those awful women were saying about him might possibly be true, and in my grief I just couldn't face it. I know I've obstructed you or whatever the word is, and I just hope you haven't lost the chance of catching my husband's killer."

Lucy could do little but suggest she was forgiven, knowing full well that there would now be nothing on the laptop of any interest whatsoever. Crafty Audrey. They were dealing with a clever one here alright.

"May I just ask, Audrey, if your diary is on here, because we do appreciate there will be private information there?"
"Yes, it's there in full. Nothing's been deleted. I know your experts could detect that. And the diary is the only thing remotely private."

The DS noticed Audrey's smarmy look, the look of the guilty, the look of the smart-arse, and she resolved to catch her out if she could. But that might be for the future.

"One last thing Audrey. That label, you know, together now together, that really meant nothing to you?" Audrey tried a feeble smirk, for which the wine was partly responsible, and lied as was clear to a detective trained in reading body language, voice patterns and facial expressions.

"No Lucy. I've no idea at all." It was Lucy's turn to smile and she hoped Audrey would be able to read *her* expression!

Over in Kemsley Willie and Hassana called time at Ray Boulchard's and headed back to base.

***

Two things happened.

Hardly had the detectives departed than Ray Boulchard returned home. And that was about the time the Magnificent Seven set sail.

Out in convoy they drove, Eric in the lead. North to the A2 and west to follow the sun through Teynham, Bapchild and Snipeshill and around Sittingbourne town centre. Using her best American accent Ananya drawled:

"We're a-coming to get you, brother Boulchard. See you at the old Kemsley corral." Molly sniggered. She'd never had any interest in Westerns and all of this had gone clean over her head, but she was as excited as all of them in Ernest's posse.

The rendezvous point was ASDA's car park.

After a check that everyone was okay Ananya, with great drama, bellowed the launch of the campaign.

"Magnificent Seven. Blue Kia Rio. Go go go." And they were off.

Early communications proved difficult, Molly struggling with the phonetic alphabet even with Ananya's help. Calling up Gerald she resorted to the simple expedient of using her own version.
Rather unnecessarily spelling the word 'park' she chose pneumatic-apple-rollo-knitting and Gerald wrote down 'narn' before realising.

Cedric didn't assist matters by using the word 'Roger' in every call, maybe a throwback to his National Service in the RAF. That was where he met Ernest. One message went as follows when they drove into Samuel Drive:

"Pussy Galore from Watson, turning into Samuel, Roger."
"Watson this is Pussy Galore, Roger received. Roger."

It was Gerald and Eric who stumbled on their possible quarry.

"Pussy Galore from Pint-Pot. Have car on radar, will check out. Address is ..." and he gave the details as Molly and Ananya whooped with delight.

Eric pulled up just beyond and Gerald strolled back. He thought about knocking and asking for a fictitious person just so he could get a sighting of Ray Boulchard but he was overtaken by events.

Toot-toot-toot. A large white van screeched to a halt half on the pavement where he was standing and out leaped the driver.

"Gelled, Gelled," the driver cried as he rushed over and hugged Gerald vigorously. It was Jokubas, the Lithuanian who had helped the stricken cyclist. "You right? You bike right? How you old friend?"

Gerald was taken aback by the hug as much as the familiarity.

"Jokubas, lovely to see you again. Yes, I'm fine and the bike is good too. Thank you so much for your help that day, it was so kind."
"No problem Gelled. Now, excuse me a mo, must deliver this parcel here." He pointed at the very house and Gerald thought it worth a punt.
"Ah yes for my good friend Mr Boulchard." Jokubas studied the label.
"Yes ... yes ... Mr boo-lick-hard," he pronounced it.

Gerald slipped behind the van and watched the front door as Jokubas knocked but was disappointed when a middle-aged woman in a dressing gown opened it, signed and took the parcel in. But he had confirmed they had Boulchard's address.

The Lithuanian came back and checked his handheld device.

"It all go Gelled. Must fly. Have to go to Middly-tunner Avy-new," he explained, meaning Middletune Avenue. "Bye Gelled. You take care. See you soon fella." Gerald winced but shook his friend's hand and wished him well, then strode back to Eric's car and sent the all-important text.

Ernest, who was close by anyway, arrived first, followed by Clayton who also screeched to a halt half on the pavement. Ernest wondered why drivers had to do that and park on the pavement to boot. Ananya was a few minutes. Gerald waited until they were all present and correct before telling his story.

"Right, well done Gerald, well done everyone. I'll call up Sergeant Broughton and let him know."
Willie's voicemail was on so Ernest left a detailed message, feeling full of disappointment. The air of anti-climax was upon them. They'd gone as far as they could go. Molly broke the spell.

"I've got some lovely home-made cakes and lots of other nibbles. You're all welcome back at my place for a, what do they call it, an unbriefing? And I've two bottles of red wine I've been keeping for a special occasion, we could open them if you like."

There was no mistaking the sensation of loss for the denouement had come and passed swiftly, and left them all empty. All the planning, the thrill of the chase, everything they'd attempted, and it was over in a flash. With heavy hearts they returned to their cars and following Eric got under way for the Dahlias in the manner of a funeral cortege.

It didn't take long for spirits to revive once back at Molly's. They were duly unbriefed as Molly had termed it and thoroughly enjoyed themselves discussing the evening's hunt. The food was delicious, there was tea and coffee for those that preferred it, and wine for those who wanted it, Clayton included. Ananya gave her blessing. She was praised for her efforts, and Gerald was roundly toasted. He himself proposed a toast.

208

"To Jokubas," he announced. "Jokubas," they all chorused.

Then Ernest was toasted. Ananya proposed a toast to Pussy Galore for running their 'communications centre' and advised them she would shortly be taking her partner back to Earth Cottage to "unbrief him!" Clayton went as red as the beetroot they were growing.

Ernest tried Willie again without luck. Oh well, never mind.

Willie had received the message but then, of course, he already knew the address, and it was nearly time to set out again. Hassana had gone off duty so the DCI had lent him Sian Stramer which was entirely to Willie's pleasure.

He knew that the job could be a relationship killer so he'd tended to steer clear of any woman likely to want more than a one-night stand. In truth, he preferred it that way. He was young and loved rifling in the market place, sampling a wide variety of the gifts on offer. By this medium he'd tackled not only young ladies in his age group but also the older woman, cougars he believed they were called.

And now he was going to Kemsley with the vacuous Sian. He did not, as a rule, date colleagues as that, he felt, could lead to tricky situations, but rules were made to be broken and he fancied DC Stramer with a longing that took him beyond his normal boundaries. But first Mr Boulchard.

They hadn't gone five miles, Sian at the wheel, before she said she wanted to take him out. He acquiesced straightaway, and his senses and emotions at once swarmed into disarray as dreams of a pleasant and rewarding evening cascaded through his mind. He grabbed occasional glances at her long legs working the pedals.

If a man can be turned on by a nylon-clad patella moving up and down then Willie was fully ignited. Unseen by her colleague

Sian was smiling, knowing she had him right where she wanted him, knowing she would physically tease him all the way to Kemsley and back and probably thereafter too.

He had to pull himself mentally together when they arrived, and it wasn't easy.

A woman opened the door and the detectives introduced themselves and learned that Mr Boulchard was home. The woman said she was Mrs Ditchmen, a friend, and showed them into the lounge.

Ray Boulchard was summoned from the rear garden by his friend who then sat next to him on the sofa. Willie didn't object. As arranged he did the talking and Sian was to look around the room, making observations of the premises.

"Sorry to trouble you sir, but you may be aware that a murder was committed near Faversham last weekend and we're following up a number of enquiries as a matter of routine. I do stress these are routine issues, nothing more.

"We reported to the papers we were interested in a blue Kia Rio seen in the vicinity of the murder Sunday morning. So far we've been inundated with responses as you can imagine. Sadly we have to check out anything that might be remotely worth pursuing.

"Someone has informed us you have such a car and you were out early Sunday morning, so we just need to ask if that's right and, if so, what you were doing. Sorry about this, it is just routine where serious crime is concerned sir."

"One of the bloody nosey neighbours, I bet," Boulchard shouted in reply while Mrs Ditchmen muttered "yes yes yes" over and over as she nodded her head and displayed a suitably disgusted look. "Can't mind their own bloody business. Bloody people."

"Is it correct sir? Were you out?" Boulchard calmed and his voice was all the softer for it as he answered Willie.

"Yes, indeed I bloody well was. I left here, I don't know, about seven thirty and went over to collect Mrs Ditchmen from her home in Bredgar. Isn't that right Poppy?" Poppy nodded. "We were back here I'd say around nine-thirty, maybe later." Poppy Ditchmen spoke up.

"Yes, that's right officer. I can't be sure of the times. It was Sunday morning after all. All very relaxed. Ray said he'd pick me up early morning and we spent the rest of the day here." It was Boulchard's turn to nod.

"Sorry to be a nuisance Mrs Ditchmen, but would there be anyone at Bredgar to verify that?"
"Don't suppose so. I'm just outside the village. Didn't see anyone I knew. Didn't see anyone at all for that matter, not until we drove through the village itself."
"Well, thank you for your time, both of you, it's really appreciated. By the way Mr Boulchard, you knew the victim's wife didn't you? Audrey Modlum?"
"Yes she was my secretary. Years ago. How do you know that?" He looked and sounded suspicious and, in Sian's view, guilty.
"We like to build up a picture of those involved and we asked Mrs Modlum about her recent life. She mentioned your name, that's all. You might have been a different Mr Boulchard. Just thought I'd ask. You've not kept in touch?"
"No, haven't spoken to Audrey for, oh I don't know, eight, nine, ten years or more."

The meeting ended soon after.

Neither detective spoke a word until they were on the road again.

"You know what Willie," Sian ventured, "I was watching him closely as I expect you were. My view is he kicked himself for

211

jumping in when you mentioned Audrey. He knows he should've played it in a more nonchalant way."

"Good point Sian, and the other thing that struck me is that he and Mrs Ditchmen had their story too off pat, like they'd been rehearsing it. And they had no idea we were going to turn up."

"Unless the neighbour Hassana spoke to told them."

"Another good point. And that would explain a well-planned story."

There was a period of reflective silence.

"That whole interview made me suspicious Willie."

"Yeah. And there's a name to play with ... Poppy Ditchmen!"

"Thin, helpless little thing, but he looked domineering and I bet she does as she's told."

"Agreed. Audrey told Ernest Pawden he was a misogynist bigot. Mind you, opens up a different avenue to Ernest's theory."

"Go on."

"Assuming she's his squeeze, how does having a new love square with the concept of him being so heartbroken about losing Audrey?"

"Some guys just can't help themselves Willie. Lose one love, find a replacement, and in this case a little old lady who is totally obedient. Fits his bill I'd say."

"A little old lady? Not that old."

"Old enough to be old Willie."

"I've never been in love Sian. No idea about the forces it creates."

"Neither have I, but I know all about the forces lust creates. We must let our forces mix on our date babes."

Willie could hardly believe his ears.

"Yeah Sian, let my force be with you!" They both laughed.

***

After hearing from Willie and Sian the DCI made her way home.

There wasn't much more to be done. Boulchard went out early Sunday morning but has an alibi which might yet have to be investigated and Sheelagh didn't want to pursue that just yet.

Poppy Ditchmen would be an accessory if Boulchard was guilty of Gareth's murder. But imagine if she was innocent? Perhaps Boulchard collected her after the killing. Sheelagh had asked Sian to go out Saturday morning and time her drive from Kemsley to the Hop Pickers Oast, on to Bredgar and back to Kemsley. Saturday was not the ideal day but hey, let's give it a try. Repeat the exercise Sunday morning when there was less traffic about if necessary.

Katie was waiting for her.

She'd been driving on Sheppey most of the day and was so happy to see her partner that a long, lingering kiss ensued. Sheelagh rarely spoke about actual cases but Katie was aware she was involved in the local murder and decided to ask.

"Any progress on that man who was killed last Sunday?"
"Yes, some my love. Sorry, some of its confidential." Katie knew that would be the situation but Sheelagh opened up much to Katie's surprise.

"Some amateur sleuth, in his eighties I ask you, has put forward a theory. He's a neighbour of the deceased and he seems to have all the neighbours working with him. You not seen anything like it! Trouble is, Kats, I think he's proving quite good at it. I'm thinking that I need to pay him a bit more attention and respect. I've appointed Willie as liaison officer and I've no idea why. Just why do I need a liaison officer to work with amateur detectives, tell me.

"I need my head examined, and Willie's none too pleased I can tell you!"

213

"He's a good man, isn't he Shee? And I expect you've done it because you have a secret admiration for this old guy and his theory."

"Yeah, you're right Kats, I do. I actually like him, and because of him I think we have a suspect. That's an admission, isn't it?"

"It is Shee, but it's not a sign of weakness, it's a sign of maturity and strength of character."

"Oh Kats you say such lovely things, I go weak at the knees. 'ere, give us a kiss."

"Anyway Shee, you've always spoken highly of Willie Broughton.   He   sounds   first   class."
"He is and I totally rely on him. I just hope he doesn't sod it all up by getting into a relationship and letting love upset his work/life balance, if you know what I mean."

"Shee you can't deny a guy his chance of love, you miserable old git. I mean, you're in a loving relationship and you haven't sodded your career up."

"True Kats. No, he's terrific."

"Anyway is your Willie popular with girls?"

"Think you'd better re-phrase that Kats!"

Later they had an Indian take-away, watched a romantic movie, snuggled up together and eventually retired full of love, joy and rum and coke.

And so it was that Kent was overrun by another Friday night.

In Kemsley Ray Boulchard was incensed. They'd found him. The newspaper said his type of car had been specified and inferred the driver could be identified. It could only be that old biddy he'd seen on his way to the Oast. She'd have to go, she really would.

"Sorry Poppy. Taking you home. Nothing personal. I'll pick you up again tomorrow morning. Just need a night to myself."

"Oh that's a shame Ray. You said you'd got some Viagra tablets and I was so looking forward to your trying them."

"Well, when we get back tomorrow its straight to bed and you can find out."

"Ray, Ray, you know how to turn a girl on, you old charmer you!"

Chapter Twenty

Nemesis

The lane had a name.

Gareth Modlum had been killed in Bald Henry Lane. For some reason the borough council had never erected any signs, yet they had done so for Blind Mary's Lane located not that far away, so there was no obvious problem. This was the country, and that's how it was. Blind Mary may have been a resident of her lane, but who bald Henry was remained a mystery.

Bald Henry Lane, narrow and bedecked with a handsome growth of grass down its centre, twisted about as if it was searching for some form of escape. But maybe it was also to take in the changing vistas and to be assured of missing nothing the area had to offer. Main roads and motorways are slaves to the speed of life generally, and thus avoid the pleasures of bucolic surroundings.

Within a few minutes drive south of the scene of the crime the North Downs sweep away towards the Weald affording splendidly scenic views for miles and miles. Above Harrietsham, Lenham and Charing the North Downs cascade sharply southwards providing a spectacular panorama.

To the north, cross the A2 and you come to the rural location of Oare, beyond it the narrow stretch of the Swale which separates the mainland from the isle of Sheppey. Here you can see Harty on the opposite shore (there was a ferry here once), and enjoy coastal walks, see incredible birdlife and simply enjoy the great outdoors.

You can eventually reach Faversham on foot from here, dodging round and along the creeks and perhaps chancing upon a wayside pub (for example The Shipwrights' Arms).

One thing is for sure, the visitor to this area may be stunned by the wealth of pleasant rolling countryside, dotted with numerous footpaths and byways, and by the quaint villages and settlements. To the hop gardens and orchards have been added vineyards as the county stretches its entrepreneurial legs and seeks to quench a thirst or two, whilst retaining the epithet 'The Garden of England'.

Some of the landscape is a little more dramatic than merely 'gently rolling'. You can gaze upon more steeply sided valleys from Doddington Place Gardens (barely a stone's throw from where Gareth met his end), at Queen Down Warren to the west (south-west of Sittingbourne), and much further afield at Crundale and above Alkham in the east. Just to name a few.

And the countryside story doesn't end there, and neither does this tale.

For Bald Henry Lane Saturday started peacefully enough.

It was mid May. The sun was up well before most of the residents with the exception of Molly Penderman. Tom was back from his nightime perambulations and had a voracious appetite which Molly sought to satisfy. Felicity watched this feeding frenzy with scorn. She would eat, and daintily so, later.

Clayton Mainstreet had awoken only to be 'unbriefed' again. Ananya had a sexual appetite matched only by Tom's craving for food. For most men, especially on a Saturday morning, that would be enough exercise to be going on with, but for Clayton, a keep-fit fanatic, the road beckoned. He just had to go out for his morning run.

Eric and Gerald, overcome by all the excitement of the previous evening, slept on soundly.

There was a slight haze about the countryside. There was stillness, there was a hint of warmth. It was going to be another

217

lovely day. Another lovely summer's day. The birds sang their wondrous tunes. The sheep and growing lambs added occasional baas. The crows, not the most musical of birds, cawed as they are inclined to do. A gull floated past on the lookout for easy food.

A breeze rustled the leaves in the orchard and in the hop garden. Kent was coming to life.

And for one lady death beckoned.

Ray Boulchard had it all planned. Up with the lark he'd selected a particularly vicious looking knife from the garden shed with which to eliminate the woman he thought might identify him. In his deranged state he could see no other way. Logic had deserted him. The sun was barely above the horizon when he set out.

And in all this Poppy Ditchmen remained ignorant and innocent.

Although it was early Ernest and Cedric decided they would go to Teynham and buy their papers. The shop would be open.

At Ospringe Audrey, Rosemary and Desmond slept. Friday evening had been surprisingly enjoyable with Desmond once again providing plenty of wine. The difference this time was that Mr Wandon was included. Liqueurs were offered and accepted in profusion, and the conversation flowed like the wine, humour added at every turn. They had retired happy souls.

Ernest had been alone, fretting about their discovery, when Willie gave him a late night call to thank him and to advise enquiries were in hand. He slept peacefully completely reassured.

Cedric helped Molly clear up and even risked a peck on her cheek as he made his farewells and headed home to the Vines, a happy chappie. He picked up *Daniel Deronda* and read a few pages but found he couldn't concentrate as thoughts of Molly occupied his mind. Later, in bed, as he turned out the light, Molly was still troubling him in a most pleasing way, and continued to do so until he fell asleep.

The object of his affections had seen nothing in that little kiss beyond two dear friends simply saying goodnight. Nevertheless that didn't stop her thinking once more about Cedric's lost love as she slipped between the sheets, gave Felicity a stroke, and snuggled down for the night. Poor Cedric. Poor Cedric.

Such thoughts were nowhere to be found Saturday morning, but Molly was exceedingly happy and carefree and was even given to humming a pretty tune, not that she could remember the words or the name of the piece. And then it struck her. It was 'Shall We Dance' from the 'King and I' and her memory flashed back to the day just past and to Yul Brynner and his hat. The humming was replaced by laughter as she recalled the fun they'd all had.

How exciting! She had no idea where the name Pussy Galore came from but had taken it to heart and treasured the idea. Looking out the back window and seeing the sun slowly clearing the shadows from the garden all sorts of agreeable recollections came to her. It had been a wonderful spring and for the first time in years she'd heard a cuckoo nearby. Even now two green woodpeckers were at play just yards from her back door.

It was all so lovely.

Tom wanted yet more food. Felicity looked at him derisively. Both ladies probably believed he'd burst if he ate any more, but more he did eat. Molly took her mug of tea into the lounge with Felicity in attendance and sat down chock full of happiness, whereupon the cat leaped into her lap for a cuddle and that made Molly feel very content. She was so awash with joie-de-vivre that she didn't even notice the car going by.

It was DC Sian Stramer on her 'timed' run. The detective was well bothered.

"I *know* he was lying," she repeated out loud to herself, "and I *know* the bastard's guilty. And I know we can't haul him in for questioning." An early call from the DCI had prepared part of the team for going forth to Bredgar on door-to-door enquiries, and another part to carry out the same task in the road where Boulchard lived. Then they might find they had enough evidence to talk to Boulchard again. Sian certainly hoped so. "Yuk, horrible bloke," she muttered as she shuddered.

Molly was so ensconced in being overjoyed with life she didn't hear the second car either.

But this one stopped.

There was a knock at the door. Molly rose and suddenly glimpsed the blue car outside. She had the presence of mind to grab her mobile phone. Of course, it could be anyone, but she was now afraid, all happiness having abandoned her leaving her pale and shaking.

"Who is it?" she called in a trembling voice as she put the chain on the door.
"Just want a little chat love. Let me in there's a good dear."
"Not so likely. I'm phoning the police right now." Her fingers fumbled hopelessly over the keys and tears came as she failed miserably to achieve the relatively easy undertaking of dialling 999.

There was a thump against the door and she knew he was trying to break it down.

Two hefty crashes later and the old wooden door gave way and Boulchard was in. Molly had backed into the lounge, still desperately trying to press 999, and was up against the fireplace. He was in the doorway, almost slobbering like a wild animal, eyes wide open and full of menace. And in his hand was a knife the like of which Molly had never seen. She screamed the most awful scream, a scream she didn't know she was capable of, a scream that might've woken the dead.

In her desolation and fear she threw the phone at him. He brushed the missile aside with a filthy laugh and took the final few steps towards her, ready to thrust the weapon into his victim. Molly closed her eyes and tried one last scream.

Just down the road Ernest was returning with Cedric. They had just pulled into the drive at Whodunit when they heard the first ear-piercing scream. It took them a split second to recover their senses.

"Ernest," cried Cedric, "did that come from Molly's?" Neither man made any further comment. They merely jumped back in the car, the vehicle being the quickest way two octogenarians could travel half a mile. They didn't hear the second and slightly quieter scream.

As they rounded the bend they saw Ray Boulchard's car and Cedric involuntarily squealed with horror. For once in his life it was Ernest screeching to a halt. He'd never driven along the lane at such a speed and he wasn't used to braking sharply. They nearly overshot. Cedric was half out of the door as the motor came to a stand but got his foot caught in the unused seatbelt and fell flat on his face.

Ernest was round in a flash, helped his friend to his feet and both men charged through the wreck of the front door. Nothing, absolutely nothing, could've prepared them for the sight that confronted them.

Molly, weeping profusely, was standing by the fireplace clutching both cats to her bosom, and lying spread-eagled on the floor was Ray Boulchard busy swearing all variety of oaths. And astride him keeping him pinned down and helpless was Clayton Mainstreet. Cedric rushed to Molly and embraced her, the pair of them with the cats in between making a kind of moggy sandwich. He ushered her gradually into the settee.

221

"Murtagh saved my life, he saved my life, Murtagh saved my life," she wailed through floods of tears. Murtagh aka Clayton was modesty itself.

"Hell no Molly. Had some help from your cats. We did it together Pussy Galore."

It transpired that Clayton had come down the lane on his run, seen the car and accelerated into a sprint that would've done Usain Bolt credit. He was almost at the door when Molly screamed. As he charged into the house, expecting the worst, Boulchard was about to administer the deadly blow when both cats, perhaps sensing the trouble their mistress was in, leaped at Boulchard clawing and shrieking. It was enough to create a distraction.

Molly ducked out of the way. Her attacker was otherwise unperturbed by the feline assault but Tom and Felicity had bought a vital extra second that enabled Clayton to throw his arms around Boulchard and wrestle him to the ground. With great speed of thought Clayton had stamped on Boulchard's right wrist forcing him to drop the weapon which the saviour promptly kicked under the settee. The assailant might've been strong but he was no match for a younger, taller and supremely fit super-hero. Clayton fell on the prostrate figure and held him there at which point Ernest and Cedric had arrived.

The former dialled 999.

The first police officer to arrive was DC Sian Stramer, there in minutes as she wasn't far away when the call went out. She aimed a violent kick at Boulchard who cried out in pain.

"Nobody saw me do that did they? My foot must've slipped. If you want some more pain Mr Boulchard, just you try resisting arrest."

Other officers arrived closely followed by Willie Broughton and a couple of paramedics, the latter checking Molly over and finding her to be in perfect working order. Boulchard, handcuffed, was escorted from the premises complaining bitterly about his treatment bearing in mind he was a taxpayer, etc.

Ernest lent Clayton his mobile so he could call home and assure Ananya he was okay.

There was some confusion in the telling of the tale as a bewildered Molly spoke freely of Murtagh's role, about Sherlock and Watson, and then tried to unravel her statements getting matters further into disorder. Clayton stepped in and gallantly offered assistance, playing down his own part in proceedings.

Molly corrected this.

"He saved my life, officer. Dear Murtagh, I mean Mr Mainstay, I mean Clayton. He saved my life." Willie noted this.

It was only a question of time before the media arrived, and there was nothing its representatives liked more than a have-a-go hero saving a lady's life.

Ananya had arrived and was photographed at his side and in his arms. Within an hour a TV crew had turned up and he was being interviewed amidst a great show of humility. Molly tried to shun the limelight but she was so keen to praise Clayton she couldn't help herself, and ended up with the TV people in her lounge.

And so it went on.

Sian Stramer was sent off to meet Lucy at the Wandons' house, Audrey now being firmly in the police sights. She stopped just down the lane and sobbed a little, just so pleased Molly had been spared. If only, if only, she thought, if only we'd been able to do Boulchard last night. But that's the way it is just as she knew it was. Unseen by other eyes Sian had revealed a hitherto unknown side, a caring human side, and a thoroughly professional side too. She'd seen through Boulchard's lies and her experiences would go towards making her a damn good detective.

More importantly she was unmistakably a different person to the one most imagined and they would come to appreciate that more in the years ahead.

The commotion lasted into the afternoon. By then the police team had departed and the news media were packing up. Contractors had arrived to secure Molly's front door. Life might be about to get back to normal, not that Bald Henry Lane would ever be quite as it was, or at least as it had been a week ago.

Gerald and Eric slept through the brouhaha and were alerted by a constant flow of vehicles including police cars going past Rose Cottage. Something was going on and a call to Ernest put them in the picture.

"What a week," exclaimed Eric. "Murder Sunday, arrest Saturday, and all sorts of occurrences in the interim. But by golly, our poor miss Molly!"
"Yay Eric. What a narrow escape. Thank God for Clayton. But I remember Ernest saying he was worried by the press story that the car driver might be identified by a witness. He thought it might put Molly in peril and he was right."
"I wonder what Audrey thinks knowing they've caught her husband's killer who very nearly claimed a second innocent victim?"
"If Ernest's summation of the saga proves correct I'd say her conscience will prick her. It certainly would've done if Molly had perished, and so horribly."

***

Audrey had been taken for questioning.

It was soon established that divorcee Mrs Ditchmen was indeed an innocent party, shocked by the news her companion was a ruthless killer, pleased she'd escaped his clutches, more than happy she was not to discover any benefits from his Viagra tablets.

Sheelagh and Willie were getting ready to grill Boulchard, while Lucy and Sian tackled Audrey once her solicitor Erica Rowhedge had been procured.

Up at Ospringe the Wandons were in a weird condition. Their guest had been whisked away and the news on the television had cut right through them. They looked in respectful awe at the interviews with self-effacing Clayton Mainstreet, they gave grateful thanks that Molly Penderman had been spared, suffered their own private pangs of guilt for no reason whatsoever save that Audrey had stayed with them, and allowed feelings of inescapable trepidation at the terror Molly must've faced to inundate their minds.

They exchanged few words for none was necessary. They were in limbo. They clung warmly to each other as if to try and stave off the horror and keep it locked out of their world. If good can come of such vile deeds then the Wandons, having cleared their personal air with each other and set their lives on a new footing, were closer than they'd ever been.

But they suffered for Audrey. Her husband slain without mercy, his body found by his wife; surely she had been through enough? They prayed she would be returned to them unharmed, that the police were merely carrying out routine interviews, that she wasn't in any way involved in Gareth's death. And they prayed some more to a God they'd never bothered with, but whose gracious mercy they now sought.

Both Ray Boulchard and Audrey Modlum were proving garrulous in their interviews and at last the whole story was out. The two versions pretty much tallied. Boulchard's confession was full and frank and it absolved Audrey of association in her husband's death, but Audrey was far from in the clear. Her laptop had been slightly more revealing than they'd hoped, especially when a contrite Audrey provided additional information.

The officers were momentarily surprised by the truth for it was not the tale they were expecting. DCI Mehedren made a decision and phoned Ernest.

As evening approached Mrs Modlum was delivered to Ospringe and fussed over excessively by the Wandons. And for once she didn't mind. It was all over, she was okay. Gareth's killer was behind bars although she herself might face a charge of obstruction. But for now that didn't matter.

Ernest Pawden was taken aback by Sheelagh's call.

"Mr Pawden, if you have nothing planned could I visit you this evening and bring Sergeant Broughton with me? I want to take a very unusual step and frankly one I should not really be taking. I would like to take you into my confidence, but what I have to say must for now be for your ears only."

"Well Chief Inspector, thank you and you would both be most welcome of course. But I would not for one moment want you to do anything for my benefit that might bring trouble for you."

"Thank you, but it's something I want to do. You see, Boulchard has not only confessed but we've learned a great deal more about this case. Not everything is as it seems, and I think you might be interested in the whole story, especially as you worked so hard on your theory which was not so very far removed from the truth."

"That's very kind Chief Inspector, and yes, I'd love to hear what you have to say. But may I please ask about the fate of my friend, dear Mrs Modlum?"

"Of course. She's back at Ospringe. She's been cleared of any part in Mr Modlum's murder but may have to answer a charge of obstruction, maybe more. But I'll tell you when I see you. Now, how does half-seven sound?"

226

"Perfect, and thanks for telling me about Mrs Modlum, that's appreciated. I'm pleased she had nothing to do with it."

At Earth Cottage Ananya was worshipping her hero and produced another couple of bottles of beer to enhance her worship.

"We might be vegans now Clay, but *you* can still have alcohol, in moderation of course. How does that sound babycakes?"

"Great, wicked, cool, everything! Get me a glass and find y'self a drink my huggybum and we'll celebrate properly."

"Cool. I'll have a lemon juice I think. Need something sharp, like, to stimulate me."

Clayton looked at her sideways and she winked.

"My boy, you can stimulate me later when I 'unbrief' you again!"

Just along the lane Eric and Gerald, having absorbed as much news as they wanted, were rejoicing and planning an al-fresco dinner, one of Gerald's specialities, and looking forward to Saturday night in front of the box accompanied by fine wine.

Cedric had helped Molly tidy up, initially assisted by Ernest and Clayton, both of whom had now departed. Eric and Gerald had popped in when the opportunity presented itself and made to feel very welcome. Molly was simply pleased to see her real friends and there were hugs in abundance. But the best hugs had been reserved for Clayton and for her cats.

Now it was just Molly and Cedric, Felicity and Tom.

The four sat on the small settee and managed to cuddle each other by turns.

"You don't seem any the worse Molly, but I wouldn't be surprised if the shock doesn't come out later." Cedric was being

227

philosophical and sounding like a doctor pronouncing diagnosis. "If you wish I could spend the night here. I could sleep on the floor downstairs. I'm at your service."

"Oh Cedric that's so kind of you, but I'm not going to be a trouble, I'll be fine just you wait and see."

"May I stay the evening, just in case you need someone?"

"Of course you may. I was hoping you'd stay anyway, but wasn't sure how to ask you."

"That's settled then. Shall I make a pot of tea?"

"Better than that, what say you if I make a nice dinner? I have a homemade chicken pie and I could do some potatoes and vegetables."

"Molly, Molly, you can't possibly go to the trouble...."

"No trouble at all Cedric. You can help me and it'll help take my mind off what's happened. Oh dear, I've just thought. What about poor Audrey?"

"I'll ring Gerald. He's got the Wandons' phone number. Maybe he's heard already."

Gerald had, and with their minds more at rest Cedric and Molly set about their Saturday evening.

Ernest sat quietly at home in the lounge of Whodunit wondering what Sheelagh had to tell him.

Chapter Twenty One

Not everything is as it seems

The detectives arrived at Whodunit slightly ahead of time.

Sheelagh, brash as ever, suggested they be on first name terms which Ernest had no objection to in the circumstances.

Teas and coffee supplied, along with a generously wide selection of biscuits, the three settled back for their discussion. The DCI, as expected, tucked into the bikkies like there was no tomorrow, leaving Ernest to wonder if he had put enough out.

"Ernest," she began, ready to warm to her theme, "I've asked you to treat this meeting as confidential. You need only do so for a short while as I'm sure the story will make good its escape fairly soon, and much will come out at the trial. We must think of Audrey. Whatever she might have done to make life easier for us she definitely had no direct connection with the crime and at first had no idea who might've committed it.

"Personally I hope she won't have any charges laid against her, such as for obstruction, but it's not up to me. I daresay the media will be hounding her in the meantime. I know you share with me genuine concern for a lady widowed in such a disgusting, heartless manner, her husband brutally attacked." Ernest nodded sagely, deep in thought. Sheelagh continued.

"My instinct told me at the outset that the murder was related to a matter earlier in Gareth's life, that is, earlier than his retirement three years ago. Gradually my conviction wavered and I became less sure that was the case, but it appears I should've gone with my first impression.

"Your theory was an excellent piece of work and headed in the right direction. You managed to get Audrey to talk in a much more open fashion than we'd been able to do. We like to build up a picture of the victim, their family and friends, their lifestyle and so on, as it can help us with our enquiries. But it seems we accepted what was on the surface whereas there was much below it. You got into hidden territory Ernest. Very helpful if I may say so.

"Your expression was search for the lady. Your document pointed out that the lady might well have been right in front of us all the time. Audrey herself. But the lady we should've been searching for has in fact been dead for over nine years. Her name was Patricia Boulchard, late wife of Ray.

"By absolute coincidence Gareth was the gas engineer sent to sort out a problem at the Boulchard's home. With his usual dexterity he rectified the fault swiftly and efficiently, promptly setting about seducing Patricia, probably with equal dexterity. She was by all accounts a very attractive well endowed middle-aged woman, ripe for plucking. As the affair grew they became rather careless so anxious were they to spend time together.

"Ray Boulchard picked up clues and finally confronted his wife who confessed. At this stage he didn't know who the man was but learned from Patricia his name was Gareth and he was a gasman. Angry and upset he needed someone to confide in, a shoulder to cry on, and devoid of close relatives and friends he turned to his secretary, a woman he'd always got on well with.

"They went out for a lunchtime drink and he poured out his story. Audrey was sympathetic until Ray mentioned the name and employment of the marital interloper. She nearly choked on her drink; it could be nobody else, and of course it wasn't. How she got through the rest of the day and drove home she doesn't know. She was shot to pieces.

"As soon as he arrived home Gareth was tackled and he came clean. He blamed Audrey because she'd had little interest in the intimate side of things, and that only enraged her further. Determined to make her reaction explosive he confessed to a variety of flings. He said it was all her fault as she'd denied him his conjugal rights, whatever they are."

Sheelagh deliberately shot Ernest a glance but his face was impassive. He was listening intently.

"Audrey found herself bent on revenge. Hell hath no fury and all that. The very next day she went into Boulchard's office and told him it was her husband who'd enjoyed all the pleasures Patricia had offered, and tendered her resignation. He wouldn't hear of it. He said they were two wounded souls. Of course she could keep her job.

"But he was already plotting his own form of revenge. He'd always fancied Audrey but regarded her as too strong-willed for his tastes. But wait a moment, what a conquest that would be! The stone-cold woman of steel tamed at last and by him, and he resolved to rise to the challenge. Slowly but surely he worked on his masterplan. However, he was overtaken by two events.

"Audrey left anyway, having persuaded Gareth, with some ease in the circumstances, that it was time she achieved her desire to be a kept woman. Shortly after that Patricia died suddenly of a stroke. Ray contacted Audrey to plead for some home comforting and she thought what the heck, might as well. Gareth was not in a position to object.

"In the fullness of time Boulchard had his evil way. As far as I can gather it was what might be termed a heavy session, and Audrey, at long last, discovered the joys of sex. Unsurprisingly Audrey wanted more and set about a long term affair with her former boss. Where you were so absolutely right Ernest was that when Gareth retired and they moved to their dream home Audrey found her marriage was more important. They rekindled their love and Audrey decided to call time on her affair.

"Being a strong woman, as you said Ernest, she accomplished the break quite easily, but an angry spurned Ray Boulchard was cut from a different cloth. He couldn't take it, but blamed Gareth for 'stealing' Patricia and then 'stealing' Audrey. He began a campaign of sheer hatred aimed at his former lover.

"Letters and e-mails arriving out of the blue. Up to a point they didn't trouble Audrey but some were noticeably disgusting and some wished ill-health, injury and death on her and on Gareth, and did so in the most obnoxious terms. She blocked his e-mails but his letters still landed on the doormat periodically. He stooped so low as to get other people to write the envelopes so she wouldn't recognise the handwriting.

"The interesting thing is that he never posted any of this bile direct to Gareth and he, apparently, remained in ignorance of it.

"Now we can explain the flowers with the message 'Together now together' – this didn't refer to him setting Audrey free, it was Boulchard's way of saying Gareth and Patricia were united in death. It was a gloat. He sent what Audrey described as a disgusting letter of condolence, hoping Gareth and Patricia would be happy back in each others' arms.

"He bumped into her in Faversham and was detestably nasty, laughing in her face."

"You were also correct about the disposal of the knife Ernest. Boulchard did indeed dislike the idea of two men living together as lovers and tried to point the finger of suspicion at them by dumping the weapon at Rose Cottage. He parked some way away in another lane and walked across the footpaths to achieve his goal.

"Oddly enough, when we thought the car Molly spotted was the newsagent and dismissed it, Willie looked into the possibility that the killer had used those footpaths to reach the Oast and murder Gareth. He didn't, but that was the way he got rid of knife.

"Audrey admitted she'd deleted tell-tale evidence from her diary, but all it amounted to were the dates she met Boulchard and the dates his vile letters arrived. She felt it important to keep that data, just in case. The diary also showed Gareth's fishing dates, the ones where he claimed to have caught nothing duly marked with a cross. The two dates Jackie mentioned were fishing dates alright, dates when Audrey knew she had plenty of time to visit Boulchard, pleasure the chief objective.

"One small and rather eerie point. Looking around the Oast I had a feeling the house was trying to tell me something. I looked again and again at the photos taken on the day of the murder. Now I know what it was. Audrey's laptop. It was in the photos but it wasn't there when we took the computer and Gareth's laptop away for inspection."

"Boulchard claims he had nothing to do with the other social media posts so they may well belong to disgruntled ex-lovers of the gasman."

Sheelagh had managed to get that far without a biscuit intake and she now made up for lost time while Ernest seized his opportunity to grab the floor.

"Basically this was about four unfaithful people. What a tangled web, but by goodness, what could've been so powerful a force to drive Boulchard to kill, and for the reasons we now know? But did he also believe that once Audrey was widowed he could rekindle the affair?"

"I don't think so Ernest. He's had other lovers. His latest, Poppy Ditchmen, strikes me as being far better suited to his style of utter dominance. She appears to be relieved she's escaped! To answer your question about what drove him to murder, well, love's a potent strength as we all know. Perhaps he did love Audrey passionately, we may never know. He simply says he's loved all the women in his life, but he's the sort of boastful macho man I loathe."

"I can't somehow reconcile Audrey as a potential conquest of such an awful man," said Ernest earnestly.

"Well Ernest, all I can say is that she knew she had an unfaithful husband, he was her one and only, so she'd never experienced the true wonders of real love and the wondrous joy in which two people can express such adoration and devotion in intimate moments. Boulchard was clever and scheming in seducing her and she may have thought she might as well, given Gareth had been playing away.

"The trouble was the occasion proved, shall we say, an eye-opener for a sexually innocent woman and excited her beyond words. The rest, as they say, is history. When Gareth retired and they moved here they found true love possibly for the first time, and I think it meant something precious to both of them. Gareth had hung up his boots, not just retiring from work, but also from extra-marital operations. Perhaps their happiness deranged Boulchard, who can say?"

"Well Sheelagh, I hope he doesn't play the mental illness card. They should lock him up and throw away the key."

"Can't say Ernest. Not up to me in any respect whatsoever. I just catch 'em. But all I will say is that he showed a sane mind planning the murder, and was dead crafty the way he decided to lose the weapon. So we can only hope, we can only hope."

More biscuits were devoured.

"Now Ernest, tell me about you. If you don't mind me saying so I think you did a splendid job and your theory wasn't very far out. You gave us plenty to think about and although we may have appeared to be ignoring you we weren't." Willie spluttered into his coffee cup. "It's just that we obviously can't involve members of the public directly in our investigative work, especially as there is much we can't disclose. But I'm proud to know you Ernest, and I thank you from the bottom of my heart." Willie coughed and then choked and finally sneezed, just managing to pull his hanky out in time. "What say you Willie? Ernest, top man to work with?"

Willie gave her one of his best contemptuous looks and spoke through near-clenched teeth.

"Yes ma-am, pleased to have worked with you Ernest. As my boss says, top man. It's been good."

Sheelagh was smiling one of her best 'caught-you-on-the-hop' grins. Ernest decided it was time to speak again.

"I appreciate your kind thoughts. In some ways I haven't enjoyed it one little bit. Gareth was a friend and he was mercilessly slaughtered right here last weekend. That's too dreadful for words. Audrey is a good friend as well, and I wanted the killer caught as much as she did. I feel heartbroken for her. What an appalling experience, and none of us should ever forget or overlook that.

"We may have given the impression this was a great adventure for all of us, but it was a facade, our way of dealing with something unimaginable. When the shock overtakes us I am certain we shall all be bereft of joy and awash with terrible sadness. None of us can begin to envisage how we might have felt if dear Molly had been killed, and I suspect you both feel that way too."

Sheelagh stopped chewing, only too aware that there might be some questions to be answered about their handling of the situation once they had found and interviewed Boulchard. But who could have dreamed that he would kill, or try to kill again, and so swiftly? They were all set to run a door-to-door in Bredgar and Kemsley to prove or hopefully disprove his alibi. Could they have done more? She chewed again, this time slowly. Willie spoke up.

"Yes we do Ernest, and we know that Clayton Mainstreet saved her life single-handed, so we are as grateful for that as you all are. Tell me, when did you first have an inkling Boulchard might be the killer?" He was trying to change the subject and Ernest was happy to move on.

"When I chatted to Audrey Thursday. She didn't know the newsagent had been eliminated from enquiries. When I told her Molly had identified a blue Kia Rio the colour drained from her face and I guessed it had given her a shock. She knew Boulchard had one. I didn't know about him then, but he materialized in Audrey's story later, and I wonder if she was unwilling to suggest him, unwilling to accept he may have murdered her husband, unwilling to face the possible truth, and settled for talking about him as a way of drawing attention to him. Who knows?

"We can't always be sure how the human mind works especially when it has been subjected to horror and emotional devastation. In her frightful state Audrey may have been unable to cope with the concept of a man she had slept with carrying out such a crime."

"Well anyway," Sheelagh broke in, "we're grateful for your skills as a private investigator, and no, I'm not taking the p-p-p ... Mickey, I truly believe you helped us no end. You have our genuine thanks Ernest."

That intervention brought the meeting to a convenient point for closure, and the two detectives left him to sit and ruminate on their disclosures and the effect they would have on him and everybody along their part of Bald Henry Lane.

There would be no chess with Cedric that evening as he was busy looking after a shaken and agitated Molly, so Ernest, having had enough of murder, set aside his books and DVDs on the subject and found an old video to watch after dinner, a delicious casserole he'd prepared Friday.

Chapter Twenty Two

Aftermath

Ernest was right.

Within days the shock set in for all of them and what had appeared at times to be a great adventure now took on a gruesome, grisly shape.

Molly was worst affected, spending hours weeping. But then she was the one who'd been faced with her own macabre death and narrowly escaped intact. She cuddled her cats incessantly, just as she hugged Cedric on his many visits. Ernest had his share of emotional embraces from her, as did Ananya, Gerald and Eric when they called.

It was when Clayton turned up that most tears fell, for they hugged each other crying with joy and crying over the memory of that outrageous attack, and did so endlessly.

But the whole event united them and made them all stronger.

And into this rural alliance they welcomed Audrey in time.

After the funeral she came back to live at the Oast with Rosemary insisting on popping in every single day. Ernest, who by this time had explained everything to his neighbours, went up and was welcomed as a true friend. Audrey was reassured by his visit.

He'd given the news to each neighbour in the way most suited to the individual being addressed.

Unanimously they'd all offered support for the widow and hoped Ernest, effectively their spokesman, would endorse their continued friendship for Audrey so that she might feel wanted back in her country community.

Expressing this he was surprised and saddened to see tiny teardrops sliding down her cheeks. There had been discreet sobs at the funeral, as befitting a recently bereaved woman, but she had held on to her inner strength with remarkable fortitude. Rosemary had disclosed to him when they were alone that the emotional breakdown came later that day, after everyone had left.

The Wandons had arranged the 'afterwards at' for their Ospringe home but mourners were reluctant to leave for some reason, when all Audrey wanted to do was, in the nicest possible way, to be shot of them.

"Ernest, bless you and bless every one of you for your kindness, and for coming and talking to me today. It is such a comfort to know that I have the support of my old friends here, and will be welcomed back and not ignored as an outcast. I behaved miserably and in an unforgiveable manner. I should've told the police all about it from the start then Ray would not have had the chance to try and murder Molly.

"I've no idea how I would feel now had he succeeded. I could've cost that poor woman her life. I don't deserve such kindness. It's no excuse to say I was mixed up and didn't want to believe the worst. I should've given the police the chance to investigate him earlier."

"Well Audrey, Molly feels for you, she really does, and attaches no blame to you whatsoever. She looks forward to seeing you, so might I be so bold as to suggest you invite her for tea? She'll be delighted I assure you. After all, without that attack she wouldn't have her hero Clayton to worship." Audrey managed a tender smile and a look of gratitude.

***

238

Despite Molly's best efforts on the day of the attack Ernest had avoided the limelight when Molly wanted to praise his detective work and leadership. Luckily for Ernest the media was more interested in Molly herself and her rescuer and concentrated their efforts there.

He thought that was just as well. The police had retained his respect throughout and he would not have wanted to emerge as a figure that had done their work for them.

Talking to Sheelagh Mehedren had been a kind of battle of wits and he'd actually enjoyed the challenge. Rather like a chess match, he'd thought. Each seemed to know what the other was thinking and were left wondering what the other's next move might be. Willie Broughton left the fray as cynically as he'd begun, never quite trusting Ernest, unable to accept that the old gentleman had in fact delivered. It amused the reluctant sleuth.

Ernest's family had responded as you might expect when you find a relative in the news, and he'd been pleasantly swamped with phone calls, but he was now beginning to tire of relating even a shortened version of the tale.

Willie's date with Sian was a low-key affair that led no further than coffee at her flat and an early night, he in his bed, she in hers. They were still too wound up after the case, but they did agree to a date at a later stage. Spending an evening in meaningful conversation Willie discovered a side to Sian he knew nothing of. Compassionate, knowledgeable, opinionated, with a very wide range of interests. They enjoyed each others' company and found talk easy. She proved herself intelligent and was not at all the empty-headed woman he rudely thought she was.

Clayton had to take a couple of days off sick so emotionally churned up was he. But wherever he went on business including, eventually, Bristol, he was feted. Ananya found herself recognised and that pleased her no end.

Gerald let his emotions get the better of him at the funeral but Eric was a good comforter. Gerald wished he'd been able to get in touch with Jokubas but a search had proved fruitless. Nonetheless the Lithuanian was toasted several times over at Rose Cottage.

* * *

Ray Boulchard was convicted of murder.

Audrey was charged with two offences but the charges were quickly dropped, and she returned to life amongst her friends in Bald Henry Lane. Gradually she became more involved and once more returned to the kitchen garden at Earth Cottage.

In fact she organised 'working parties' of neighbours to gather the fruit and veg, and in September Ananya and Clayton threw a Harvest Party for all of them, Rosemary and Desmond included. No doubt encouraged by a decent intake of drink they all decided that their little community needed a name and they settled on Clayton Corner. Ananya announced amidst much mirth that it couldn't be a ham-let, they being vegans, it had to be a small village.

After the bash Audrey was sure she'd seen Molly and Cedric walking home hand in hand. Rosemary and Desmond were staying the night at the Oast and they also walked back hand in hand, for they were a couple re-born.

Ernest's sister's daughter Naomi and her husband Richard had also been at the party as they were spending a few days at Whodunit and had helped in the garden. In fact gardening had become a common feature in which they all helped each other, Audrey lending her expertise as needed, and it made their summer blossom and bound them closer together.

Tom and Felicity had been treated to the life of Riley following their contribution to Molly's rescue.

"You know Cedric," she once observed astutely, "those two rascals knew I was in trouble and reacted accordingly. Cats are far more intelligent than some give them credit for."

The following year Eric and Gerald married and did so at Shepherd Neame's brewery, with a good time being had by all. Clayton, as best man, said in his speech that Gerald had indeed proved he could organise a drink-up in a brewery.....

THE END, BUT ....

... if you've enjoyed this book and haven't read '*The Chortleford Mystery*' do try it. Set in an imaginary village lost in the glorious Kent countryside it starts with the murder of a well-loved local gentleman. There's a wide diversity of characters as you might expect in such a village. Gossip takes hold, the police seem baffled, a too-clever-by-half local reporter gets involved, and then there's another murder.

The Chortleford Mystery is available from Amazon as an e-book and in paperback, and has been described by one reviewer as a 'nice easy read, good storyline, well written. Midsomer Murders comes to Kent.'

Author's afterthoughts

Bald Henry Lane is a fictional location, the suggestion being it lies "somewhere" to the south of Faversham, a real and lovely historic town in the borough of Swale, Kent. Blind Mary's Lane is also quite real!

The fictional location could be almost anywhere in Kent. There are still hop gardens in the county so I placed one next to the Modlum's Hop Pickers Oast; close by are orchards and fields full of sheep. This is no imaginary rustic idyll however, as such quiet country lanes abound in the 'Garden of England' and I wanted the setting to be obviously Kentish.

These days I could easily have added a vineyard as the county is an impressive wine-producer!

As I mentioned in *'The Chortleford Mystery'* the county is still remarkably rural and you really can get away from it all. Spectacular views lie in wait amidst some very pleasant rolling countryside and even the relatively flat Romney Marsh has a beauty all of its own.

Set aside (with the greatest respect) major tourist cities like Canterbury and Rochester and there are attractive old towns dotted here and there awaiting your exploration. Faversham is one of many and is so worth a visit. The countryside to the south and south-west is an area of astonishing beauty where you will indeed chance upon quiet narrow country lanes.

Most of the other places mentioned in the text are real (Sittingbourne, Kemsley, Ospringe, Teynham, Doddington, Eastling, Stalisfield, etc.). But again I must make it absolutely clear that the police officers in this work are fictitious in every respect. Their ranks, behaviours, procedures are products of my imagination to suit the story and nothing more. I have the utmost respect for Kent Police and there is no intended reflection on them.

There are, however, some degrees of satire throughout the story aimed at various people, situations and concepts. No offence is intended, my words written without malice.

I had the honour and privilege to work with a young Lithuanian woman for a short while, a lovely, cheerful, warm-hearted, hard-working, conscientious and inspiring person indeed, and she has a mention as you may have noticed.

Ernest's recollections of his early life and wartime Detling are based on a real person's actual experiences, someone who was indeed born nearby and lived on a farm close to the aerodrome, and to whom I am grateful for far more than I care to reveal here.

By the way the Teynham newsagent in this story is imaginary!

Ananya and Clayton had initially decided their form of veganism would exclude alcohol altogether which was their personal choice, despite some drinks being acceptable to vegans.

I mention in the text Brambles B&B at Eythorne, east Kent. Check out the website. It's one of the best I've ever stayed in, luxury as standard and incredible breakfasts to die for. Astonishing and imaginative evening meals available too! Handy for the quiet Kent countryside, as well as Dover, Canterbury, Sandwich, the White Cliffs and a host of varied attractions, and plenty of lesser known ones. Many walks nearby in unspoilt Kentish countryside, such as at Wootton, just the other side of the A2. Your hosts Claire and Mike will make you very welcome.

You could spend a year on holiday in Kent and not see it all. And yes, there are miles and miles of unspoilt countryside into the bargain.

Other books by Peter Chegwidden

Peter writes across various genres so there's bound to be something for almost everyone. Kent features in most of his works. If you've enjoyed Death at the Oast you may like its forerunner The Chortleford Mystery.

The Chortleford Mystery

Murder comes to the Kent countryside and a quiet little unassuming village.

Everyone knew who the killer was, so why didn't the police *do* something?

A lovely old gentleman is slain in his back garden and everyone was sure his wicked stepson, Michael Martyn, carried out the dreadful deed. And Martyn has plenty of secrets he wants left hidden.

But it transpires there are other secrets in this rural settlement.

If you like your murder mysteries in a more genteel and cosy vein, tinged with humour, set in glorious bucolic surroundings, and with just enough sauce added to make it spicy, then this tale's for you.

No obscene language, no gory details.

Village gossip takes hold, the police seem baffled, a too-clever-by-half local reporter gets involved, and then, inevitably, another murder takes place. And secrets are uncovered.

One by one.

Two new works coming soon

SOULS DOWN THE RIVER

A very English excursion

From high in the hills of Countryshire the river Flemm flows down to a lush valley where it meanders past quaint little villages and hamlets such as Much Blather, Bordham Witlass, Sharpe Corner and Sawe Bottom on its way to the distant sea.

And in each settlement there are stories to be told.......

Our journey takes us down the river at a gentle pace, stopping off at each village in turn to hear a tale or two unfurl, tales of sauciness and frivolity, of muddle and mayhem, of romps, scandal and rustic charm, with poignancy and pathos and a little satire, all anecdotes to cheer, all told with warmth and humour and without malice or unhappy endings.

There is heroism, adventure, stupidity, deception and love. And plenty of sauce to make it spicy.

Welcome to rural England. Welcome to Countryshire and the Flemm valley and its inhabitants.

THE MASTER OF DOWNSLAND

A drama set in north Kent during the 18th century

Disinherited for marrying the girl he loves David Grayan leaves family wealth and status behind. With what little money he has he embarks on various business ventures that eventually reap dividends and earn him his fortune.

He buys a handsome house in North Kent, and earns the respect of the country folk. But he is largely shunned by his own class particularly for his unconventional views and practices.

Then tragedy strikes.

His beloved wife, Marie, dies in childbirth. Unable to come to terms with his dreadful loss, he throws himself into his business affairs and retreats into a dark, solitary state where even his few close friends cannot help him, an emotionally broken man.

Then a new maid starts work at his Downsland Hall. But can a mere maid, a lowly servant, provide any medium by which he might emerge from his darkness into the light? And could he love again?

A dramatic tale of romance and love set against a backdrop of tragedy, family feuds, loyalty and betrayal, revenge, enduring and fickle friendships, bigotry and the constraints of society's conventions in the 18th century.

***

Books (e-books and paperbacks) available from Amazon now

Kindale

It is the late 18th century, in the reign of George III.

Major events such as the American War of Independence, the French Revolution and the Napoleonic Wars belong to this era. Indeed even now Napoleon is rising to power.

The fear of war is bringing uneasiness to Kent as it is elsewhere.

Now the mysterious Oliver Kindale is on his way to Dover.

His destiny is aligned to the activities of a Frenchman and an English outlaw. Threatening developments in France seem to be at the centre of his critical mission.

But Kindale is not an officer of the law, nor is he a military man. Indeed, little is known about him.

The east Kent coast has been a hotbed for smuggling but Kindale is not pursuing the free-traders, although their paths will inevitably cross. Which side of the law does Kindale operate on? What are his motives? Why is he in Kent at all?

And what of the man himself?

Death hangs in the air. These are dangerous times and Kindale will face danger and other challenges, some that will test him heart and mind, body and soul.

Could the very fate of England be in his hands?

No Shelter for the Wicked

Three unexplained, seemingly motiveless murders in different parts of the country. No clues, no murder weapons, no meaningful DNA, no useful forensic evidence. Nothing to connect them.

Then the police discover a bizarre and tenuous, wafer-thin link. But how to progress it with nothing to go on? Or is it all coincidence? The police don't think so.

A private eye, an ex-cop, doesn't believe in such coincidences either. He's a suspect in one of the murders, and by chance he becomes more deeply involved in the investigations. In a remarkable set of circumstances he forms an unlikely alliance with a supposedly disreputable woman, an ex-con, who is desperately seeking her sister, and they set out on a quest that eventually leads to peril.

And a terrible shock for this woman he has befriended.

The trail heads from Kent to Hertfordshire, Suffolk, the Derbyshire Dales, north Devon and the Lake District, and eventually to a life or death situation and heartbreak.

A tale of murder, mystery, of love and passion in many guises, of deceit, betrayal and vengeance, played out across the country as the tension mounts inexorably towards its horrifying climax.

Peter Chegwidden has written a crime novel of many separate threads entwining as the thrilling denouement approaches, and has done so with his own style of humour and pathos, satire and poignancy.

Tom Investigates

This is intended to be a simple, charming little fun story about cats.

These cats are not cartoon cats, or any sort of animated cats, they are just the neighbourhood cats we come across every day. Perhaps even your very own cat! They are cats behaving like cats just as we see them behaving every day.

But in this tale we allowed into their world. We hear them speak and learn what they are thinking.

It is a kiddies tale for adults. Just sit back, relax and enjoy!

Admittedly the adventures are very far-fetched but otherwise there would be no story. There are several interwoven threads and several very happy endings.

There is no bad language or anything to offend.

So come with us and get in touch with your feline side.

Tom Vanishes

The sequel to Tom Investigates sees the tabby accidently kidnapped and taken from the Isle of Sheppey to a mainland supermarket.

The story follows Tom and his efforts to get back home. His feline discover by chance what has happened and devise plans for his rescue with chaos ensuing.

Along the way Tom strikes up an alliance with a stray cat that will lead him into unforeseen difficulties. Meanwhile the Minster Moggies get themselves into all kinds of tangles as their rescue operations founder.

So is there a happy ending? Of course there is, well, several in fact.

Tom Vanishes is available as an e-book only.

Sheppey Short Stories

Eighteen short stories all based on Kent's Isle of Sheppey about the year 2014.

All kinds of tales from the humorous to the sad, the satirical and the ghostly, the romantic and the saucy, tales of heroism and tales of despair, but mostly stories to warm you. Great fun!

Here's one of them, entitled: **Infrastructure** – *a tale of meaningless words and expressions*

"Infrastructure," Martin intoned with mocking expression, "when them politicians, planners, developers, gawd knows who else, starts talking *Infrastructure* you know y'in trouble!"

And to emphasise the last point his finger, which had hitherto been poking about in the air, prodded his mate firmly in the chest, just to make sure Simon got the message.

"You see, Si, if they knew what infrastructure meant they wouldn't be building all them hundreds of homes up Thistle Hill and leave that three-quarter mile stretch of Lower Road, Barton Hill Drive to Cowstead Corner, like it is, a meandering country lane, where it's dangerous to walk let alone cycle. And they'd have done it before the first brick was laid.

"Don't tell me it's complicated. It ain't. Look, Si, if they wanted to build a six lane motorway through my house they'd bloody do it. Compulsory purchase. Knock me house down, motorway built. Simples.

"Know what, Si? In this country we solve yesterday's problems tomorrow, never build for the future." Simon nodded throughout the dialogue but was content to offer no comment either in favour of his friend's views, or by way of providing an alternative argument.

"Infrastructure, Si, suggests joined-up thinking, don't it? Well, don't you believe it mate! Start using words like that and it's a cover up." Simon nodded some more in his contented fashion.

"Robust. There's another. Robust strategies, robust this, robust that. Know what, Si? Look it up in the dictionary, mate, means *sturdy*, sturdy construction. So what's wrong with a *sturdy* plan? I'll tell you what, most robust strategies turn out to have feet of clay." And once more Simon's chest was the recipient of various fingertip prods. And once more Simon nodded. It was almost as if Martin was pressing a button on Simon's front that caused him to nod.

"Mart?"
"Yerss."

"What's regeneration then?"

"Another one of them words what hides a multitude of sins, and is loved by politicians. You see, if you're a developer and you want to build loads of homes and make packets of money all you have to do is say you're regenerating a place and bingo, everyone's on board. You see, you just promise to build all kinds of other stuff, like a community centre, school, kiddies playground and the like, and add, very important this, Si, add that it'll create X number of jobs and wallop. Yer in.

"You don't have to necessarily make good on all your promises. Shop, pubs and restaurants sound great too, but I think people have rumbled that one. They know the shops they want ain't gonna turn up. Marks and Sparks ain't gonna open up in a housing estate.

"Regeneration, Si, the art of building money-making homes especially when you know local people would object and be against the idea. You promise all them extras and that it'll all create jobs and objections just get bulldozed. Just like my house. If my house, my home sweet home, was in the way it would be knocked down before you could say Jack Doings. No problems you see, Si, nothing stands in the way then, there's no complications. Easy-peesy.

"So when they say something's very complicated it's stalling tactics, that's all. Like the Lower Road, mate."

"Oh, I see," Simon responded although his tone of voice suggested he was only marginal clearer in his understanding. At this juncture he felt moved to make a comment.

"Can't see why they use all these meaningless words, Mart."
"They're buzz-words, Si, very popular. People come up with all these crazy words and expressions then they become sort of trendy. Like 'thinking outside the box' .... I ask you, did you ever!"

251

Simon followed the safest of his options and returned to gentle nodding.

"And 'clear skies thinking' ... that's another. I reckon they all start out in America and we gotta copy them," Martin added with a single laugh which vanished almost as soon as it appeared. Warming to his already glowing theme he continued,

"Remember, not long ago, our boss used to come up with ideas? He used to say we'll run 'em up the flagpole, see who salutes them. The ones nobody saluted he did anyway cos he thought they were good ideas and they all lost money! We gave 'em a salute, didn't we, Si?"

Both men chuckled.

"Never mentioned it since, Si, no more flagpoles. He does what he thinks is best and them ideas still lose money and get scrapped. And we, you and me, come up with a brainwave, Si, he says it's no good then about six months later launches it was his own scheme and, guess what, it makes money!"

"Yeah, Mart, and he takes all the credit."
"Got it, Si, and claims a bonus into the bargain. And when they've paid all the bosses their bonuses and given 'em pay rises money gets a bit tight and one of us plebs gets redundant. Remember Geoff last year? Doing well, three years under his belt here, not long married, kid just born and he's out on his ear."

Simon considered all the evidence that Martin had placed before him, decided that it was all very unfair, that somebody should do something about it, but refrained from commenting on it. He settled for a vigorous nod. Then another, as if to ensure that Martin appreciated his acquiescence.

"Talking of the boss, he'll be back from the pub in a mo, so we'd better get cracking me old son."

Simon nodded.

That evening, at home with his wife and their teenage son in Sanspareil Avenue, Simon was trying to enjoy an after dinner cup of tea. There was nothing wrong with the tea, it was just the ambience he was drinking it in. Nathanial had a computer game on the widescreen tv, and was noisily trying to kill off all manner of monsters amid a dreadful cacophony of sound at what Simon assumed, probably inaccurately, was playing at around a million decibels.

Eventually it became too much for him and he asked Nat to pack it up or turn it right down. Nat explained that losing most of the sound took all the fun out of it, but he turned it down anyway without further comment from his father.

As his mind slowly returned to normal Simon found himself considering the name of his road. *Sanspareil*. That, he felt, was not that far removed from *Infrastructure*. Wonder what Sanspareil means? Just like *Infrastructure*, he reasoned. Possibly meaningless! And his recovered mind wandered further afield.

'Perhaps I should have a *robust Sanspareil*. Maybe when they build new houses they should have a complete *Sanspareil* in place!'

Later that evening, when the curtains were drawn, the tv had been switched off with the day's soaps and game shows watched, Simon made enquiry of his wife.

"Lynne, is the *infrastructure* in place for us to go to bed?"
"What on earth are you on about? Infrastructure for going to bed? You're round the bend, Si, you don't even know what it means!"
"No, but you don't have to. People who use the word infrastructure don't have to know what it means, it just sounds good, y'know, a buzz-word."
"Do you have to train hard, Si, to be as stupid as you or were you born that way? Is it a gift?"

Simon cackled, and Lynne smiled.

"I wish," she said, "there was infrastructure in place for keeping Nat quiet and off those bloody games of his."
"Yes," commented Simon, "he needs a robust Sanspareil to get him organised."

Seeing Lynne's eyes were out on stalks, and then rolling skywards, Simon rose, yawned, stretched and said he was off to bed, was she coming? Indeed she was, and they paused at Nat's door, not to say goodnight, but to tell him in unison to keep the bloody noise down.

Next morning Nat set off for school bellowing a tuneless song which presumably echoed the noise ripping through his earpieces and the wires that connected them to his life support system, his mobile music centre, whatever it was called. Lynne never could remember.

He somehow looked scruffier than when he first got up and *that* wasn't the sort of picture of a loved one you would want to cherish. Now he looked a slob. Simon had muttered something over breakfast about wanting to dismantle Nat's entire technological infrastructure, but she was beyond trying to fathom out what her husband was waffling on about.

They didn't really have a proper sit down brekky. Lynne, still in her nightie and dressing gown, would provide whatever was required, which usually wasn't much anyway, as Simon dashed about, running late as normal, and Nat did the exact opposite, late but not dashing.

In between she'd manage a yoghurt maybe, a Ryvita probably, a few sips of coffee possibly, and then have a clear up once her family had departed.

"I need to change the infrastructure here," she said quietly to herself, and granted herself a mild chuckle. "I need other people involved in my infrastructure, like Si and Nat f'rinstance." And her rueful little chuckle evolved into a hearty laugh. "Si, you idiot; infrastructure indeed!"

Swiftly forgetting all that nonsense she cleared up the house, made the beds, and got herself ready for her own part-time job. She sniggered. A cleaner! A right home from home job. But the seeds of rebellion had been sown in her mind and her mind, being a fertile land for examining new ideas, did not let the matter rest.

Over the next couple of days Lynne's mind cradled and nurtured the new idea that had been born there. Gradually the idea developed and Lynne christened it the 'concept' as she thought it ought to have a title more in keeping with Simon's buzz-words! And, my goodness, he'd come out with a few. That Martin, he's got a lot to answer for, thought Lynne.

Eventually she put pen to paper and from a tangle of ideas, thoughts and considerations her 'concept' took a more material shape. By committing her feelings to the written word she found she could build up a solid picture where alterations could be adopted and their effects examined. She changed this and she changed that and in due course a clear programme emerged.

I have a robust plan she decided, and further decided that the formation of such a project warranted a massive grin of self-satisfaction. My *infrastructure*, she mentally concluded, has indeed thought of everything, taken every angle into account, allowed for every degree of reasonable flexibility, and it takes a woman to do this. The last part changed the grin into a laugh and then a guffaw she didn't even know she was capable of.

This'll show 'em, she thought.

That weekend Lynne called a meeting much to the surprise of her family.

"We sit round the table and we are going to talk strategy," she'd explained, adding the words, "*My* robust strategy," for more dramatic effect. Nathanial and Simon looked at each other and neither spoke.

"And, by the way," she'd continued, "I'm giving up my cleaning job, got a part-time post in an office. Should enable me to fulfil my duties at home. All part of the revised *infrastructure* for this family."

If Simon was utterly baffled Nat was off the planet, "Duh?" his only comment.

And so the meeting started.

It transpired that Lynne had compiled a programme so that all aspects of basic housework were shared equally, and she saw off protests by saying that she would still take the lion's share. But weekends were to be a little different. Nat didn't go to school, Simon didn't go to work, so she expected them to be more involved in running the family home Saturdays and Sundays.

There were going to be quiet periods when the telly was off and the use of potentially noisy technology was to be banned. Mobile phones off. Any conversation would be between the three of them, but two at a time was acceptable! No music, nothing.

Nathanial was so overwhelmed that he was rendered speechless. His mouth made some odd little movements, as if to suggest words were on their way, but clearly his brain was nowhere near engaged enough to participate.

Lynne had printed out copies of the next week's schedule which she handed out to her amazed and dumbstruck audience.

"Any questions? Good, right, we start Monday morning and Nat I'd like two Weetabix and a slice of toast and marmalade, please, oh and a cup of tea. You'll see you're on breakfast

Monday so get up nice and early, right? In any case you'll need plenty of time to make your bed."

In her discourse Lynne deliberately left no time for any questions, so there were none.

"You'll see we have a quiet period for an hour Tuesday night...."
"But ... but ... but there's football at 7.45," stammered Simon.
"Fine, we can move the quiet period to start at 6.45. Agreed?"
"But mum, mum, I like to have a couple of games before the football..."
"Well, you can't on Tuesday, Nat, so there you have it."

The conversation, if it could be called that, did not proceed very much further, especially as Lynne was in the driving seat and handling the navigation too. Simon had to agree that it all seemed quite fair. In fact, after the meeting, when Nat had gone upstairs to indulge in a particularly noisy computer game, possibly out of vengeance, Simon pointed out with a wink and a knowing grin that she had left one activity off her schedule.

"Does that mean we don't, you know, anymore?"
"Depends babes, depends. If between us we have all the infrastructure in place, and in your case it had better be very, very robust, and Nat is nowhere to be seen, then we can enjoy a damn good Sanspareilling together. *When* there is the time in our hectic schedule."
"Can you see a window of opportunity?" queried Simon, snuggling up to his wife and smirking.
"If you're a good boy then there might be later tonight," said Lynne as she returned his smirk.

They kissed and hugged and Simon mentally resolved, very light-heartedly in all respects, that he would probably punch his friend Martin for starting all this infrastructure nonsense. But even he had to admit that if it helped overcome Nat's growing pains (as he called them) then it had to be for the good, as indeed it turned out to be.

Takes a woman to sort all this out, Lynne knew. And they won't ever take me for granted again!

Sheppey Short Stories is available as a e-book only.

Deadened Pain

A parody of the crime novel genre

The story starts with the investigation into a robbery at a local garage, in which very little was taken, and gradually gathers momentum as the crimes become more serious and involve kidnap and murder.

It is only as the tale unfolds that the very serious nature of some of these crimes and their terrible connections and consequences become apparent.

Detective Chief Superintendent Luke Fuselage works for Birkchester CID and it is probably as well for the good citizens of the area that serious crime is rare if this particular DCS is the best they have.

However, things are about to change and more dramatically than anyone could've imagined. In a quiet village a long way from town a body is discovered, a body that is horribly mutilated. Thus starts to unravel an extraordinary chain of events that will test the local police force to the limits as the body count increases, and result in a race to find a killer or killers before he, she or they strike yet again.

Sound familiar? Yes, it's the stuff of all good crime fiction, naturally. But most crime fiction doesn't feature someone of DCS Fuselage's ability at the helm. There are red herrings, and probably some of different hues, and there are twists and turns. All sorts of characters wander in and out of the story. Unsurprisingly.

Join Fuselage on this voyage into the dark unknown as he pieces together the clues that will lead him to the perpetrator. But first he must find and identify those clues. It's a case that will require all his ingenuity, experience and expertise. And somebody is keeping one step ahead of him and seemingly outwitting his team at every opportunity.

And his squad has all the elements that are needed in any successful team: togetherness, love, loathing, jealousy, incompetence, admiration, stupidity, efficiency, cliques, aggression, shyness, lust, sensitivity, contempt, cleverness, nastiness, cunning.

The private lives of some of the police officers become caught up in the story as each person is swept along by their own emotions and events at work. Fuselage's team is comprised of a curious mixture of personalities all bubbling along in their own ways trying to achieve an ultimate goal. As matters get worse additional members are drawn into this team and it seems that there could be an internal issue none has bargained for.

Expect the unexpected. The unimaginable can be the reality. The truth may be startling.

Deadened Pain is available as an e-book only.

Printed in Great Britain
by Amazon

19886076R00149